THE
BARROWHOUSE
INCIDENT

71 of 100

Also by Martin G. Naylor

Secrets of Hightower

www.secretsofhightower.org

Commended – the Sheffield Children's Book Award 2010

THE
BARROWHOUSE
INCIDENT

MARTIN G. NAYLOR

Matador
5 Weir Road
Kibworth Beauchamp, Leicester
LE8 0LQ
Tel: (+44) 116 279 2299
Email: books@troubador.co.uk
Web: www.troubador.co.uk/matador

ISBN 978 1848766 136

British Library Cataloguing in Publication Data.
A catalogue record for this book is available from the British Library.

Map by Anne Haslam

Typeset in 11pt Palatino by Troubador Publishing Ltd, Leicester, UK

Matador is an imprint of Troubador Publishing Ltd

Printed in Great Britain by the MPG Books Group, Bodmin and King's Lynn

For Michael and Sarah

Thanks once again to the usual crowd for their help and support. Also to Terri, the first person to read Barrowhouse.
– Plus a huge thank you to
Hannah Adams
and Christopher Hattersley

CONTENTS

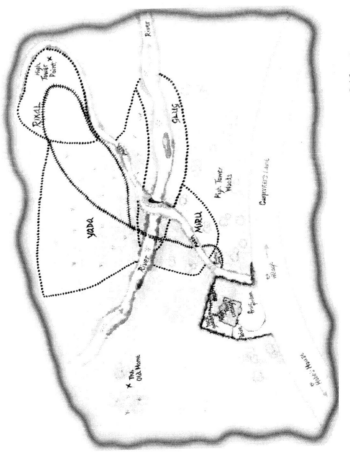

Highwater

Chapter 1

REUNION

It was no warmer in the dark, gloomy corridor than it had been outside and the feeling that they were walking into a trap grew with each step towards the flickering light from the open door ahead.

He glanced at the two figures at his side. Their wary faces reflected his own unease and as he nodded to each in turn he hoped that he looked a lot more confident than he felt.

At the door they stopped, the echo of their boots on the hard floor fading away.

With a trembling hand he pulled out the dagger strapped to his belt.

"There'll be no need for that," said a familiar voice harshly.

For a moment he hesitated before replacing it.

"Thank you. Now it would be a great honour, a truly great and wonderful honour, if you would kindly step into my humble abode."

The voice had taken on a softer tone but the words were spoken in a mocking, yet demanding way and he knew that this was a command, not a request. With a deep breath he stepped into the room, the others following, but at a discreet distance behind.

The room was bigger than he expected. At one time

it must have been quite elaborate with its high ceilings, panelled walls and huge marble fireplace, but now, even with only firelight to illuminate it, the dimness couldn't disguise the shabbiness and neglect. The wood panelling was rotting, the paint on the ceiling flaking, and there was a stale fustiness about the place.

In an old leather chair to the side of the fire sat a figure, little more than a silhouette against the firelight. The long, thin legs were crossed at the ankles, the bony fingers drumming casually on the arms of the chair.

He was about to reply to the figure when a sudden movement in the cracked mirror above the fireplace caught his eye. He spun round. In the shadows of the farthest corner stood six tall, hooded figures, the features of their faces hidden in the blackness. Only the whites of their pupil-less eyes shone out in the gloom, giving them a fearful, spectral appearance.

"Deebers!" He hissed, his hand grabbing for the dagger once more.

"Relax Napoleon. They won't hurt you," said the voice from the chair.

For a moment there was silence. He slowly turned back to the figure.

"Hurt me? Hurt me? It's more what I would do to them Tritus," he bellowed confidently, keeping a cautious eye on the mirror.

Tritus cackled and leaned back in his chair.

"Some things never change do they Napoleon? Even now, four months after being banished from Rixal, four months after all your brave army deserted you, except for these…" he made a mocking, elaborate effort at counting the figures lurking by the doorway, "er… two fine specimens, you still remain as feisty and pompous as ever."

Napoleon's nerves subsided as his anger sparked.

2

"My army shall return. I shall return. My time is coming," he said grandly.

"Rubbish. You live in an old plant pot on the edge of Rixal. Oh how the mighty have fallen. You can't do anything or go anywhere for fear of being mocked. I know all about you Napoleon. You are one of the ones I keep an eye on."

"And what about you then Tritus?" roared Napoleon as the spark of anger became an explosion. "Stuck here in the old home. Not exactly got an abundance of friends yourself have you?"

"I at least am making plans to change things. Unlike you my friend, who appears to have simply given up."

"Making plans?" Napoleon threw back his head and laughed, his pony tail swinging back and forth as he did so. "Making plans with what? This huge army of useless Deebers? I don't know whether you've noticed, but apart from the fact that they're not exactly wired up right in the head, they're only any use in almost complete darkness. Now excuse me, but any army that has to hide if someone sticks anything brighter than a candle near their nose doesn't exactly make an elite fighting force in my book!

I've heard nothing, absolutely nothing, from you since *that* day. Not until last night when a message was left for me. So don't think I'm expecting any great plans from you in the old 'we're going to take over the entire world' department!"

"And why do you think you've heard nothing from me in all that time?"

If Napoleon hadn't been so angry he'd have picked up on the sudden ice cold edge in Tritus's voice.

"Because you're running scared. You're in hiding knowing that if you step foot outside this mausoleum you'll be arrested."

"No!" The voice wasn't particularly loud but it resounded around the room and Napoleon took a startled step back.

"This is why you have heard nothing from me," Tritus hissed as he struggled to his feet, fumbling for a cane propped against the chair as he did so. As he staggered forward the light from the fire cast a glow over him and the men in the room gasped.

The whole of the left side of his face was horribly disfigured where skin tissue had burnt away. The mouth was pulled down in a grotesque leering grin. There was no left eye, only a dark empty socket. The top half of the left ear was completely missing. Even in the dismal light the texture of the skin looked blistered and raw.

"This is why…" he said again as he stumbled toward Napoleon, his bony hand grabbing Napoleon's arm for support.

"You see why now huh?" The hideous face peered down into Napoleons, a trickle of saliva dribbling down over the blackened gums where once there had been a lip. Napoleon thought he could smell something resembling burnt, charred flesh, but maybe that was just his over active imagination.

"This is what happened to me on *that* day. I struggled to fly back to the old home but the bird was too damaged and I crashed on the way in. The Deebers saved me. We understand each other now."

Napoleon glared into the one good eye. There was a strange vagueness about the look. He felt no sympathy, just revulsion. The hand gripped harder on his arm.

"But now I am feeling stronger. Now I am getting better. I want us to work together. I need your help my friend."

"And in what way do you need my help?" asked Napoleon cautiously.

Tritus relaxed his grip on Napoleon's arm and stood in the middle of the room, leaning heavily on his cane and swaying awkwardly.

"Revenge," he growled.

"Revenge?" repeated Napoleon. "On who?"

The vacant look in Tritus's one good eye instantly disappeared.

"On our overseer. On Master Dominic Oliver Collins. He was the one that did this to me. He was the one who destroyed all my plans. I was so close to my ultimate victory, flying back with my mission completed. He was the one who engaged me in battle. But the boy used his one and only power to grow to his full, human size and I was lucky to fly out of reach of those giant hands…if living like this could be called lucky!"

Napoleon let Tritus rant on, but he did feel a glimmer of interest. After all, on that same fateful day, the Collins kid and his friends had been responsible for his own downfall.

"So what's the idea," he said, stroking his thick, bushy beard.

"We watch and wait."

The glimmer of interest began to fade.

"Wait? Wait for what?"

"For an opportunity. I have our overseer under constant surveillance."

"Great. So we're looking for something but we don't know what, but when we find it we'll do something… but again, we don't know what."

"Patience," said Tritus placing an arm round Napoleon's shoulder. Napoleon wasn't sure if this was an act of friendship or just support. "You underestimate me. I have something else that will help."

He turned Napoleon to face the Deebers.

"Oh, the Deebers," said Napoleon looking distinctly

unimpressed. "I've already said the Deebers are not going to be any…"

His voice trailed away as the Deebers stepped to one side, revealing a familiar figure standing in the corner, smiling contentedly.

Napoleon's mouth opened and shut in quick succession.

"You?" he stammered. "What are you doing here?"

Tritus smiled a massive, humourless, lop-sided smile.

"This is the person who will help us in our quest," he said triumphantly.

"A robot surely?" replied Napoleon, frowning. "As a designer you've always been good at these."

Tritus shook his head.

"Oh no. Not this time. I'm not going down that line again. This is the real thing. Our friend here is very eager and willing to help us, and the beauty of it all is that young Master Collins won't suspect anyone so close to him until it's too late."

Napoleon felt a tinge of pleasure at the possibilities opening up before them.

"So, we'll lure Dominic Collins here," he said thoughtfully. "Then we'll kill him, and with no overseer we'll be able to move in and take over Elverey."

Tritus turned towards him. The side of his face that was still recognizable looked flushed and excited.

"Oh no my dear Napoleon. I really don't want him killed." For a few seconds his breathing became shallow and he doubled up in a fit of coughing. When he straightened back his eye was almost burning with a renewed intensity.

"I don't want him killed at all. You see, what you and I will plan for him will be far, far worse than that!!"

Chapter 2

BARROWHOUSE

"Would Dominic Collins please go to the Barrowhouse reception desk situated at the front door, Main Street, where his mother is waiting for him."

Nick stared at his reflection in the window of the sports shop. The figure facing him was wide eyed and open mouthed, and he could feel his face reddening, starting at the neck and creeping up to his forehead.

Then things got worse!

There was a sudden hiss of static followed by a rumbling sound from the hundreds of speakers throughout the shopping complex. The girl's voice appeared again, this time sounding more distant and confused.

"But Mrs.Collins, we don't usually give out..." the voice faded into disjointed mumbling. Nick glanced round nervously. The crowd of shoppers seemed to pause, waiting expectantly.

"Would Dominic Collins of Hightower Cottage please go to the Barrowhouse reception desk situated at the front door, Main Street, where his mother is anxiously waiting for him."

It might have been Nick's imagination considering his mortified state, but this time the words seemed to be spoken much more slowly and with a great deal of heavy sighing.

He pretended to be absorbed in the contents of the shop window, desperately hoping that no one he knew had heard the announcement. He'd only been at his new school a few months and hadn't really managed to fit in yet so the idea that, come Monday morning everyone would know that twelve year old Nick Collins had got lost shopping and had to be called by his mummy, positively filled him with dread.

It wasn't as though he could even deny it was him. They hadn't only called out his name, but for good measure repeated it and added where he lived!

There was always the chance that his full name wouldn't be recognized. After all, his mum was the only person who called him Dominic, a name he hated, but it seemed a bit of a forlorn hope.

The crowds surged onwards once more but he felt as though everyone now knew who he was and were nudging each other, pointing and sniggering, so he counted to ten very slowly before turning and walking away as casually as possible, hands in pockets, whistling tunelessly.

Nobody took any notice of him of course, and as he weaved through the crowd on his way toward Main Street, his embarrassment began to turn to anger. How could his mum show him up like that?

He turned a corner by the computer games shop where he spent many hours, (and a considerable amount of money) and there they were...his mum with her latest boyfriend, Dave.

They made an odd couple. Marion, a large, well built woman in her usual bizarre outfit of swirling oranges and reds, and Dave, a small, stocky figure with a thick neck and bald head.

Nick neither liked nor trusted Dave. He'd turned up some weeks ago to sort out a sudden appearance of wasps at Hightower Cottage. At that time it had been late October and Dave had made big noises about how dangerous wasps could be so late in the year. He'd promised that, as the best pest control operative in the area, he'd soon find their nest and then quickly sort them out. But now it was December and he'd managed to do neither. Strangely, for the time of year, the wasps were still there. So, for that matter, was Dave!

Marion had seen Dave as yet another possible conquest. Dave had seen Marion as someone quite wealthy. So it had come as no surprise to Nick to walk into the lounge one evening and find them sitting together, holding hands and watching television, Dave with his feet up on the coffee table, a half drunk bottle of beer at his side.

As Nick marched up to the reception desk Marion made an exaggerated gesture of looking at her watch. Dave watched him carefully, a self satisfied grin on his face.

"Why did you have to go and put out a call on that... that thing?" said Nick, when they were within yelling distance.

"Twelve o'clock I said. On the dot I said," Marion replied, tapping her watch vigorously.

"You could have phoned me," he snapped, pulling out the 'all singing, all dancing' phone he'd bought a couple of weeks ago.

"You know I haven't got a phone."

"No, but he has," said Nick nodding at Dave.

Dave held his arms up, the thick gold bracelet Marion had bought him glinting gaudily on his chubby forearm.

"Hey, I've not got it on me." The tone was carefully controlled but those steely blue eyes bore into Nick. "I've left it in the car."

"Oh very secure," muttered Nick under his breath.

"Couldn't be more secure," said Dave, the control wavering. "Not with Duke in there."

"Yeah. Good old Duke," Nick hissed sarcastically. For a moment they stared at each other in an icy stalemate. Nick broke first and peered down at the floor as though intensely interested in the laces on his trainers.

Marion looked at them both in turn then rubbed her hands together.

"Well I'm glad that's sorted," she said brightly, making one of her usual sudden mood changes. "Now I don't know about you two but I'm starving. Let's go and get something to eat."

*

"Thank you David," cooed Marion as Dave slid the tray onto the table.

"Thanks," mumbled Nick, grabbing his burger. He gritted his teeth as he noticed Dave slipping the change into the pocket of his jeans, despite the fact that his mum had paid for the meal — again!

He leaned back in his chair and stared up at the intricate tubing and girders of the food hall ceiling with its huge domed glass centre piece so high above. A modern, square framed chandelier hung down from the centre of the dome, dazzling spotlights countersunk within its shiny wooden veneer.

In the middle of the hall was a gigantic silver Christmas tree, resplendent with hundreds of tiny blue lights, its tapering topmost branches piercing through the square chandelier. A large silver star perched at the very top, almost touching the apex of the dome.

Nick placed a lump of gristle from his burger into the polystyrene container and sighed. He felt somehow detached from this fast, modern world. He glared at a kid at the next table, perhaps two or three years older than himself, who was showing off to a couple of pretty, giggling girls, and envied the simplicity of the boy's life.

The weight of the world seemed to press down on his shoulders, but that was hardly surprising, because in reality he did have the weight of a world on his shoulders... the huge responsibility of a vast miniature world back home at Hightower.

The kid nearby was talking more seriously now and the girls were staring at him, hanging onto every word he was saying. Nick smiled grimly and wondered how impressed the girls would be if they knew about some of the things that had happened to him. After all, not everyone had been stuck in a spiders web, travelled in rats and cats, fought huge hooded monsters, or been attacked by vicious killer birds. Not many people could claim they'd saved an entire world either!

But then, not everyone had inherited a cottage with enormous grounds which just happened to include a world populated by hundreds of thousands. This was the world of the Elvereys, where everyone was smaller than half the size of his little finger. A world he had to look after in total secrecy. A world that only he could shrink down to and visit.

He sighed again. Thinking back, things had been somewhat hectic, but now they'd settled down and become almost dull in comparison. As overseer he often travelled round the four separate regions, attending meals in the grassland area of Yada, presiding at official openings of new businesses in the tree shopping areas of Miru, and pretending to be impressed when shown around mining developments in the mountain region of Rixal.

Some things were great fun though, like sailing in twig boats down on the river near the market at Glug with Jed, his best friend in Elverey.

It was funny, after the unbelievable shock upon discovering the Elvereys at Hightower, followed by the fear and excitement during those first incredible adventures, everything had settled down to be almost mundane. Strange how the human mind could accept such things, then transform them into an almost accepted normality.

A chubby finger was prodding his shoulder and he jumped.

"I said snails…"

"What?" asked Nick irritably.

The finger pointed to the wooden chandelier.

"Snails. Up there. Found hundreds of em. Well, quite a few anyway. Dumped em in the lake outside. Now how do you reckon they got all the way up there? Must of taken months." He laughed and a gold filling flashed in the light from the spotlights.

Nick shrugged but said nothing.

"You must have a wonderful head for heights David," said Marion, looking suitably impressed. "I couldn't go all the way up there."

Dave smiled at her in a modestly humble way that didn't quite work.

"Oh, it's nothing. Just part of the job. It was really the rats that I was contracted to sort out here. Pretty much done too. I'm back here tonight to do the rounds and make sure." He rubbed his thumb and forefinger together and winked. "Bit of overtime like. But I can confidently say that there are no rats here in Barrowhouse anymore."

"Then why…?" Nick's voice trailed away as he sat up in his chair. Next to him was a large blue pot containing a tall, plastic tree. He stared down into the shadows at the base of the pot and could hardly believe his eyes.

There, staring at him was the most enormous rat he had ever seen! But it was the odd look in its eyes that stopped him responding further to Dave's remark.

There was something familiar about the way the thing just stood there, staring at him intently, that made him hold his breath and sent a shiver down his spine.

Suddenly the rodent turned and slipped away into the darkness behind the pot, but it was the way it turned, smoothly and deliberately, that confirmed Nick's initial feelings.

A rat! It looked like a rat, but it didn't quite act in the same way as rats he'd seen before. Nothing he could put his finger on, but it just didn't seem right. Memories of where he'd seen that sort of thing came flooding back and the thoughts both confused and excited him.

He stared at his mum and Dave but they were too engrossed in each other to have noticed anything.

When he looked back down at the pot there was nothing there and he began to wonder if he'd actually imagined it all.

*

Later that afternoon, in the spotlessly clean and freshly scented toilets, Nick was still thinking about the rat as he washed his hands and turned to the hand dryer. The soothing music was temporarily drowned out by a roar of hot air.

The dryer clicked off. He looked in the mirror and brushed the hair back from his eyes. The only other occupant coughed loudly and spit into one of the basins before leaving.

Charming, he thought as he turned to follow. The music changed, but sounded pretty much like the last tune. He walked to the exit door and pulled on the handle.

Nothing happened.

He frowned and pulled again but the door wouldn't budge.

"What the?" he muttered, pulling for the third time. A ripple of concern fluttered in his stomach and he subconsciously touched his phone, wondering just who to ring to say he was stuck in the toilet!

Just then the music faded.

He backed into the empty room, the sudden silence making him feel nervous. Tilting his head slightly he thought he could just about hear something. He held his breath and listened harder.

"*Help us,*" called a tiny voice from the speaker in the ceiling.

"Who are you?" he replied, his voice trembling.

"*Dominic Collins. Please help us.*"

"Who are you?" Nick repeated.

"*Only you can help us.*"

With a ferocious thud the toilet door bounced in its frame.

"Come on," shouted a voice from outside. "Stop messing about. Open up."

Nick stared at the door, then back at the speaker, totally unsure what to do.

"*Go to the hobby shop by the food mall.*" The words were hurried now. "*Look in the window and wait. You'll be shown what to do.*"

"Come on. Open up."

"*Please help us.*"

"OPEN UP!!"

"*Go. Go now.*"

Everything seemed to happen at once. The music came back on, there was a click from the door, and a large man in green overalls fell in, obviously surprised at suddenly gaining access.

"What do you think you're playing at jamming the door shut," he demanded, glaring at Nick who just stood there feeling totally bemused. "What have you been damaging in here. We have enough trouble with kids like you."

"Nothing," protested Nick, forcing himself into action. He dodged round the man and leapt through the doorway. Before anyone could stop him he sneaked through the inquisitive crowd gathering outside, thinking that for the second time that day his face must be the colour of a tomato!

Thankfully though, Marion and Dave were just finishing off their cup of coffee and hadn't witnessed his latest brush with total humiliation.

"Right," said Marion, shuffling ample amounts of sugar sticks into her handbag from the tray in the centre of the table. "I think we've had enough of this place for one day. Let's get going."

Nick stood there hopping from one foot to the other. He really didn't know how to handle this.

"Er... Mum," he said cautiously. "Can I go to the hobby shop? I just want to look at something before we go."

"The hobby shop?" replied Marion, looking up in surprise. "But you don't like places like that Dominic."

"I know. But… but it's something I want to…to look at. It's Jamie's birthday soon," he added with a sudden burst of inspiration.

"It's your friend's birthday in four months time if I remember rightly, and you hardly ever see him since we've moved here."

"I know, but I think there's something he particularly wanted in there. I may not see one again."

"But Jamie only likes computers."

Nick clenched his teeth. "Well, this is sort of a computer type thing."

"In a hobby shop?"

"Yes," spluttered Nick, feeling totally frustrated.

Marion shrugged her shoulders.

"Well it's up to you. I'll stay here and have another coffee. Do you want to go with him David?"

Nick put his hands behind his back and crossed his fingers.

Dave, who'd been watching this interaction with an amused grin on his face, shook his head.

"No my sweet. I'll stay here and get us another drink. Have you got any change?"

Nick's spirits rose.

"But don't be long," yelled Marion.

"No."

"And don't go spending all your..." but the words faded into the general melee as he rushed away in the direction of the food hall.

*

The hobby shop appeared strangely out of place in a modern shopping centre with its mock old fashioned window panes and heavy wooden door.

Nick gazed at the display in the window. In one corner was a large, remote controlled car, in the other an assorted group of planes. In the centre was a bewildering array of model cars and behind them a group of figures from various science fiction films. Some he recognized, some he didn't.

He stared from one model to another but there seemed to be absolutely nothing out of the ordinary in any of them. Occasionally someone would come over and scrutinize the window's contents, then walk away. He tried to look interested but it wasn't easy when there was nothing for him to be interested in.

He'd been standing there for a good five minutes, feeling hugely self-conscious when something in the middle of the display caught his eye.

He glanced round furtively to make sure he was alone then peered closer.

One of the figures in the shadows behind the cars suddenly leapt forward. Nick was so taken aback he nearly jumped out of his skin. The tiny figure looked like some sort of ancient warrior, wearing a startling white robe adorned with gold braid. His golden hair was immaculately swept back, his golden beard perfectly trimmed. On his feet were golden sandals and in one hand he clutched a long, slender spear. In the other hand however, he held a battered black bag that rather detracted from the overall impression.

The warrior bent down and shuffled around in the bag before grandly pulling out an old fashioned scroll. He unrolled it and held it up dramatically for Nick who once more glanced round cautiously before leaning so close to the window that his nose was almost touching.

He squinted at the tiny scroll and frowned. There was nothing to read.

The warrior leaned forward, looking puzzled. He stared at the parchment for a moment, then with a flourish, turned it round and held it aloft.

Nick peered again. With a heavy sigh he shook his head.

For the second time the warrior scrutinized the scroll. This time, with a sheepish smile, he turned it the right way up.

Nick's nose squashed against the glass. He could just make out some words.

'We despratly need your help.
Take me with you to Hightower – NOW
A matter of great urgensey!'

Despite his utter astonishment Nick couldn't help but smile. Spelling had never been the Elvereys strong point!

The warrior was standing absolutely still once more and Nick suddenly realized he was no longer the only person looking at the display. A little boy was standing next to him. He stepped back and pointed vaguely to one of the planes in the corner.

"They're my favourites," he said, trying to get the boy's attention as far away as possible. "Those … jet type things. I like them best."

The boy looked at him in a confused way and shuffled away without saying a word.

Nick turned back to the window and nodded, to which the warrior, quick as a flash, folded the parchment back into the bag, dragged open the door of a bright red sports car and with a dramatic wave of his hand, proceeded to squeeze inside, head first.

The whole affair didn't go too slickly however, owing to the fact that the car was on a smaller scale than the figure, whose robe was riding up as he pushed into the rear seat, revealing large, very un-warrior like underpants as he did so. When he was finally in place, an arm probed back out and dragged the bag in with equal difficulty. Finally the spear was squeezed in, though the first attempt at shutting the door left the somewhat sharp tip sticking out. It took three more attempts, one of which he caught his finger on the tip, before the door would finally shut.

When all this action was finally completed his head appeared in the tiny back window. The hair looked a lot more dishevelled and he was sucking blood from his finger, but his expression looked dramatically triumphant at such a successful operation.

Nick just stood there, fascinated by the events but unsure as to what to do next.

He pulled himself together. There was only one thing he could do, so he checked he had sufficient money, and with a deep breath entered the shop.

A little bell jingled as he shut the door behind him, drowning out the noise outside. Inside the smell of plastic and glue was overpowering in such cramped confines.

Thankfully, the only person in the place was the assistant, a thin, lanky man with an enormous crooked nose.

"Afternoon. May I help you," he asked with a withering smile.

"Er…yes," replied Nick anxiously. "I'm after a model. A car. The car in the window." He pointed at the sports car.

"Ah, the GT 420. I'll just get you one from the storeroom."

"No, it's all right," said Nick, his heartbeat quickening. "I'll take that one."

The assistant's eyes narrowed.

"But that's the display model. You need one that's already boxed up."

"No," said Nick a little too hurriedly. "I'm perfectly happy with that one. I… I don't need a box for it. I… I want to play with it now."

"Play? But it's not a toy. It's a model. That's a GT 420 with fully integrated…"

"Please," snapped Nick, "I just want that one there."

"You'll not get any reduction for it being on display," replied the assistant, eyeing him suspiciously.

Nick sighed. "I know. I just want that one."

The man thought for a moment, then shrugged his shoulders and grabbed the car from the display.

"Careful," yelled Nick, snatching the car from the astonished assistant, who jumped back as though expecting to be attacked.

Nick laughed in a nervous, embarrassed way as he cradled the car in his arms, keeping it as level as possible.

"That'll be £29.95," the assistant muttered, his eyes fixed on Nick, a wary, confused frown on his face.

Nick placed the money on the counter.

"Would you like a bag for that?"

"Uh?"

"A bag?"

"Oh…yes please."

Keeping a discreet distance between them, the man leaned forward and passed the bag over, his frown deepening as Nick very, very carefully placed the car inside.

"Thank you," said Nick, trying to smile.

"A pleasure," came the cautious reply, a look of sympathy replacing the earlier concern.

Great, thought Nick as he walked out. What a day! Half this place thinks I'm a mummy's boy, the rest think I'm either some weirdo type of toilet vandal or that I'm just stark, staring mad!!

*

"It seems such a shame that it's all got to be destroyed," said Marion sadly as they were walking back through the car park.

"Progress," replied Dave gruffly. "It's impossible to find an empty parking space here. Getting rid of that lake and a few trees is the best thing that could happen."

Nick glanced over at the railings bordering off the rather pretty little lake. There was a tiny island in the centre and a couple of swans floating on its rippling water.

Standing ominously by the railings was an excavator.

"I suppose you're right," said Marion, shaking her

head. "Those poor swans though, losing their homes like that."

"Yeah terrible," replied Dave, stifling a yawn.

"Shouldn't they have gone now? You know, mitigated for the winter?"

Dave chuckled. "You mean migrate?" The chuckle turned into a nasty laugh. "If they do, they'd better hurry up and do it. All that lot will be gone in a few days."

He pointed his key at a large black four by four with shiny alloy wheels. With a high pitched beep the lights flashed and almost immediately the vehicle began to rock as Duke, barking thunderously, leapt from side to side behind the heavy mesh grill in the back.

Dave wrenched his door open.

"Shut that racket up," he yelled as he settled in behind the wheel.

The dog stopped barking but kept prowling round and round in its tiny space, carefully watching as Nick edged into the back seat and gently placed his new purchase on the seat beside him. He took the receipt out and glared at it. £29.95! For something he didn't even want! He threw the receipt onto the seat beside him.

In the back, Duke snarled menacingly.

He disliked Duke as much as he disliked Dave. The creature was an unbelievably huge, ugly and vicious black brute with no redeeming qualities. It always seemed to be snarling, or barking, or eating vast amounts of food. Everyone was frightened of the thing, a fact that Dave seemed immensely proud of.

Today, Duke seemed even more hostile than ever. As they roared out of the car park he growled and clawed at the mesh, saliva dripping from his mouth as his eyes stared down at the bag on the seat. The mesh rattled in its frame as the animal threw its weight against it and

Nick was worried whether it would actually hold.

"Duke, settle down," shouted Dave. Marion, sitting next to him, glanced round nervously.

The dog snarled and banged the mesh again.

Dave's eyes glared furiously in the rear view mirror.

"DUKE! Settle down. NOW! I really don't know what's wrong with you today."

Nick picked up the bag and carefully placed it on the floor out of sight. The dog reluctantly settled down.

He looked out of the window. Fog was coming down. Inside, a drowsy wasp flew slowly from the glass and disappeared under the seat. Typical, he mused with a vague feeling of satisfaction. Dave thought he'd got rid of the rats but obviously he hadn't, now he couldn't even get rid of the wasps!

His thoughts drifted. Even by his standards it had been an unbelievably bewildering day.

Not one tiny world, but two!

Did that mean that somewhere there was another overseer, someone he could talk to about his secret? Someone who could travel with him to these incredible places?

But was he doing the right thing taking this complete stranger into his world; the place he was sworn to protect?

Did he have a choice?

Deep down, he thought not.

He leaned forward and stared into the bag on the floor. It was too dark to make out anything inside. He hoped the warrior was all right.

As he peered down a thrill pulsed through him, washing away the earlier thoughts that things were starting to get a little too mundane. Somehow, he had a feeling that mundane was going to be the last thing that life was going to be!

Chapter 3

HERCULES

Nick raced up the stairs two at a time and barged into his bedroom. He carefully placed the bag on the desk next to the cage containing his strange communication system, Polly the parrot, and without stopping to take his jacket off, bent down as close to the cage as possible.

"Who's a pretty boy then?" he whispered, keeping a close eye on the bedroom door and thinking, as always, what a ridiculous way to make contact that sentence was!

Almost immediately a crackling sound came from the bird.

"Nicky, you're back. How did the operation go? Did you form a pincer movement to cut off their 4th division and leave their right flank exposed."

"Not now Church," snapped Nick. "Tell the rest of the committee we have to meet, now, down at the cave. Tell them it's an emergency."

There was a moment's pause.

"I certainly will captain. I'll organize all the troops to assemble at...er, seventy three hundred hours. They'll parade in full..."

"NOW Church!"

"Now," repeated the voice. "Oh, we'll be there sooner than that sir."

The crackling noise intensified for a second and then was gone.

Nick peered into the bag. There was no sign of movement inside the car and he was worried that the figure might have suffocated or been crushed to death somehow.

"Hello," he whispered, feeling rather self conscious at talking into a bag! "I'm going to take you to meet the others. I'm sorry I can't get you out of there yet but it's too dangerous."

He paused as footsteps trudged upstairs and went into the bathroom. He was aware just how often his mum would walk into his room unannounced, no matter how many times he complained about this lack of privacy.

"Not long now though," he added comfortingly.

He checked his pocket and took out a tiny stick, feeling that familiar sense of relief, knowing the shrinkage post was always in his possession. After the troubles in the early days he no longer thought it wise to keep the thing down at the cave where anyone could take it. After all, losing the shrinkage post meant losing the most important contact with Elverey. Not that anyone else could use it. As overseer, he was the only one it would work for.

The bathroom door clicked shut and the footsteps went back downstairs.

He waited a few moments, then grabbed the bag and rushed down to the kitchen.

Marion, with hands on hips, glared at him still in his jacket.

"Dominic, for heavens sake, you're not going out there again. It's cold and dark and the fog's coming down."

"Won't be long Mum," he answered, reaching for the back door.

"No more than thirty minutes then," she replied with a stern look. "Tea will be ready and poor David's got to go back to work."

"Yeah, poor David," muttered Nick as he leapt out into the cold and raced down the garden. With a furtive glance over his shoulder he dragged the bushes aside down by the shed to reveal a narrow path winding through the trees beyond.

He picked his way down the steps in the gloom, acutely aware of the huge number of Elvereys living their everyday lives, wandering the corridors in the overhanging branches above and shopping in the enormous arcades in the tree trunks, for this was the region of Miru, the main shopping area of Elverey.

Before he reached the stream and the old stone bridge that contained the housing complex in the region of Glug, he turned off the path, brushing his way through the undergrowth before squeezing through a tiny opening in the rock wall. Inside was a small cave that was light, fresh and warm. A curious, contented feeling of returning home overcame him.

He took the car out of the bag and placed it on the stone floor, then fumbled in his pocket and took out the shrinkage post. He stared at it for a second and held his breath. He never liked this bit and as always his heart was beating very fast as he turned the ring on his thumb around till it could connect easily with the top of the post.

He pressed the two together.

Instantly that familiar screeching sound pierced his brain and his body felt like it was being ripped apart from the inside. He closed his eyes tight shut and clenched his teeth till the pain subsided and he stood there trembling, leaning heavily on the cane that moments earlier had been a tiny stick.

His senses took some moments to adjust to their new surroundings. The cave was now a huge hall. Tiny stones were now large boulders. The red sports car now looked almost like a real car.

Almost, but not quite! It was slightly smaller than a real car. Its metal looked a little too thick, its wheels a little too heavy. At this size and at such close quarters the whole thing looked a bit crude and poorly built.

Nick put the shrinkage post down and ran to the car. His hand was on the door, ready to drag it open when a peculiar hissing noise behind him made him pause.

Very slowly he turned round, his hand frozen to the door handle.

In the shadows at the far corner of the hall something was squeezing through a tiny crack in the wall. It was difficult to make out at first, just a large, long flowing shape, sliding ominously forward.

The loud hissing noise filled the hall.

Nick tried to swallow but his mouth was too dry. His mind now recognized only too clearly what it was he was looking at.

"No," he muttered hoarsely as the snake slithered towards him, its tongue flicking in and out as its tiny black eyes homed on its prey.

He just stood there, unable to move. Somewhere at the back of his mind was the knowledge that insects and rodents couldn't hurt them when inside the boundaries of Elverey. But did that apply to reptiles?

The thing slithered closer and closer with incredible speed. Nick stared anxiously at the ground where the shrinkage post lay. Already it was too late to make a grab for it. The snake was upon him. It was so big that he had to look up towards the ceiling as it towered over him, its head wavering from side to side, the scales looking huge on its shiny, silver body.

Suddenly the head lunged towards him. He leaned back against the car in terror as it opened its mouth revealing huge white fangs. Its breath felt warm and smelt sour. The tongue flicked forward, then the forked edge just dropped to the floor and the whole thing became totally motionless.

"Nicky hi," said a figure emerging from behind the fangs.

Nick put his hand to his chest. His heart was thudding against his ribcage.

"Ayisha? Oh, hi," he replied, his voice trembling.

Ayisha bounced down the tongue, looking radiant in a flowing red dress, her hair swirling round her pretty face.

"Sorry if we startled you a bit," she said brightly, giving him a hug.

"Me? No, not really," he replied dismissively with a vague wave of a still trembling hand.

"Nicky. Church... Royal Engine Noses, reporting for duty as ordered sir."

Nick glanced over Ayisha's shoulder at Church marching down the tongue, dressed in a baggy military outfit with generous amounts of blackening covering his face.

"Royal what?" asked Nick, looking puzzled.

"Royal Engine Noses," repeated Church with a sloppy salute.

Nick scratched his head and thought for a moment before bursting out laughing.

"Church, I think you mean Royal Engineers, not Engine Ears or Engine Noses!"

"Oh, I get it," replied Church, but it was pretty obvious from the vacant expression that he didn't.

"Have you been watching war films?"

The little Elverey nodded. The whiteness of his eyes

seemed unnaturally bright against the blackness of the camouflage.

"Got to be prepared for any eventualities sir. So, what do you think of the new snake-mobile? It'll be absolutely unbeatable in snow."

"If it doesn't break down again," giggled Ayisha.

"It just glides over the terrain, using my revolutionary new Optimum Overland Proceeding System."

"Or OOPS for short," replied Ayisha, the giggling getting louder.

"Nicky! How are you," yelled a voice from above.

Nick looked up to see a much older figure, with short grey hair and a trimmed grey beard, leaning heavily against one of the fangs.

"I'm fine Varn, and how are you?" he enquired mischievously, knowing full well what the reaction would be.

As if on cue the old Elverey bent double, convulsed by a sudden spasm of violent coughing. Church rushed back up and gently escorted him down.

"Oh you know me. I'm not one to complain but the old chest isn't as strong as it was; and the palpitations seem to be getting worse. The muscle ache appears to be improving but now it feels like it's going into the other arm."

By the time he'd finally reeled off the remaining ailments the four of them were standing facing each other and Nick had quite forgotten about their new visitor.

Forgotten that is, until a loud banging noise suddenly erupted from inside the car.

"Whatever's that?" muttered Varn, wiping his watering eyes on his checked shirt.

Nick wasn't quite sure whether he meant the noise or the car.

"That?" he replied anxiously. "Well, apparently that's a GT 420!"

"A what?"

"A GT 420."

"But what's it doing here?"

Before Nick could answer the car shook violently and the white underpants appeared at the side window as the warrior used his backside to push the door open.

With a considerable amount of grunting and cursing the figure squeezed out of the tiny opening backwards. He then pulled the bag out and threw it to the ground, before leaning back in and, with great difficulty dragged the spear out, a difficult manoeuvre as it seemed stubbornly wedged between the windscreen and the back seat.

Nick, Ayisha,Varn and Church all stood in open mouthed fascination as with a roar, followed by a yell of pain the newcomer wrenched the spear out of the car at the fourth attempt, the blunt end catching him just above the eye. As he staggered backwards he tripped over the bag and landed in a heap on the cave floor.

He immediately leapt to his feet and turned to face them, grabbing the spear and smoothing his hair back into place before striking a pose of composed self importance.

There was a long awkward silence.

Just as Nick was about to speak the warriors eyes widened and his muscular body tensed. In his right hand he held the spear, ready to throw. His left hand he raised, imploring those before him not to move.

"Stay exactly where you are," he yelled theatrically. "For behind you has crept an enormous dragon. I shall strike it to the very earth before it devours you all."

The mouths of the four of them opened still further. Nick found it difficult not to laugh. He reckoned this medieval looking character might well be some great warrior but observation obviously wasn't one of his strong points. It had taken him quite a while to notice Church's huge snake-mobile towering behind them!

"It's all right," he said reassuringly. "That's our...our form of transport."

The figure relaxed.

"Your chariot?" He turned to the GT 420. "You mean, like mine?"

"Sort of," replied Nick, smiling.

There was another prolonged silence, then everyone seemed to talk at once.

"Who are you...?"

"Where are you from....?"

"Why are you here...?"

The warrior held a hand aloft for silence.

"I..." he said slowly and dramatically, "... am Hercules!"

The others looked at each other in bemused silence.

Hercules obviously thought the mere mention of his name was sufficient to answer all their questions.

"Well, hello Hercules," said Nick at last. "I am..."

"I know who you are," he replied pompously. "You are Dominic Collins of Hightower cottage."

"I prefer Nick or Nicky."

Hercules stroked his perfectly trimmed beard as if giving the name a great deal of consideration before nodding gravely.

"...And these are members of Hightower's overseer committee, Varn, Church and Ayisha."

A curt nod to each one was followed by a lingering, appreciative gaze and a knowing smile for Ayisha who appeared far from impressed by the attention.

"So, what exactly were you doing at that shopping complex today?" asked Nick. "Are you from another group of Elvereys or something?"

"Another world?" spluttered Ayisha amidst gasps from the other two.

Hercules bent over the bag and pulled out another parchment with a flourish.

"I am Hercules," he repeated grandly. "I am on the overseer committee of Barrowhouse."

"Barrowhouse?" whispered Church.

"I have been entrusted with the greatest and noblest of tasks. It is my duty. It is my quest. I have sworn to succeed or die trying. I shall strike my enemies to the very earth in order to complete my work. It is why I am here today."

"Er…right," said Nick cautiously. "But what exactly is this task?"

Hercules unfolded the parchment with great deliberation.

Nick wasn't surprised when he had to turn it the other way up, an operation that took some time as the paper creased and got caught in the folds of his robe as he did so.

The audience waited patiently.

"I am entrusted with the task of reading this message to you from the Elvereys of Barrowhouse."

Nick stood there transfixed. Another Elverey world! He could hardly believe it. By the expressions on his friends faces it was obvious they felt the same way.

"We, the Elvereys of Barrowhouse, desperately need your help. Our world will soon be destroyed forever. We cannot trace our overseer. We are alone. In the next few days we will either all be dead or our world will be discovered. Neither possibility can be allowed to happen. Please help us!"

Hercules slowly rolled up the parchment and placed it back in the bag.

"But why?" was all Nick could think of to say.

Hercules clasped his hands together, a deep frown creasing his forehead.

"I am entrusted with returning you, and anyone who wishes to go with you, to Barrowhouse so you can see for yourself. All your questions will be answered there."

"Back to Barrowhouse? When?"

"Now! Time is of the essence."

"But I can't just…"

"You have to. There is no time."

Nick sighed and glared at the others. An eager excitement radiated from them that was infectious.

"OK," he said cautiously, "but how could we get there at this time?"

"What about your chariot?" replied Hercules, pointing at the snake.

Varn shook his head.

"Too slow," he said.

"It'd break down anyway," muttered Ayisha.

"How about flying there?" asked Church eagerly. "We could go in Polly."

"Not tonight," replied Nick. "It's getting too foggy. We'd never find our way."

He wished that Paul and Laura were around. They had been entrusted with the secret of the Elvereys and had helped him out of scrapes before. They lived close by, just up the lane in fact, but they were away for the weekend and wouldn't be back till late tomorrow.

He glanced at his watch. It was time to go. His tea was ready and there would be all kinds of trouble if he wasn't back on time. It was a thought that brought with it a sudden inspiration.

They were having an early tea so Dave could go back to work…at Barrowhouse!!

"Church," he yelled triumphantly. "If I can sort out our transport, can you sort out how to get the team to it?"

"No problem sir," replied Church with a smart salute. "You just tell me where and what time and the troops will be there."

Hercules nodded approvingly.

"This fellow is obviously of a strong military background. Professional, reliable and competent, just like me."

Ayisha stifled a giggle.

"Right," said Nick, thinking furiously. "Dave will be leaving in the next hour. We're going with him; in his car!"

"Dave?" replied Church coldly. The Elvereys disliked Marion's boyfriend almost as much as Nick did.

"Yeah. I'll make sure its open for you to sneak in. I'll have to sort myself out because the timings going to be difficult. I'll get in, shut the door, shrink down and meet up with rest of you. You sure you can sort yourselves out?"

There was much nodding of heads.

"Don't worry Nicky," said Church happily. "I'll sort us out."

Nick looked dubiously at the little Elverey,

"Look, I've got to go," he said anxiously. "Hercules, will you be all right with the others?"

"Of course," he replied with a look of maddening superiority. "I shall protect you all."

He leaned confidently on the car, which rolled backwards and he fell, banging his head on one of the headlamps.

A furious droning sound suddenly erupted above them. Nick glanced up to see an enormous dragonfly, with its thin, tapered body and sparkling, delicate wings, hovering near the ceiling.

Hercules staggered to his feet, spear in hand.

"Stand back," he ordered. "I shall fight this demon. I shall strike this devil to the very earth."

As the dragonfly circled lower, Nick could just make out two shapes, one in front of the other, sitting on the insect's body.

Unlike the appearance of the snake he didn't feel concerned by this apparition.

"Hold on," he said to Hercules. "I don't think it's going to attack us."

As if to confirm Nick's words, as the dragonfly banked in for its landing, the figure sitting behind waved down to them.

The droning noise increased as the insect slowed, its wings vibrating at incredible speed as it hovered downward before gently dropping to the ground, the delicate legs soaking up the impact.

Even before the four wings had ceased vibrating the second figure jumped down and began running towards them.

"Jed," cried out Nick. "What are you doing here?"

Jed pushed the old fashioned flying goggles up over his ruffled hair and grinned at his friend.

"Old Mr.S heard your call to the others through Polly and asked if I wanted to come over."

Nick was amazed at how much Mr.Scoggins, Jed's guardian, had changed over the last few months. In the early days he'd been rude, uncooperative and generally obnoxious, but Nick had stood up to him and gradually, partly because he was the overseer, Mr.S had started to show him some grudging respect. He'd even been invited on occasions to their grubby little house inside a tree on the edge of the woods. As a lookout Mr.S had proudly shown him the insects he used to warn the Elverey world of any approaching humans.

Nick enjoyed seeing the hornets and the bats and how the whole warning system worked. He didn't however, enjoy the various culinary delights that Mrs.S tried to force him to eat and which always made him heave!

"Hi Jed," said Ayisha brightly. "Is Goldie not with you today?"

Nick shuddered. Goldie was Jed's pet beetle. He dragged it round on a lead. Despite being an ugly black brute of a thing it was quite placid. Trouble was, it was always getting in the way and everyone kept tripping over its legs!

"Nah," Jed replied. "Can't get on the dragonfly. He's back at home eating some of Mrs.S's fungus shoots."

Nick shuddered again.

Jed surveyed the group and his eyes widened.

"Hey, who's the strange guy in the frock?"

Hercules bristled. Nick hurriedly pulled Jed to one side, draping an arm round his shoulder. It wasn't easy, as despite being the same age, Jed was slightly the taller of the two.

"That's...that's..." he spluttered, trying to find a way of quickly explaining these new events, but time wasn't on his side and he gave up. "Look Jed, I've got to go, but if you're up for it, tonight could be very interesting."

Jed looked puzzled.

"The others will explain. See you later huh?"

Without waiting for an answer he grabbed the shrinkage post and with a cheery wave turned to leave.

"Well, well, well. Nice ter see yer again."

The voice made him pause.

"Yes, right... Nice to see you too Mr.Scoggins," he said politely.

The figure standing before him was still wearing his flying goggles, something as a blessing really as it disguised part of his ugly, scruffy face. The eyes narrowed as he squinted at the crowd near the snake.

"Somethin' goin' on then?"

"Er…yes," replied Nick, trying not to breath too deeply in such a close proximity. "They'll tell you about it. Jed may want to come with us later if that's all right?"

"S'pose so. So long as 'e tells me what's goin' on. I am one o' the lookouts after all."

"Of course Mr.Scoggins. Now I really must go."

Nick turned and ran. As he did he pressed the ring and the top of the shrinkage post together. He'd gone no more than two paces before his whole world began to scream and distort once more.

*

Nick ate his meal in silence, his thoughts totally immersed in recent events.

Afterwards he sneaked out to Dave's big car and opened the rear passenger door just enough to allow access for the others. He knew it wouldn't be locked. Dave didn't bother when he parked in the countryside.

Then he went up to his bedroom, telling his mum that he wanted to use his computer for a while before turning in for an early night.

Marion sighed but said nothing. This was, after all, quite normal behaviour as Nick always seemed to spend an awful lot of time on his own.

In his room he put on his warmest winter jacket before taking a head and shoulders model of himself from a secret compartment behind the wardrobe. He placed it on his pillow with the sheets pulled up as high as possible and pressed a switch behind the ear. The thing began to make soft breathing noises, interspersed occasionally with a low, rasping snore.

His mum rarely checked on him when she came to bed but it was always best to make sure. If she did speak to him, the Elvereys watching from behind the bedroom walls would send a reply via the model. He really didn't like the idea that the Elvereys could get access to his private room through the numerous invisible doors in the bedroom wall but at times like this it was somewhat useful.

He glanced out of his bedroom window. The back garden and the grounds beyond were pitch black.

It always seemed incredibly strange to him. Down there in the darkness, the Elvereys were living their lives. Even in the back garden of Hightower cottage there were some residents. Mr.and Mrs. Crumble and their two children lived in a plastic watering can hidden down in the far corner amongst the weeds. Inside, their home was clean and comfortable, though the big, high ceilinged rooms were rather strange shapes!

In the other corner, a wizened old lady called Mrs.Bloggwatch lived alone beneath the base of an ancient, gnarled rose bush along with her pet centipede Norbert.

Beyond the garden of course, the main population lived much closer together in their four distinct regions. Thousands upon thousands of them...and what strange people they were!

Nick's thoughts drifted back to one of the strangest days back in the summer when Jed and the overseer committee had taken him to Yada, the grassland area, to see the world famous (Elverey world that is!) Tary Arena.

They'd travelled up in a convoy of frogs, a hot, uncomfortable journey made worse by having to be tightly strapped in because of the bounce from the back legs as the things leapt forward in short, sharp bursts.

The moment Nick had squeezed out through the exit in the machines slimy side and jumped down, he'd immediately faced the immensely long stadium which was sunk down into the ground. The yellow sides were extremely steep, with row upon row of wooden seating interspersed by lines of wooden steps that descended to a large sports area below. At one end there was a silver circle with a domed silver door, which Nick assumed was where the competitors climbed up into the arena from. Above this, at the highest point of the narrow end and slightly off centre, the word 'TARY' stood out in fading black letters.

It took half an hour to climb down the steps and reach the arena floor, by which time a lunch had been laid out for them all. Not that he ate much, for he was much too pre-occupied by the spectacle around and above him. He made himself dizzy staring at the line upon line of steps and seats receding upwards into the distance.

An extremely tall, thin Elverey slowly approached the group, wearing what looked like a purple tracksuit that was at least two sizes too big for him, and a purple baseball cap, two sizes too small. The cap was turned so the peak was at the back and it perched precariously on top of long, greasy ginger hair.

The members of the overseer committee seemed totally in awe of him. They all shook his hand and Ayisha looked as though she was going to faint when he smiled at her.

"So pleased to meet you," he said slowly in a high pitched, vaguely irritating voice, when it was Nick's turn to shake hands.

"Thank you. It's a lovely stadium."

"It is. You must come to see the snail racing. Thursdays. That's the day the snail racing takes place. One race. Takes all day. Six snails. Sometimes the lead changes as many times as twice during a race. It really is exciting."

Nick doubted it, but nodded politely.

"Or, if you prefer something a little faster, there's worm racing on Tuesdays. Usually two races. One in the morning and, if there's time, one in the afternoon. Now that really is very exciting."

He plodded back to the others. Everyone gathered around, eager to hear more from the great man.

"Now, let me tell you some of the wonderful history of Tary stadium. Built in the seventies and developed over…"

But that was about as much as Nick could listen to. The next hour seemed like an eternity in the heat and the dust. Not that anyone else seemed to be bored. They all just stood there enthralled. Not a blink of an eye, or a movement of any sort as they soaked up every word.

"…and there is so much more to tell, but that will have to wait for another day. I've taken enough of your time already."

You can say that again, thought Nick as the rest of the group broke out in spontaneous applause. Finally, they said their goodbyes and started the long climb back up the steps.

Jed was virtually beside himself at having shaken the great man's hand. Nick couldn't understand it. Twice he asked Jed exactly what he was famous for as they made their way back to the frogs. Neither time did he get a satisfactory explanation; just something to do with worms and snails. In the end, Nick reckoned that in the odd world of Elverey sport, the scrawny purple weirdo was one of those characters that was just famous for being famous!

The sound of Dave's voice downstairs dragged Nick's thoughts back to the present. He slipped out of his bedroom and into the bathroom to wash his face and hands. Turning the tap, the water swirled into the yellow washbasin. His gaze drifted to the words;

JAMES HARDWYN AND SON
FINE SANITARY WARE

-written in faded letters just above the overflow outlet.

He had to smile.

Behind him, the bath was white and relatively new. The old yellow one had been replaced many years ago and his grandfather, when he'd been overseer, had put it in the ground up in Yada, hidden behind weeds and bramble bushes. The Elvereys had converted it into the very large, very impressive stadium. Over the years the words had faded till only the letters 'TARY' from the word SANITARY were still visible.

He was still smiling as he crept quietly down the stairs and sneaked out the door.

Dave's big four by four stood in the drive, swathed in mist. The air was fresh but cold and he pulled up his collar as he rushed to the back door and slipped inside. He didn't even have time to check if the others had made it before a ray of light pierced out of the cottage and footsteps crunched down the gravel path.

With a dull click he shut the door and the tiny interior light went out.

He knelt on the seat, holding his breath, his heart pounding as he pressed the ring and post together.

The transformation always seemed to take an eternity whenever he needed it to happen quickly. By the time the screeching noise had subsided and his senses were returning to normal Dave had reached the car.

He grabbed the shrinkage post and ran across the heavy fabric, frantically searching for somewhere to hide. There was nowhere, so he crouched down in the shadows at the farthest corner of the seat, feeling open and vulnerable.

"Come on Duke my lad. You can sit behind me. Better than being squashed into that cage huh?"

"Oh no," muttered Nick, fearfully. He stared up at the enormous door as a spectral black figure engulfed the entire glass screen. He tried to squeeze further back but there was nowhere to go. He was trapped!

The door swung open and the inside light flicked on. He blinked despite the weakness of the beam. His limbs were trembling, his body numb with dread.

A gigantic black bag came flying towards him. He closed his eyes and covered his head as it crashed down onto the seat and he braced himself, waiting for it to topple over and crush him.

There was a moment's silence. He unfolded his arms and looked up cautiously. The bag towered over him like some huge dark wall. He relaxed just a fraction. At least here there might be some protection.

But the feeling was short lived. As he stared up a silhouette suddenly appeared above the bag.

Nick gasped and his blood turned to ice as a paralysing terror gripped him.

It was at that moment that Duke spotted the tiny figure of Nick huddled in the farthest corner of the seat… and when he did, all hell broke loose!

*

Chapter 4

DUKE

Everything happened in a flash. Nick saw the huge mouth with its vicious, razor sharp teeth and felt the stench of the hot, raw breath. There was a deafening roar of barking and snarling. Somewhere beyond came the vague sound of a man shouting.

In that split second numerous thoughts flashed through his terrified mind. Hide! Escape! Run!

Touch the shrinkage post!

If he did, he could never explain any of this to Dave. But he had no choice. In a fraction of a second he'd be eaten alive or torn to pieces. With trembling hands he reached for the top of the post. As he did, Duke lunged again, his fangs snapping so close he could feel the draught, spittle flooding from the demented dog's mouth.

The liquid engulfed him in one huge, pounding wave, knocking the post from his grasp and covering him in thick, slimy, evil smelling glob!

The man's voice screamed out again and the chain lead clanged taut. With a howl of angry frustration the head recoiled and the dog was finally dragged from the vehicle.

"What... is... wrong... with...you?" yelled Dave furiously above the incessant barking as Duke circled excitedly, furiously searching for a way to get round his master and renew the attack on his quarry.

To Nick, all the sounds seemed muffled and distorted, trapped inside his dribbling bubble of thick, gooey liquid. He could hardly breathe and panic swelled in his chest as he clawed at his nose and mouth, dragging thin white strands of the sticky mess from his face as his legs kicked out in an effort to break free. With a final lunge he rolled out into fresh air, coughing out lumps of the awful smelling, acrid tasting saliva.

"So, what were you after then boy? Let's see what that was all about." The voice was much sharper without Duke's drool as insulation.

Dave's shadow loomed over the interior light and Nick glanced round desperately. He struggled to his feet, his trainers slipping with the oozing moisture coating them. Without daring to look up he scanned round for the shrinkage post. It lay close to a piece of paper, engulfed in its own little globule of Duke's spittle.

He had no plan. He just grabbed the post, leapt under the paper, and crouched down.

The light brightened above him as Dave momentarily lifted the bag from the seat. The thin paper offered scant protection and he felt terribly vulnerable. He peered up anxiously but could see nothing apart from the huge figures '£29.95 – Thank you' on the white sheet covering him.

"Well I can't see…"

There was a brief pause. Nick closed his eyes tight shut, waiting for the moment of his detection.

"… Oh… DUKE!! Well, I'll tell you what. There's no way your sitting in this seat now boy. You're going in the back."

Nick opened his eyes and hesitantly peered under the paper. A huge blue monster was furiously sliding towards him, then away from him, then towards him, then away again. It made a harsh rasping sound as it rubbed across the small, sharp bristles of the seat.

He suddenly realized that the monster was an enormous blue cloth!

"How many times have I told you about slavering in this car?"

The rasping sound finally stopped. The barking stopped. The door at the back clunked open and Duke leapt into the rear compartment, making subdued noises that alternated between a whine and a growl.

Nick breathed a sigh of relief and his thudding heartbeat slowed. He cautiously slipped out from his paper hiding place and shuffled over to the relative safety of Dave's bag.

As he slipped into the shadows he thought he heard something near the open side door. It sounded like a shuffling or pattering noise, though considering the state of his battered senses it could have been nothing but his imagination.

But was it the others? They obviously hadn't been around when he'd had his little altercation with Duke, so where were they? Surely he wasn't going to end up going all this way on his own... and for nothing!

The back door slammed shut. The side door slammed shut. The front door opened...then slammed shut!

The engine roared into life.

Finally, they were on the move.

*

Tritus listened till the engine faded away into the fog laden night and smiled his mirthless, lopsided smile.

This was the first time he'd felt well enough to venture out of the old home. Considering recent events it had been well worth the effort.

He breathed in the cold, moist air and closed his one good eye, savouring the clear freshness of the outside world. In his pocket was the folded paper. He sighed contentedly.

A hooded figure emerged from the shadows and held out a crystal glass. The wine inside looked like blood in the darkness.

"Thank you my friend," whispered Tritus, noting with some satisfaction that the thin, bony hand bearing the glass was trembling.

Fear perhaps?

He took the glass and sighed again. Things were starting to come together. All the waiting he'd endured. All the work he'd had to do. Finally it was starting to pay off.

His thoughts turned to Napoleon. Just how much could he trust him? Enough, he reckoned, to complete his task. After all, didn't they both have the same common enemy?

Dominic Collins!!

Just the name was enough to switch his mood. He felt a surge of rage well up from deep within.

"A straw," he screamed, staring at the glass in his hand. "How can I drink this without a straw?"

With all his strength he flung the glass to the ground. The shards scattered into thousands of pieces, the liquid splattering across the floor like black tentacles.

He turned to the Deeber cowering in the shadows.

"You do this deliberately huh? You want to see me pour wine all over myself? You think it funny that I can't drink properly?"

In terror the figure slid to the floor and covered its head with its claw like hands.

Tritus paused. His chest was rising and falling in a fast, angry rhythm. He tried to breathe slowly in an effort to calm himself.

The plan, he thought. Concentrate on the plan.

Subconsciously, his hand went back to the pocket containing the paper. He felt soothed by its touch. Soon, he'd be able to use the person he'd shown to Napoleon.

But what absolutely no one knew was that there was now a second person to help him gain his final revenge over the boy.

He pulled the paper from his pocket, unfolded it, and stared at the name written on it with intense satisfaction.

…Mindi Pankhurst!

*

They'd been travelling for less than ten minutes and Nick was lying down to stop from rolling about, his body as close to the huge wall that was Dave's bag as possible. He was still trying to calm himself down from the earlier adventures when Duke's whining became a louder, more insistent growl as he tried to poke his snout through the wire mesh. The dog had obviously seen, or sensed something.

Through the mirror Dave glared at him.

"Don't start again boy," he warned.

The dog didn't seem to take any notice and Nick could feel himself tensing.

Suddenly, ahead of him, over the vast expanse of the seat, two paws emerged, followed by the tips of two pointed ears. The ears merged into the top of a head. As the head rose further, two bright eyes came into view.

A cat!

But not any cat.

Patch!

Nick scrambled to his feet and ran forward as Patch's

head rested on the front edge of the seat between the two paws.

As he approached, an arm waved to him from Patch's left ear. Behind him Duke's growl erupted into fully blown barking once more.

He leapt quickly onto the cat's nose, pulling himself up by the whiskers, and climbed up to the ear.

Church grabbed his hand and pulled him through the opening into the control area that was Patch's head. He beckoned Nick into the left seat, leapt into the right one, and began flicking switches and checking dials on the control panel. With a hefty pull on a lever, the view through the two screens in front of them began to change to a dark, shadowy world as Patch slid back down to the floor.

Nick sank back in the seat and sighed deeply. "Thanks Church, but for heaven's sake, turn the sound down."

Church beamed and fiddled with another switch in the bewildering array in front of him. Thankfully the deafening roar of Dukes barking softened to a muffled, more bearable level, along with the yells of 'Duke, SHUT UP' from Dave.

"That's better. Are the others here?"

Church nodded.

"Good. Let's go and sit with them. We've got plenty of time till we reach Barrowhouse and we've got to make a plan."

Church's smile managed to get even bigger.

"A plan. Of course. How about a three pronged pincer movement to cut off the enemy's left flank?"

Nick gave Church a withering look and jumped down the four steps into the cabin.

Although there were twelve seats in all, set out in pairs, Hercules was sat in the front pair, squeezed in next to Ayisha, who was looking distinctly uncomfortable.

The others, Varn and Jed were spread out in the remaining seats. Nick noticed, with some trepidation, the huge shiny black body of Goldie, Jed's pet beetle, lying on the last seat, numerous furry black legs hanging into the aisle.

Nick sat down in the other front seat, opposite Hercules. Church, the fifteen medals emblazoned across his chest rattling and clanging, sat in the one behind.

"Hi Nicky," said Ayisha, frowning. "You look all wet."

"And you stink..." added Jed.

"Yeah thanks," replied Nick, feeling self conscious. "Had a little trouble with our four legged friend out there."

"Is it catching?" asked Varn anxiously.

Nick ignored the question.

"So," he said with a heavy sigh. "Could someone tell me just who thought it was a good idea to come in Patch?"

"Me sir," replied Church with a vague attempt at a salute.

"Good military sense," agreed Hercules, sniffing and pulling a face at Nick's sodden clothes.

"Good sense?" repeated Nick incredulously. "You've come in a cat when we've got the dog from hell out there?"

No one spoke.

"Hasn't it occurred to anyone that cats and dogs don't actually get on. In fact, they positively hate each other?"

Still no one spoke.

"So Patch was probably the worst possible idea anyone could have come up with."

"Don't worry," said Church, still smiling. "We've made a contingency plan for the dog."

Nick felt even more worried as the Elvereys plans usually meant trouble.

"Contingency plan? What contingency plan?"

Church tapped the side of his nose. "You'll see," he said secretively.

"It's doozin' brilliant," cut in Jed.

"Truly excellent," agreed Hercules, frowning at Jed's language.

"Really very good," said Varn, dissolving into a fit of coughing.

Nick turned to Ayisha who seemed too pre-occupied with repelling the attentions of Hercules to be able to join in the conversation.

"OK," he said, giving up on the contingency plan. "But what about if we break down?"

"Break down?" repeated Church, feigning a look of hurt, yet still managing to smile.

"Yes, break down. Patch hasn't exactly got a great record in the reliability stakes. If I remember rightly, this thing breaks down like, every five minutes!"

"Church's sorted it all out. Worked really hard too," said Jed, leaping up on his seat.

Church nodded. "Perfectly reliable now. Total refit you see."

"Perfectly reliable," agreed Varn, wiping his brow. "Church, I think I'm getting a temperature. Can you turn the heating down a bit?"

"Sorry Varn I can't. It's broken."

Nick slapped his palm on his forehead in frustration.

"Look," he said as calmly as he could. "Whatever happens when we get there, we do nothing till I say, right?"

There was much nodding of heads.

"We want Dave and that dog out of the way. We stay here till they've gone. I'll slip out of Patch, use the shrinkage post, unlock the car, then come back to you. Understand?"

"I could deal with that dog," bellowed Hercules, making them all jump. "I would strike it to the very earth."

To emphasise the point, he banged his spear on the ground, nicking the edge of his sandaled toe as he did so.

"Er, yes," mumbled Nick. "But under these circumstances, I think we'll stick to the first plan. We'll need you to show us the way in. If you know it."

"Of course I know it," snapped Hercules, rubbing his toe.

"Hush," said Ayisha suddenly. "I think we're stopping."

Nick concentrated. It was true. The rocking sensation in the cabin had stopped.

"OK, looks like it's time to go."

Church grabbed a tin hat from the seat beside him and strapped it to his head.

"Action stations. Scramble. Every man for himself…"

"Church shut up," yelled Varn. "I'm getting a headache."

"Nice hat soldier," observed Hercules.

"Here," replied Church, handing another one over.

The large Elverey looked positively ridiculous as he perched the tiny tin hat on his huge head. Things deteriorated still further when, upon trying to fasten the strap under his chin he got his beard stuck in the buckle.

"Heaven help us," muttered Nick as he followed Church back up into the cat's head. These days he was used to the strange ways of the Elvereys, but they still had a remarkable ability to exasperate him!

*

50

"Can you see anything yet?" whispered Hercules over Nick and Church's shoulder as they stared out through the twin screens that were Patch's eyes.

"No more than the last couple of times you asked," replied Nick irritably.

"Let's see if we can see the door," mused Church, chewing on his lower lip in concentration as he pushed a tiny blue lever forward.

The cat's head swung slowly. The view was still vague but Nick could just make out the lower part of the rear passenger door.

A clunking noise suddenly echoed through the speaker and the screens lit up, momentarily dazzling them.

For a second Nick couldn't understand what had happened. The door was no longer there. He looked at the top of the screen. An enormous arm was bending down to pick up the bag on the seat above them. It blocked out some of the light for a moment, then both arm and bag withdrew.

"The light's still on," hissed Nick. "He's left the door open."

"Not very security conscious is he?" said Church.

"He's getting Duke out the back. Doesn't really need much security with that brute."

Hercules straightened up, banging his head for the third time.

Good job he's got the tin hat on thought Nick.

"Now is the time to make our escape," Hercules roared, deafening them both. "Onward. I shall show you the way. Onward on our valiant quest."

"No," snapped Nick. "We'll wait till it's safe."

But Church was like a coiled spring, desperately waiting for action.

"No," warned Nick again.

"Onward," repeated Hercules.

Church looked from one to the other, a momentary pause of indecision then, with a gleam in his eye he yelled, "Seventh cavalry...CHARGE," and slammed two levers in opposite directions.

Nick was thrown back in his seat. Hercules was thrown into the back wall. The screens in front of them showed the open doorway getting wider and wider till they suddenly plunged out into the fog shrouded car park.

"Which way?" cried Church.

A hand gripped the back of the seat and Hercules' head appeared between them, his tin hat at an angle, his golden hair sticking out in all directions.

"The left," he yelled, "towards the lake. No...no... To the right."

In frustration Church swung Patch first one way then the other. Screams and yells came from the cabin below.

"Yes... This way," roared Hercules, pointing to the left.

Church slammed the biggest lever forward and Patch picked up speed. The movement became much smoother once the cat got into its stride.

"Or is it the other way," muttered Hercules hesitantly.

As Nick and Church looked at him horror stricken, two things happened at virtually the same time.

The speaker above their heads picked up the familiar sound of barking...and Patch decided to break down!

"Great," yelled Nick, slamming his fist on the control panel. "I told you to wait. Now look at us."

"Let's see what's happening," said a subdued Church, pulling back the tiny blue lever.

"I think we know what's happening. Our pal Duke's seen us."

"Let's just check this out."

"…And our ultra reliable Patch has broken down. Like you said it wouldn't!"

The screen turned.

Through the mist they could see Dave's vehicle. The back door was up. Duke was barking madly and straining at the leash and Dave was struggling to hold him.

"We may need the contingency plan," said Church hurriedly. "Nicky, would you and Hercules help Jed. I've shown him what to do. I'll stay here and get Patch working."

Nick was so furious he couldn't think of anything else to say. He and Hercules leapt down into the cabin. Jed was already at the back, squeezing up into a compartment high up on the back wall.

It was an even tighter squeeze for Hercules to get through. Nick averted his eyes. He'd seen quite enough of the great warrior's underpants for one day!

When it was his turn he forced his way in and found himself in what looked like a small storage room. It was gloomy and smelt musty. What little light there was seemed to come from a large hole at the back. Through it he could see the car park. Unfortunately, through it he could also see Duke… and at that moment Duke, still wound up from his earlier confrontations, broke free from a startled Dave and began hurtling towards them, the chain sparking as it bounced off the ground.

"The plan?" he screamed at Jed. "What's the plan?"

With a confident nod, Jed pointed to a large, long shape on the floor behind Hercules.

Nick leapt over and grabbed one end. Hercules grabbed the other. They heaved it up. It felt heavy and smelt sickly sweet.

"Jed? What is it?"

"It goes through here," replied Jed, pointing to the hole. "It's a bone," he said grandly.

Nick's stomach felt like it had fallen through the floor. The great contingency plan! A bone!!

As they hauled it across the room he saw out the corner of his eye that the dog was about to strike.

"You really think...pushing a...bone through a...cat's bottom...is going to...stop that...thing?" he spluttered between gasps for breath as they heaved the thing into the opening.

...But incredibly it did; for a few moments anyway.

Whether it was the sight of a bone coming out the rear of a cat, or the weird aroma of the bone itself, Duke hesitated, then stopped. He eyed Patch furtively as he sniffed the bone and one ear pricked up when he heard his master calling his name. For a moment he seemed uncertain what to do, then the ear flicked back into place and with a disdainful look at the bone, he let out a deep, vicious growl and leapt at the cat.

But those few moments had given Church time to patch up Patch. As the dog leapt, the cat shot off, leaving Duke clutching nothing.

The sudden movement caught Nick off guard and he almost fell through the opening. Only Jed, grabbing his arm, saved him from a fall to the ground and another meeting with Duke.

"Thanks mate," he mumbled and Jed grinned happily.

It was no easy task to get back up to Church. Nick struggled through the violently rocking cabin, clinging onto seats for support, tripping over Goldie's legs and grabbing Ayisha's hand, before pulling himself up the steps.

Church was still strapped in his seat, concentrating hard as his hands flashed across the controls, but he managed a weak smile when he saw Nick.

Nick staggered into his seat, fastening the belt as he stared at the screens. The main doors of the shopping complex were getting closer and closer. They swished open and suddenly they were inside, rushing down enormous corridors, the shuttered shop fronts flashing past.

"Which way?" cried Church.

"Dunno. Is Duke still with us do you think?"

Church twisted another dial and barking immediately blasted from the speaker above them.

"Yep," they both said in unison.

"We need to get out of here," yelled Hercules from behind. "Not that way.To the right."

The cat streaked round the corner and Hercules grabbed the back of Nick's seat.

"Now the left," cried Hercules.

The cat skidded to the left and Hercules grabbed the back of Church's seat.

"Uh oh," said Hercules awkwardly.

Nick felt that wave of panic again.

"What's 'uh oh' mean Hercules?"

"I think we've gone the wrong way."

Ahead of them was the eating area with the huge Christmas tree in the centre. People visiting the cinema still occupied one or two of the tables. They looked on in startled bewilderment as an old cat, chased by a huge dog, raced across the tiled floor. The cat, its legs a blur at such speed, tucked its tail low to keep it from the thrashing jaws of the dog as it took an enormous leap into the lowest branches of the tree. Baubles scattered across the floor as it grabbed for the next branch, slipped, and fell back to the ground.

It turned and faced the dog.

The dog stopped and eyed the cat.

If a dog could ever exude an air of victory, this one

did. It surveyed its prey, savouring its moment of success.

"Oops," said Church softly as they stared into the face of Duke. "Forgot I'd taken the climbing programme out when I did the re-fit."

Nick stared at the screen. Behind Duke he could see the people rising slowly from their seats. They looked unsure and frightened. Nobody wanted to tackle this beast.

Strangely, he felt calm. All his senses seemed to have been drained. The shrinkage post was at his side but he couldn't use it. If he tried, maybe he'd rip Patch apart as he grew, but maybe Patch would retain him and he'd be crushed. When the dog attacked they might be thrown out and he could save his friends. Maybe...

Through the speaker he heard a strange buzzing sound. It reminded him of the hornets Mr.Scoggins would send out to warn the Elvereys at Hightower of approaching humans. But these weren't anything to do with Mr.S. This was way too far out of his territory.

Suddenly, four wasps shot into view. They buzzed around Duke's head, flying into his ears, hovering round his nose. He snapped at them, flinging his head from side to side as he backed off, snapping and snarling.

"Come on Church," bellowed Nick. "Let's get out of here while we can."

Patch shot off once more, dodging round Duke and leaping down the corridor towards the front door. They swung round a particularly tight corner ...

"Look out..." yelled Nick as a pair of familiar black boots flashed onto the screen. They lurched to the right, leapt over the boots, and scampered through the exit doors before a bewildered Dave had any chance to react.

But it was obvious that Duke had escaped his tormenters, for the ominous barking sounds were blasting through the speaker once more.

"Doesn't that thing ever give up?" said Nick.

"That way…over by the trees," yelled Hercules.

Considering Hercules navigating skills Nick was dubious but Church turned towards the trees. As he did so, he leaned forward in his seat.

"Whatever are those?" he stammered, frowning at the screen.

Nick squinted into the gloom. Four indistinct white shapes stood in front of them.

"Yes…" cried Hercules, raising a fist in the air.

The mist cleared a little and the lake came into view. The shapes, standing at the waters edge, became more distinct.

"Swans?" whispered Nick, bemused.

"Swans," agreed Hercules triumphantly. "Keep going Church. Stop this chariot in the middle of them."

Church shrugged and manoeuvred Patch between the swans. He swung the cat's head to face Duke who was thundering towards them.

The dog slowed, hesitated, and eyeballed the newcomers. The first two swans waddled forward a couple of paces, leaned their necks forward, and hissed menacingly.

Duke's head recoiled in surprise. He looked at each swan in turn, head cocked on one side as though deciding what to do, then down at Patch, and with one last growl, turned and padded away.

The swans watched carefully as the dog melted into the mist, tail between its legs, looking totally exhausted.

From the cabin below came a loud cheer. From the speaker above came Dave's voice screaming furiously at Duke.

"Well that went well I thought," said Church cheerfully.

Before Nick could think of a reply, one of the swans

bent down to Patch, its head wavering on its long, thin neck. Gradually, the head descended lower and lower till its beak was resting on Patch's ear.

Nick and Church heard a thump and a bang by the ear. They looked at each other, puzzled.

"I think someone wants to come in," observed Church.

Nick shrugged. "Well seeing as they've just saved us, I suppose we'd better let them."

Church grinned and pressed a button.

Almost immediately a shadow appeared in the ear doorway.

Hercules stood up, banging his head yet again.

"Hello Hercules," said a female voice. "You do realize we should have all touched base two hours twenty seven minutes ago. Honestly, it's totally thrown my schedule out. I've had to cancel two important meetings already."

Hercules stood with hands on hips.

"My quest was fraught with danger. Had I been able to get out, I would have fought that monster. I would have struck it …"

"…to the very earth; yeah, yeah," the stranger replied disdainfully, stepping away from the entrance and out of the shadows.

Nick was taken aback. The newcomer looked somewhat different to most Elvereys. She was short, with black hair, scraped back from a severe, humourless face. Her suit was black and smart, with a crisp white blouse. Hooked to one ear was some sort of phone system that constantly flashed an irritating blue light. In her left hand she carried a lap-top in a case. In her right hand was another mobile phone. It looked like she was just stepping out of some high powered executive meeting.

"Well we're here now," Hercules said huffily.

Not much thanks to you, thought Nick.

"Anyway," continued Hercules, turning to address Nick and Church. "May I introduce you to my fellow overseer committee member...Mindi Pankhurst!!

*

Chapter 5

MEETINGS

Nick didn't like heights, so he definitely didn't like travelling vertically up the outside of a huge glass wall, squashed inside a snail with his new friend Mindi Pankhurst.

To make the whole thing worse, the entire shell of the snail appeared, from the inside, to be made of glass. This provided a fabulous panoramic view all around them. Unfortunately, it also made Nick feel extremely sick!

Not that he'd noticed too much to begin with. As the snail had turned upwards and the seats had swung to remain in a level position, Mindi had swept a seven page document and a pen under his nose.

"Disclaimer," she announced brusquely. "Health and safety. Please read pages one and four. Complete pages two, three and six, then sign pages five and seven. It's not rocket science, but it needs to be filled in on journeys like this."

Nick had been so pre-occupied with ticking boxes and shading squares that they were almost halfway up the building by the time he'd finished. When he did look down, his stomach did a sort of double roll.

"How... how long will it take to get to the top?" he asked weakly.

Mindi was frenziedly texting.

"Approximately fourteen minutes and thirty seven seconds," she replied, her eyes never leaving the screen.

"Oh." Nick tried to swallow but his mouth was dry.

The snail was moving faster than a real snail would, but not fast enough to draw attention to itself. He forced himself to look out. Peering into the building they were travelling up, he could make out some of the closed shops and the corridors they'd rushed through in Patch.

Mindi finished texting and slipped the phone in her pocket.

"There, that's done," she said with a smile. It didn't make her look any less severe. "Just needed to make sure they're all singing off the same hymn sheet so to speak."

"Oh," said Nick again. He didn't bother asking who 'they' were.

"So, what do you think of our snail lift then?"

"It's… it's impressive."

She tapped the glass.

"A window from the inside but…"

"…From the outside it looks like a snail. Yeah, we have the same thing in Hightower. Trees and animals and stuff are like that."

The phone went again. Mindi shuffled in her pocket.

"Sorry about this," she said in a conspiratorial way, "but you know how it is."

Nick hadn't a clue how it was!

"Yes?… Well I can't help that… We'll just have to exercise some blue sky thinking on this one…"

Nick glanced back down at the car park. The fog was lifting and he could see the lake with its little island in the centre. It all seemed so far away. Dave's 4 by 4 looked like a toy from this distance.

"…OK, so we'll run it up the flagpole and hit the ground running so to speak. Bye."

Mindi leaned over to see what Nick was looking at.

"Ah, the lake. You see the island? That's where most Elvereys live. Unfortunately, it's just not big enough."

Nick glared at the excavators at the waters edge.

"And it's not going to be there much longer?"

"I'm afraid not."

"So where do the rest live?"

Mindi waved her hand vaguely at the building.

"In the shopping complex. High up out of the big ones' way. Bottom line is, it's not ideal. Too much chance of being seen. The big ones were doing some maintenance or something the other day and found a load of our snail lifts…"

Nick thought about what Dave had said about dumping snails in the lake.

"…poor old Egberth nearly drowned. We had to call out the emergency trout rescue service. Took days to prioritize the paperwork for that incident!"

"So," said Nick, "the complex is too dangerous, the island's too small…and in any case, it won't exist soon."

"Correct. You can see our predicament."

"Just how many Elvereys are there here?"

"At a rough guess, twenty thousand, three hundred and seventeen."

Nick knew that was a tiny figure in comparison with Hightower, but it was still a lot when they had no home.

"So what about an overseer. Isn't there one here?"

Mindi held a hand up.

"I'll bring you up to speed with Barrowhouse when we get to my office. Then we'll do some brainstorming in order…"

The phone in Mindi's ear started buzzing.

"Sorry about this…" Nick held his breath and dared

himself to lean over and look straight down. It made him feel even more sick and dizzy. Below, he glimpsed the snails containing the others, gradually sliding upwards in the wake of their own slimy trail.

"It's a pity we couldn't help you earlier than we did."

Nick jumped. He hadn't realized Mindi had finished her conversation.

"Sorry?"

"In the cat. Sorry we couldn't get the swans to you quicker. So difficult you see. Had to fill in a form B47103LT... In triplicate. Takes ages to get the authorization before we can hit the ground running, so to speak."

"That's OK," he said, smiling. "You saved us with the wasps anyway."

Mindi frowned. "The what?"

"The wasps"

There was a long silence.

"Didn't have anything to do with that. I hear what you're saying but there's no authority on wasp intervention. Ah, we're at the top. Nearly there now."

Nick hardly felt a thing, his seat swinging level on its support bar as the snail bounced up over the ledge and continued lumbering along the flat glass roof.

The thing he did feel was a lessening of his nausea, but that was only a temporary reprieve. When he peered out the side and looked down, he saw the food hall way below, the tables and chairs making tiny, scattered patterns on the floor. In the centre the Christmas tree looked like a huge, towering rocket, and his face went ashen again.

Mindi glanced at him sympathetically.

"Not far to my office now," she said, placing a comforting hand on his shoulder. "Then we can really start to push the envelope on this problem so to speak."

The phone in her pocket went off again...

*

Mindi's office was extremely plain. The walls were white, the desk and chairs black. The only picture was a strange red and purple abstract that could have been hung upside down and no-one would know.

Nick and Jed stood at the window, looking down over the food hall.

Way below Dave strolled across the floor, Duke held tightly at his side.

"Doozer," muttered Jed. Nick couldn't help but agree.

They were inside the huge wooden chandelier, overlooking the topmost branches of the Christmas tree. A scent, like summer flowers, hung in the warm air. Nick felt more relaxed than he had done in ages.

Suddenly the door opened and Mindi swept in, followed by a short, round little figure with pointed ears and thick round glasses that made his eyes look enormous. He carried a clipboard and looked like a professor in his startlingly white coat.

"Attention everyone," cried Mindi importantly, gesturing everyone to sit down round the desk.

There was much mumbling and shuffling. Hercules squeezed as close to Ayisha as possible, despite the generous proportions of the room. Ayisha moved closer to Varn. Church saluted before sitting. Nick and Jed sat in the final two seats.

On the table were six sheets of paper headed –

Itinerary:- *The Barrowhouse Dilemma*,

– followed by a lot of serious looking writing that nobody bothered to read.

"Now, we haven't much time," continued Mindi. "I have a strategy meeting in twenty minutes with some very…"

"Oh, get on with it," growled Hercules, picking his teeth with the point of his spear.

Mindi glared at him.

"…Yes…Well. May I introduce to you, Mr.Spack."

Nick covered his mouth with his hand to hide a smile as she pushed the little figure to the head of the table and grabbed his clipboard.

"Mr.Spack will tell you a little of the history of Barrowhouse."

"Great," muttered Jed, stifling a yawn.

"…Whilst I will sit in the corner and take the minutes."

Mr. Spack pushed his glasses higher up his nose, making his eyes look even bigger.

"Er, thank you Mindi. For those of you who have only just learnt of our existence, Barrowhouse has been here for many, many years, in two separate, but connected areas. One was on the island at the centre of the lake, the other was just over a wall in the garden of a private house. This house, along with a number of other houses, was destroyed quite recently to make way for the Barrowhouse shopping complex."

"Excuse me," said Nick, holding his hand up. "This house? Did an overseer live there?"

Mr. Spack opened his mouth to reply.

"They did," interrupted Mindi. "The last one was Richard Slater, a really nice man. He died, along with his wife in a road accident three years ago."

The words 'road accident' were said with great deliberation as if to emphasize her views on the matter.

"Thank you," said Mr.Spack, smiling insincerely at Mindi. "The Elvereys from the garden moved in with those at the lake on a temporary basis but it was a terrible squeeze. Eventually, they moved into the complex, but this is far from ideal. Transport is very difficult. Unfortunately, the rats and snails have been observed on occasions. The roads through the inner girders and indeed, some of the accommodation could always be accidentally discovered, especially when the big ones are doing their routine maintenance."

"OUCH," came a sudden shout. Everyone turned round. Hercules was hurriedly wiping blood from the corner of his mouth and the tip of his spear. "Sorry," he mumbled sheepishly.

Mindi's glare darkened.

"However," continued Mr. Spack manfully, "the strangest incident occurred during the removal from the garden area when the house was being demolished. In order to ensure that nothing incriminating was left, everything had to be moved. During that move, certain documents were unearthed that had been hidden for many years. They proved that when the Elvereys first arrived on Earth, they came in at least three separate craft."

"Three?" spluttered Varn amidst the general melee of gasps.

Nick sat up in his chair, suddenly intensely interested.

"Oh yes. One of them, the main one, came down somewhere much further north. Another one was mentioned as landing at Hightower, but until now we had no idea where that was. Apparently, the main craft, the one up north, kept in touch with us for a while. For reasons unknown, the contact was finally lost.

For the first time, we realized we were not alone. Considering our present problems, there's little wonder that we have been so desperate to make contact."

There was a long, deathly silence. Everyone was too amazed to speak. Nick's mind was churning with questions.

Suddenly everyone seemed to have questions of their

own. The room erupted into a yelling frenzy. Mr. Spack and Mindi raised their hands.

"Please," Mr.Spack implored. "We can tell you no more on this subject. Until today we have simply not been able to make that contact."

The room quietened.

"OK. On another subject, what about your power supply?" enquired Varn. "Do you have your own engine-hearts?"

"I'll address this issue if I may," replied Mindi, getting to her feet. "The Barrowhouse craft was small. It had only one power unit. The engine-heart, as you call it, was sufficient to provide power for both the garden and the island region."

Nick was pleased there was only one engine-heart. If two or more were too close together, their combined power allowed a terrible, evil force to overpower people's minds. That force was what had stranded the Elvereys on earth hundreds of years ago. It was also the reason why the four areas of Hightower were so far apart.

"But is your engine-heart still used?" asked Ayisha.

"Absolutely. It powers the island twenty four seven. The power for those in the complex comes from the big one's supply although, at the end of the day, that does give us, and them, some problems."

"So..." mused Ayisha hesitantly, "in theory, the one you have would most likely go with you, wherever you went."

"Most likely, yes."

"Now hold on a second Ayisha," said Varn, looking uncertainly at the rest of the group. "You're thinking about Rixal?... right?"

Ayisha nodded.

"Since Tritus stole theirs, they've had no power," she said excitedly.

Nick shivered at the mention of that name and he glanced down at the scar on his hand where the vicious bird Tritus had been piloting had attacked him. He'd been lucky to win the battle, and even luckier to come away with his life. He only wished he could have prevented Tritus getting away with Rixal's engine-heart.

"But would Rixal want an influx of newcomers in their district?" asked Varn.

"There's not many of them left since the engine-heart was taken," said Church. "Who wants to live somewhere with no power?"

Ayisha nodded eagerly.

Varn fell silent. He touched his chest and winced dramatically.

"Well," said Mindi, rubbing her hands together. "I think this has been a most informative session. We've established some new, multi platform purpose formats..."

"Some what?" muttered Jed.

"...and I propose we create a series of multi task workshops to..."

"Mindi. We've only got one week before those digger chariots move in," cried Hercules impatiently.

"Yes...Absolutely. Well I'll send you all minutes from the meeting and we'll set the next one for say, Tuesday at ten fifteen. Venue to be arranged." She smiled at the group and clasped her hands together.

"May I ask something?" said Nick slowly.

The smile vanished.

"Yes, but please make it quick. I'm due to touch base with my next group."

"How come you found me? How come you knew my name? It can't have been mentioned in some old documents."

"It wasn't," replied Mindi, appearing surprised by

the question. "When your name was called out today, so was your address. We picked up on the Hightower bit, did some thinking outside the box, and hoped it wasn't just a coincidence. We were going to follow you to find out where Hightower was, but when you arrived at the reception area we did a long range scan. It revealed you were carrying a reduction stick…"

"A what?"

"A reduction stick."

"You mean shrinkage post."

"Shrinkage post; reduction stick…whatever you like to call it," said Mindi with an irritated frown, "the bottom line is; nothing on earth has ever been made from those materials so you had to be an overseer."

"Right…" said Nick, scratching his head, his mind racing ahead with hundreds of questions. "So what about the overseer. The one who died with his wife. Did they have any kids?"

Mindi sighed and turned to Hercules. Hercules, deep in thought, leaned back in his seat and nearly overbalanced.

"They did," he said, slowly stroking his beard. "Twins I believe. They'll be nine or ten years old now."

Nick felt a tremor of excitement. Twins! A bizarre question popped into his head. As the eldest was generally the only one able to use the shrinkage post, in their case, would both be able to use it?

"Do you know where they are now?" he asked, trying not to sound too interested, but the idea of teaching someone how to be an overseer was somewhat appealing.

"No, but to be perfectly honest, it wouldn't be difficult to find out," replied Mindi, glancing at her watch. "Perhaps you would like to make that your project for our next meeting? Now I really must be going."

With that, she swept up her lap-top, phones, clipboard and pen, and staggered from the room.

"Right," said Hercules, grabbing one of the papers from the table and throwing it in the bin.

"So exactly how do we get back to Hightower?" inquired Jed.

"Oh, …We'll take you back in a swan," said Mr. Spack. "The fog's lifting nicely now."

"But what about Patch?" asked Church.

"He'll go into the swan without any trouble. They're big freight carriers you see. We use them a great deal in our search for the missing craft in the north."

"Hope it's not too draughty," grumbled Varn. "No good for my arthritis."

The voices faded as Nick thought about what he'd just learnt. In one day he'd discovered not just one new Elverey world, but possibly two!

But this one needed help quickly. He knew exactly who would give him assistance with his project; and it was the project that really excited him. By the time of the next meeting, he was sure he'd have some of the answers the Barrowhouse Elvereys so desperately needed.

*

"I'm so pleased you came back early," said Nick for the third time as he sipped his tea the following morning in Paul and Laura's comfortable kitchen with its beamed ceiling and pine furniture.

"You might be, but we're not," grinned Laura. "Paul's driving has never been that good, but running into my sister's brand new car has taken it to a new level."

"It was only a little scratch," said Paul sheepishly. "I don't know why they took it so seriously."

"Little scratch? You nearly took their door off!"

70

"The way I look at it, I've done you a favour."

"Me?...A favour?"

"Yes. You didn't want to visit your sister's family in the first place."

"Well, considering the huge argument we all had, it's hardly likely we'll ever be invited back again."

"That's true. What a shame!"

"Try and say that without sniggering, you totally useless driver."

Nick glanced from one to the other as they spoke. He liked being in Paul and Laura's company. The fact that they were watchers helped of course. Watchers, nominated by the overseer were useful in helping to keep Hightower a secret from the outside world. It meant that they were the only people he could talk to about the Elvereys, and they'd helped him out of many scrapes in the past.

He sipped the tea. It revived him a little. Although he'd slept in late, he was still tired. Not surprising really, considering all the previous day's incredible events and the time he'd finally got to bed!

Paul turned to Nick.

"What was the name of that couple again?" he said. "The ones killed in the car accident?"

"Slater. Richard Slater. I don't know his wife's first name."

Paul wrote the name down and stared at the paper thoughtfully.

"Hmmm. What about the twin's names?"

"Sorry," replied Nick, shaking his head. "I don't know."

"I still can't believe it. Another world!" said Laura absently.

Ever since he'd arrived and told them the story about Barrowhouse, Nick could see how deeply it had affected

71

them both, despite the light-hearted act they tried to portray. Laura in particular, who usually spoke so much it was impossible to get a word in edgeways, seemed distant and thoughtful.

He stared at them both as they stood together. They looked so different, yet appeared so perfectly matched. Paul had long, dark hair and the beginnings of a beard. He wore dark clothes that were always creased and unkempt. Laura on the other hand, had short, blonde hair, a pretty face, and usually wore bright, new tracksuits.

Paul picked up his mug of coffee and slurped the contents.

"Look," he said thoughtfully. "I'll see what I can do Nicky. There must be news clippings about the accident. Maybe I can get some information from them."

"Thanks Paul."

"I know you need it quickly. I'll see what I can do tomorrow."

"What do you think will happen to them?" said Laura. "The Barrowhouse Elvereys I mean."

Nick swept the hair back from his eyes and shrugged.

"Dunno. Perhaps they will have to come here. If we can't find their overseer that is."

He suddenly brightened.

"Hey, if they did have to come, how about letting them live here, in your back garden. Wouldn't that be awesome?"

Paul and Laura exchanged glances and looked for something to throw at him.

"Only kidding guys."

Paul placed his hands on his hips.

"I just hope you are," he said, feigning seriousness. "We have enough trouble with your Hightower crowd. We don't want any of our own thank you very much!"

*

When Nick stepped into the living room that evening, a premiership football match was playing on the huge new TV that Marion had recently bought for Dave.

Dave himself was slumped in the armchair in front of the TV, feet up on the coffee table and a can of beer in his hand. Marion, in a fluffy pink dressing gown and fluffy pink slippers, was sitting on the settee with a cup of coffee, trying to look interested in the game.

"Don't you go telling me the score," warned Dave, without taking his eyes from the screen. "Your mum recorded this for me earlier."

"Don't know it," he replied sulkily, stepping over Duke. The dog looked up and growled softly, a trickle of saliva dripping from the corner of his mouth.

Nick shivered at the sight and turned his attention to the screen as he sat down next to his mum.

But he didn't really see the game. For once, he wasn't interested in football. His mind was swirling with the events of the last twenty four hours. Would he find the twins? Was it likely that Barrowhouse and Hightower would become one? Would Barrowhouse find their own new home? One thing was for certain. He wouldn't find out from the meeting on Tuesday. He wouldn't be there because he'd be at school, but that didn't bother him. He didn't think he could manage to sit through another of Mindi's meetings!

The room started to become a blur and he closed his eyes.

Time drifted on.

"Yessss," yelled Dave, cracking open another can.

Nick opened his eyes. The final whistle had just blown. Dave was obviously happy with the result and

Marion, yawning profusely, was obviously tired.

"You going to bed then?" said Dave, flicking the remote at the TV. The football changed to boxing.

Marion nodded and picked up her empty cup.

"I am," she replied, rubbing her eyes. "Dominic, don't you be long now. It's school tomorrow."

"I won't Mum. Goodnight."

"Oh, and Marion?" said Dave, grabbing her sleeve. "Take these empty cans into the kitchen will you?"

Without another word the gaudy pink apparition swept the cans from the coffee table and trudged out of the room.

"Thanks sweet pea. Goodnight."

'Sweetpea!' mused Nick with a grim smile.

Dave belched loudly.

"You like boxing huh?" he asked, when they were alone, his eyes still on the screen.

"Not really."

"You like football though?"

Nick shrugged. "Yeah. It's like, something I'm pretty good at."

There was a long, drawn out silence. Duke stood up, stretched, and padded into the kitchen. On the TV, one of the boxers was going in for the kill.

"But you don't like me." It wasn't a question but a statement. Dave turned and stared at him icily.

Nick was taken off guard. He shrugged again, but could think of nothing to say.

"You're not going to get in the way of me and your mother kid." The words were barely a whisper but the menace couldn't have been more obvious had he been screaming. "Soon I'll be living here permanently...and things will change."

Nick stared at the TV. He didn't want to look into those icy, grey eyes.

One of the boxers was starting to stagger.

Dave leaned closer. The beer on his breath smelt stale.

"When I do, we'll sell this place and I'll make myself some serious money."

"You can't. My Dad held it in trust to me." Nick's voice trembled but he wasn't sure if it was from fear or anger.

Dave sat back and swigged the last of his beer.

"Maybe so, maybe not," he said calmly. "But even if it can't be sold, it can be built on."

Nick's heart sank.

"What do you mean," he said anxiously.

Dave stood up, squeezed the can till it cracked, and threw it in the bin.

"Think I might persuade your mum to let me build a hotel on this site. Use some of the collateral in this place. There's plenty of room. Dig up the grounds. Build it all up. Nothing to stop me improving your inheritance. Remember, there's always a way, so don't cross me… ever. Goodnight kid."

On the screen, the staggering boxer crashed, unconscious, to the floor.

The door slammed shut and Nick just sat there, horrified. The idea of Hightower being ripped apart felt all too close to the awful events of Barrowhouse.

At that moment, he realized that something had to be done about Dave.

Chapter 6

THE TWINS

On the Monday, Nick had a dismal time at school and was glad when it was time to leave. He hadn't been able to concentrate on anything and hardly heard a word anyone said all day.

Memories of the incident with Dave the previous evening still pressed down on him, making him feel miserable. He'd thought about telling his mum about what had happened but knowing what she was like, and how she felt about Dave, it was unlikely that she'd believe him. Worse still, she might even think that the awful hotel proposal was a good idea! She'd changed so much since he'd arrived. She'd become subdued, almost meek in his presence and had started to agree with everything he said and did.

No, talking to his mum was the last thing he reckoned he should do.

So instead, he'd spent most of the day trying to think up ways to get rid of Dave. Most involved varying degrees of violence and the higher the level, the more he liked it!

Different ways of getting a car to crash (with him inside) was a popular theme, as was dubious work accidents that left him being rushed to hospital. Even more centred round home accidents, with the old trip wire at the top of the stairs giving him a great deal of satisfaction! The most bizarre of the ideas saw Nick with magical powers that simply lifted Dave (and Duke) from the cottage and sent them kicking and screaming, up and away over the hills.

None of these were practical of course and however much he liked the magical flying routine, all it did was get him in trouble for daydreaming in English!

His mood brightened a little when he saw Paul and Laura's battered old estate car waiting outside the school gates.

He waved to them and ran over to the car. Dragging the back door open wasn't easy but it finally conceded with a horrific screech.

"You come for me?" he asked hopefully, bending down to peer inside.

"Yeah," replied Paul. "Hop in."

Nick slipped inside, noting with some apprehension that Paul was driving. He carefully fastened the seatbelt.

"We've found your twins," said Laura brightly. "Or rather, Paul has," she added hastily as Paul narrowed his eyes at her.

"There was a piece about the accident in the local paper," he said, starting the engine. The old car shuddered into action.

"Paul found it in the archives. Took him ages."

"But it gave the names of the two kids. Matthew and Emily. They went to live with Richard's brother and his wife."

"Matthew and Emily," repeated Nick under his breath. "Matthew and Emily." Did you get an address?" he asked eagerly.

"Course he did," said Laura. "My husband's a genius."

Paul, with white knuckles gripping the steering

wheel and nose pressed up against the windscreen, pulled slowly away from the kerb. A car screamed past, its horn blaring.

"...Just not good at driving," she added.

They juddered into the traffic and moved slowly off up the hill.

"I got the address from the telephone directory," said Paul, his eyes fixed nervously ahead of him. "It's not far."

"Thank goodness," muttered Nick under his breath. He leaned back and stared out the side window. It felt better not watching the road ahead.

Laura glanced round anxiously.

"Are you all right Nicky? You look subdued."

"Yeah."

"Bad day at school huh?" said Paul.

"Well, ...yeah, something like that."

He slouched down further into the seat. For some reason he really didn't want to go over what had happened with Dave.

Not yet anyway.

They turned down a tree lined road, bordered on either side by small semi- detached houses.

"What number are we looking for?" said Paul, his hands gripping the steering wheel even tighter as he tried to glance at the house numbers.

Laura looked down at the crumpled bit of paper in her lap.

"Paul," she said grinning. "It's number two hundred and sixteen, right at the other end, so I think you can go a bit quicker than ten miles an hour!"

Paul tried to relax and pushed the car up to fifteen miles per hour. They counted the numbers off, very slowly, till they came to 216.

The house didn't look as well cared for as its

neighbours. A couple of slates were missing from the roof and the old windows could have done with replacing. An old car was standing on bricks in the unkempt garden, pieces of engine strewn around it in the weeds.

"Hmmm. Doesn't look very salubrious to me," whispered Laura.

"Look very what?" said Nick.

"It's the only big word she knows," said Paul to Nick.

Laura elbowed him in the ribs.

"So what now?" she asked.

Paul sat back and drummed his fingers on the dashboard.

"I think it might be better if you went Laura. You and Nicky might not seem so intimidating."

Nick's heart leapt. He was eagerly looking forward to this. What would the twins be like? How would they handle such knowledge?

To that end, what exactly were they going to tell them? *'…Well hello there Matthew and Emily. We know your parents are dead but hey, congratulations! You've just inherited a little world of tiny people and you've got to look after them. Oh, by the way. Ever flown in a swan before??.....or travelled around inside a cat for that matter?'*

Nick scratched his head. He was so looking forward to teaching the kids all about being an overseer, but how were they going to get over this first part?

Paul and Laura seemed more confident. They'd obviously discussed this confrontation well before he'd got into the car.

"OK," agreed Laura. "You coming Nicky?"

"Too right I am," he said, banging the stubborn door open.

As they walked up an uneven path to the front door,

a bitter wind swirled round them and Laura pulled the collar of her coat up to her neck.

She knocked hesitantly on the door and a dog started barking inside. Nick took a step back, thinking of Duke. He shivered, but this time it wasn't because of the cold wind.

"Shut up Rex," yelled a man's gruff voice.

Laura and Nick exchanged glances. She tried a comforting smile but it just made her look more tense.

A key rattled in the lock and the door swung open to reveal a tall, bald man of about thirty. A smell of boiled cabbage drifted out from the hall.

"Yes?" he said, glaring at them.

"Oh, er… hello," began Laura. "I was wondering…"

"We don't want ter buy nothin."

A fat kid, about eleven years old, with hair so short he almost looked as bald as his dad, sidled up to the door and stared out at them. With a vacant expression, he wiped his snotty nose on the back of his sleeve.

Matthew doesn't look too dynamic, thought Nick.

"I'm not selling anything," persisted Laura. "I just…"

"Don't want nothin' religious neither."

He was about to slam the door when a thin, lanky woman appeared behind him, wiping a plate on a scruffy towel.

"What's all this then?" she said curiously.

"We're not selling anything," repeated Laura, appealing to the woman. "We just wondered if you could help us. We're after some information."

"Information BAH! They're doin some sort er survey," said the man, turning away. The kid followed.

The woman though, stayed, looking vaguely interested.

"This is nothing bad," said Laura quickly, trying to hold her attention. "We're hoping to contact Matthew and Emily Slater who came here about three years ago."

The woman stopped wiping the plate and stared hesitantly back inside the house. The man and the boy had disappeared into the front room and the television was blaring out.

"What about them?" she said suspiciously.

"We're trying to find them because...because we think their parents, or maybe their father...er, left them something."

Left them something, thought Nick. Oh yeah, he certainly left them something!!

The woman glared at them in a quizzical manner for a long time before making up her mind.

"Sorry," she said abruptly, one hand on the door, ready to push it shut. "Can't 'elp."

"Oh, please," said Laura imploringly.

"Can't 'elp," repeated the woman.

"Why?"

"Coz they're not 'ere, that's why. Those kids couldn't stand livin' round 'ere after what 'appened to their parents. Nice kids they were too." She stared into the distance. "Remember 'em well. One was left 'anded and the other was right 'anded. 'Appens a lot with twins you know. One left, one right 'anded."

"But what happened to them," cut in Nick, a feeling of dejection sliding over him.

She looked back at them.

"They left. Whole family, a few months ago. We moved in 'ere after they left."

The door started to close.

"And went where? Do you know?" Nick's voice was barely a whisper.

The door stopped.

"Oh I know," said the woman with a smile. "But it won't do you no good...They emigrated see? Went as far away from 'ere as they could."

"To where?"

"Australia!"

The door finally slammed shut.

*

If things had started to get hectic over the last few days they took on a whole new pace from late Tuesday afternoon.

Nick was slumped on the settee in the front room with his arms folded and his head resting on a cushion. There was no one else in yet and he should have been upstairs doing his homework. It was starting to build up but he couldn't be bothered. He knew he'd be in trouble tomorrow but that was the least of his worries.

He stared at the huge screen without really seeing anything.

The fact that he would never be able to share the overseer's secrets with Matthew and Emily had affected him more than he'd expected. He was once more alone in the overseer's role, and that disappointed and saddened him deeply.

In short, Nick was feeling intensely sorry for himself.

He munched on a biscuit. Crumbs slithered down into his lap and he brushed them onto the floor. No doubt his mum would give him a grilling for that later. Either her or Dave, but he didn't really care.

Not that Dave could talk. He left empty beer cans, mugs of tea, plates and knives and forks lying around all over, yet nothing was ever said about that.

He absently pressed the remote and the picture flicked from a cartoon to something about fishing, with two blokes standing on a riverbank in the pouring rain. Nick subconsciously swept the hair back from his eyes and sighed, immersed in his sullen thoughts.

He suddenly became aware of two new figures on the screen. They seemed almost superimposed onto the river scene. One was short, with an enormous floppy green hat and even more enormous green wading boots that seemed to come right up to his chest. The other was taller and older wearing a dark brown coat with the collar turned up. Both were vaguely familiar. The shorter one was excitedly waving a long fishing rod around in a most unprofessional and downright dangerous way.

Nick sat upright and put down the remnants of his biscuit.

"Varn? ...Church?" he said incredulously.

Both figures smiled and moved forward till the other two men on the riverbank were totally blotted out.

"Nicky," said Varn grandly. "What do you think to our new communication system?"

Nick was astounded.

"Can...can you hear me?" he stuttered.

"Of course," replied Church, pushing the floppy hat back out of his eyes. "We can hear you and see you perfectly."

"Well it's certainly better than using Polly, but you'll have to be careful. We can only use it when my Mum or Dave aren't in."

"Of course," said Varn.

"We'll be careful," agreed Church. "You can rely on us."

Yeah...right, thought Nick.

"It's my BUMS," said Church cheerfully.

"Your what?"

"I call it the Binary Unilateral Mergerlating System," continued Church. "You see, we're actually in the communication studio in the main tree at Miru. It's fitted with..."

"Not now," cut in Varn irritably. "We need to tell Nicky about the meeting we attended this afternoon… and besides," he added, with a dramatic cough, "we really can't stay in this studio too long. It's too cold. Not at all good for my lungs."

"Ah yes, the meeting," said Nick with a sulky air of disapproval. Although he hadn't wanted to be there, it was still frustrating not being involved in something so important.

"Mindi was in charge of the proceedings," said Church, waving the fishing rod around with renewed enthusiasm.

"I'm sure she was," muttered Nick.

"…and she came up with… What did Mindi say it was Varn?"

"An optimised, multi lateral format, I think."

"A what?"

"Exactly…CHURCH, stop messing with that thing. That's the third time you've swiped me on the arm. I'm going to have to get that bruising seen to."

"Sorry," said Church, placing the fishing rod carefully on the floor. "What do you think of my outfit Nicky? Saw it on a programme today. Going to take up big game fishing…"

"Church, I'm not bothered about fishing," said Nick, clenching his teeth. "What happened at the meeting?"

In the distance the outside door clicked shut and footsteps thudded across the kitchen floor.

Varn rubbed his hands together and grinned.

"We've come to an agreement. Barrowhouse is going to move into Rixal as we'd previously suggested."

"It is?" said Nick, staring at them both.

"There wasn't anything else we could do. After you'd told us that the overseer thing wasn't going to happen there was nowhere else they could go."

"There wasn't?"

"It's too dangerous for them to stay where they are. We really couldn't say no."

"We couldn't?"

"So the agreement was made."

"It was....? So when's this all happening then?" added Nick, thinking his conversation was getting a bit repetitive!

Church jumped forward till he was nearly taking up the full screen.

"They're starting to move out from Thursday. It should all be done by the end of the weekend."

"...And we'll have the Barrowhouse engine-heart," said Varn, pushing Church to one side. Both figures consumed the whole picture now, making Nick feel dizzy as they jostled each other for room.

"So Rixal will have power once more," beamed Church.

"By the week end," muttered Nick anxiously. "Can it be done in that..."

The door suddenly banged open.

"What's this rubbish then? ...And why aren't you upstairs doing your homework like your mother asks you to?"

The two figures squashed together on the screen froze in horror as Nick jumped up, trying to cover the television.

"Oh, hi Dave," he stammered. "I'm, I'm just...just watching something on fishing."

"Fishing?" roared Dave, pushing him out of the way to look. "What do you know about fishing?"

"Well...I..."

They both stared down at the screen.

Varn and Church looked worriedly at each other, backed away from the screen a little till the view of the river could be seen, then turned confidently to face their audience.

"Yes Charles," said Varn grandly. "Catching gloopy fish at this time of year can be particularly rewarding, even for the most practised of anglingers…"

"Most rewarding Herbert," replied Church. "The gloopy fish is a difficult critter to catch, perhaps even more difficult than the er… drimblebob fish!"

"Oh dear God!" groaned Nick quietly.

Dave looked totally bewildered as he glared at the screen.

"Well whatever rubbish it is, it's going off," he said, grabbing the remote and flicking it to the sports channel. "And as for you me lad, you can go upstairs and leave me in peace."

"Anything you say," muttered Nick sarcastically, feeling mighty relieved that Dave knew nothing whatsoever about fish!

"Oh, and tomorrow night, you can stay in your room if you don't mind. Me and your mother'll be having a bit of a celebration."

Nick's hand froze on the door knob. Visions alternated between his mum in a white dress and her and Dave sipping champagne outside a huge hotel complex.

"Celebration?" he spluttered anxiously. "What sort of a celebration?"

"Sorted out that rat problem at Barrowhouse," said Dave, sliding into the chair and putting his feet up on the coffee table. "Got a meeting there twelve thirty tomorrow. In the boardroom no less. The works done, the rats are gone…and I get paid big time."

"Oh… right," said Nick, feeling relieved, but trying to sound casually disinterested, as he quietly shut the door.

But disinterested was far from how he really felt.

He leapt up the stairs two at a time. Once in his bedroom he grinned at Polly the parrot in a cage in the corner.

He had an idea.

It was time to re-establish communication with the Elvereys!

*

Chapter 7

PAY BACK

Nick squeezed in through a small hatch located between the ears and slid down into his seat in the tiny, cramped control room next to a very efficient young woman in green overalls, who was hurriedly checking switches and inspecting dials.

The air was heavy with the smell of oil and the throbbing vibration of the engine made his head hurt.

"Welcome aboard," shouted the woman before turning back to the array of dials before her.

"Thank you," spluttered Nick, wedging the shrinkage post down at his side and strapping himself tightly in, but his words were drowned out as suddenly the noise increased still further and the whole cabin began to rock.

He peered cautiously at his new companion. It was difficult to make out much as she had enormous headphones strapped over her curly black hair and, despite the gloom, she was wearing sunglasses.

She said something, but in the noise it was impossible to make out the words. He frowned and leaned even closer till their arms were almost touching. She passed him some headphones and gestured for him to put them on.

It was a relief when the thick pads covered his ears and the sound became a dull drone.

"Is that better?" said the woman's voice brightly through the speakers.

"Much," he said. "Thanks."

The woman adjusted her microphone and beckoned him to do the same with his.

"Good. Now, let's show you what we at Barrowhouse can do. You just sit back and enjoy the show. After all, you organized it!"

Nick gave a thumbs up sign and smiled. He felt proud of himself but slightly apprehensive. Yes, this was his idea, but just how would it go? Were the Barrowhouse Elvereys anything like the Hightower Elvereys when it came to things like this?

He hoped not! The Hightower crowd, lovable as they were, were not exactly great when it came to efficiency, and yet they usually managed to stumble their way through.

He tried to relax but the fear of the unknown made him shudder inwardly.

"12-61, this is Whitey. We are ready to roll," said the woman, leaning forward in her seat and flicking a couple of switches above the tiny, round window in front of her.

Nick looked directly forward and peered through his own little round window but in the darkness there was nothing much to see.

"Ok Whitey," came a sudden sharp voice through his headphones. "12-61 here. Take your group out and proceed to the rendezvous point."

"Thank you 12-61."

Nick's stomach lurched as the cabin suddenly rolled, first sideways, then upwards, then forwards. Even through the headphones he could hear the distant roar of noise that seemed to increase or lessen with each loping sway as they thudded forward.

Gradually they settled into some momentum and Nick relaxed a little, easing back into his seat.

It was terribly hot in such a tiny area. He swept his arm across his glistening forehead and sighed heavily. Through the little round window he could just make out the shape of a long, narrow corridor.

"Bent Whisker to Whitey," yelled a crackling, harsh voice. "Reckon we'll make rendezvous point in five minutes. What do you think?"

The woman re-adjusted her microphone yet again and scrutinized one of the myriad of gauges.

"Hi Bent Whisker. Yeah, five minutes should do it. How are the others?"

There was a moment's pause.

"All following you and looking good. Tails End had a bit of trouble starting one of his engines but he's OK now."

"Good. Just all stay close behind me."

"Will do Whitey. You know how much we like to watch your rear end!"

"Yeah, right. Less of the cheek," replied Nick's companion with a grin.

"You OK?" she asked, turning to him.

"Fine. Can I ask; why do they call you Whitey? Is that your name?"

The grin broadened.

"Heavens no. My name's Angel. Well, actually it's Angela, but everyone calls me Angel. It's a long story. Anyway, you'll be able to see where the Whitey part comes from in a moment."

Before she had finished speaking, the cabin suddenly became engulfed in light. It was so bright that Nick wished he had some sunglasses. He squinted and peered at the window. As his eyes adjusted, he could see that they were travelling along a much wider, silver corridor.

"If you lean forward and look to the side, you'll see what I mean," said Angel.

Nick eased forward, pulling at the straps of his seat, and leaned over the control panel till his head was almost inside the round lens of the window.

He looked to the side and gasped. The silver wall was bright and shiny and acted almost like a mirror. Though the vision was somewhat distorted as they flashed down the corridor, in the reflection he could just make out his head peering out of the little glass eye bubble. What he could distinctly see however, was the broad swathe of white fur that ran from the bubble right back to the rear.

"We're in one of the big one's electrical conduits. Makes a great mirror don't you think?"

"It sure does," he replied, easing back into his seat. It didn't matter where he went or what he saw in the Elverey world, there were times, many times, when he still had to pinch himself to make sure he wasn't dreaming!

"Here we go. The rendezvous point," said Angel as they came to the end of the corridor.

The cabin suddenly lurched to the right. Nick stared at the scene before them and subconsciously pinched his leg.

"Well?" said Angel, "What do you think?"

"Awesome," muttered Nick, his mouth hanging open. "Simply awesome!!"

*

Oh, Dave felt good. This day had been a long time coming but as he knocked hesitantly on the door, listening to the murmured babble of voices inside, he prided himself on a job well done.

He stared at the large brass plate with the words BOARDROOM emblazoned upon it. A wasp hovered round him for a moment before lazily droning away. He'd never been in this hallowed room before and he nervously kept alternating between hurriedly brushing the sleeves of his old jacket and straightening his tie as he waited.

The door swung open and a tall, grey haired man in an expensive looking suit stood there with his hand extended. His smile seemed warm but not terribly sincere.

"David…Dave. Good to see you," said the man. "Come in."

Dave stepped forward, shaking the man's hand and trying not to grimace too much as his hand was enthusiastically crushed.

"Thanks Mr.Denton," he stuttered.

Mr.Denton didn't seem to notice. He was too busy bustling around in a whirlwind of self important energy.

"I don't know if you've ever met the others here," he said, waving vaguely at the other six figures in the room.

Dave hadn't … and he certainly didn't take in any of the names of the three men and three women, equally smartly dressed, as they politely smiled and introduced themselves.

He nodded back and glanced around. The boardroom was smaller than he'd expected. There were no windows and the dark, wooden panelling gave it a sombre appearance. Each wall was lined with pictures of Barrowhouse at various stages during its construction. In the centre of the room was a heavy, ornate table surrounded by plush, green leather chairs.

Down one wall was another table, draped by a white cloth. On it was a bewildering assortment of sandwiches, crisps, sausage rolls, cakes and fruit, bordered by tea, coffee and various fruit juices.

"Would you like anything to eat, or drink?" asked Mr.Denton.

Dave surveyed the table. He wouldn't have minded a beer or two, but there didn't seem to be any on offer.

Mr. Denton rubbed his hands together enthusiastically.

"This is one of our little celebrations. Christmas sales have been good so far…"

He patted Dave on the shoulder and laughed. As if on cue, the others politely laughed.

"…and you could say that some of that's down to your help. Getting rid of our little 'friends' has certainly encouraged the customers to come flooding back…"

The others hastily agreed amidst more polite laughter and much nodding of heads.

"…so we thought we'd have a bite to eat before we started our busy afternoon agenda. Are you sure you wouldn't like anything?"

Dave could see the mouth moving but wasn't really taking in the words. All he wanted was his money and to get out of there, so he just shook his head and held up his hands in a gesture of submission.

"No?" said Mr. Denton. "Very well, we'll get back to business then."

As one, the others put down their half eaten sandwiches and sat at the table. Mr.Denton sat at the head of the table of course and beckoned Dave to sit next to him.

Dave edged into his seat and started to relax. In front of him was a white envelope with his name on. He felt like ripping it open right there and kissing the numbers written on it.

"Final payment," said Mr.Denton, nodding appreciatively at the envelope. "We've added a little bonus for a job well done. I'm sure you'll be most satisfied."

The others nodded appreciatively too.

I'm sure I will, thought Dave, licking his lips and staring at the envelope.

"Please, tell me," said a thin woman with a huge beaked nose. "Was this a particularly difficult job? There seemed to be so many rats before we called you in."

"So many," agreed a bald man with glasses balanced on the tip of his nose.

"...and so potentially damaging to our trade," said Mr.Denton.

They all looked at Mr.Denton and nodded at such wise words.

"Well..." said Dave, rubbing his chin and leaning back in his chair. "It was one of my more spectacular successes I suppose you could say. There were so many rats and with rats it's so difficult to try and find their lair; especially in a place of this size."

He looked at each of them in turn. They stared back at him with intense concentration on their faces.

"...And of course, it wasn't just rats. I had to dispose of a great deal of snails as well."

He nodded at the envelope and smiled knowingly at Mr.Denton.

So you'd better have put a bit of something special in for that Denters me old mate, he thought.

Mr. Denton smiled back. The others smiled. Things were going well.

"But it was the size of the rats that was the thing about this operation," he continued, warming to his theme and feeling happier and happier as they eagerly soaked up his every word.

"I've never seen anything quite like it before. Some of them were as big as this..." He held his hands apart. Quite a lot further apart actually than what any of the rats had really been!

Beak nose gasped.

The bald man peered over his glasses at him with undisguised admiration.

"...So there's no wonder it was such a long, difficult job. There's no wonder I had to work such long, awkward hours..."

There's no wonder I'd better have a nice big bonus in that envelope he thought, glancing triumphantly at Mr.Denton, but Mr.Denton wasn't looking at him anymore. He was looking toward the table of food...and his eyes were widening.

Not that Dave was bothered. He was enjoying his moment. OK, maybe he was going on a bit, but why shouldn't he? He was just as good as this lot in their fancy suits.

"...Oh yes. It was a long, difficult job," he repeated, "but it was worth it. I can confidently say your problems are over. There are no rats anywhere in Barrowhouse anymore. The rat problem is finally over and..."

His voice trailed away. The others, as always, were following Mr.Denton's lead and were looking at the food table.

Puzzled, Dave too turned to look...and the blood in his veins froze!!

There, on the table amidst the sandwiches and the cream cakes, sat an enormous black rat, casually rubbing its whiskers with its front paws.

Before anyone could speak another leapt up...then another.

"What the....?" spluttered Dave, mortified.

Beak nose screamed and leapt from her chair. Havoc ensued. People jumped to their feet. The bald man's glasses fell to the floor. Voices rose in a crescendo, interspersed by screams and shouts.

There were rats running across the floor now. Rats

climbing onto the table. Big ones, small ones, black ones and brown ones. Dave gawped at them, his mouth hanging open.

Everyone else was rushing for the door, fighting to get out. Mr.Denton was the last to leave the table. He rose to his full, impressive height, his eyes like thunder.

He grabbed the envelope from under Dave's nose and slammed a fist down hard on the table. The rats made a slight detour but carried on scurrying around.

"YOU…" he yelled, "You, can get out of here. I never want to see you again."

With a deft movement, he tore the envelope in half and marched to the door.

"I'll get a proper firm to do this job," he roared, leaving Dave, head in his hands, the only one left at the table. Indeed, the only one left in the room!

The rats continued scampering around on the floor. Gradually, their numbers receded till only a few were visible.

One big one, its fur streaked white down either side, had the audacity to actually crawl over his foot, and it was this action that finally stirred Dave into life.

The shock drained from him, replaced by a sudden, surging anger that flooded through him as he watched the white sided rat casually scamper to the corner.

How could this happen? How could these things, these evil, foul things ruin his life?

With a howl of rage, he leapt to the food table, grabbed a knife from the tray, and with strength heightened by anger and accuracy intensified through hatred, he hurled the knife at the rat, pinning it to the wooden floor.

The rat's legs struggled desperately but it was no use. It was held fast by the knife, the blade skewering it just below the head and slicing straight through the body.

For one moment, Dave savoured this triumph, then with gritted teeth, fury took over once more and he strode over to the rodent, his boot hovering over its quivering body, ready to crush it to its final death.

Suddenly he felt a pain in his left leg. He struggled backwards and swung round.

He could hardly believe his eyes. From behind the table a small flap in the wooden panelling was open and rats were pouring back out. There were hundreds and hundreds of them. So many in fact, that the floor was becoming a writhing, searing mass. He glanced down at his leg. A huge rat was staring up at him, its black eyes bearing into him, its razor sharp teeth ready to plunge into his leg.

Others were crawling over his boots and starting to scramble up his legs.

Now anger dissolved into fear. With a last, lingering look at the white sided rat flailing on the knife, he hurriedly turned and leapt for the door.

Without turning back, he dragged the rats off his legs and grabbed the handle with trembling hands.

In an instant he was out the door and running, terror stricken, down the corridor.

*

Nick's hands were shaking so violently he found it hard to unstrap the harness supporting him.

He was still feeling groggy and only half aware of where he was, and when he coughed, the acrid smoke made his throat hurt. Around him was a fizzing, crackling noise from wires that hung down like streamers. Nothing was actually on fire but everything seemed broken. The whole cabin was lying sideways, making it difficult to move.

He'd vaguely seen the huge figure of Dave advancing towards them through the cracked, splintered screen and he'd witnessed their rescue by the hordes of Barrowhouse rats that were now swarming around them.

"Angel? ...Angel?..Are you all right?" he called out into the gloom in a panicky voice. The straps finally gave way and he lifted himself from the seat, carefully flexing and testing each limb to make sure that no bones were broken.

Angel, in the other seat, groaned. He looked at her. She had a nasty cut on her forehead and her face was dusty and dirty.

"My sunglasses," she muttered irritably. "I've broken my sunglasses!"

"Yeah," grinned Nick, feeling relieved.

From above came a sudden cracking sound and bright light surged in, bringing with it glorious fresh air.

"Nicky?" called Ayisha's worried voice.

"Are you OK?" cried Church, sounding equally concerned.

Nick looked up, squinting against the light.

Four or five heads were peering down, all eagerly pushing each other out of the way in order to see through the little hatch.

"Oh my," exclaimed Church, looking stricken.

Nick followed his gaze and looked behind his seat where a huge silver wall was now located, lodged against his head rest.

"Church? What exactly is that?" he asked, puzzled.

"That Nicky, is the knife that Dave threw. It's what's pinning your rat to the floor."

Nick felt physically sick. Just a fraction further forward and neither he, nor Angel would be alive.

"Church," he said, trying to stay calm and think. "We've all got to get out of here; fast. They'll be back soon. Can we get that knife out do you think?"

Church shook his head.

"It's stuck in too deep. That was one pretty angry bloke."

"Yeah," agreed Nick with a grin. It was the first moment he'd had to savour the satisfaction of getting one over on Dave. But he hadn't time to dwell on it.

He grabbed Angel's arm and together they dragged themselves from the wreckage of the cabin and jumped down, thankfully breathing in the fresh air as they did so.

As he surveyed the scene the feeling of nausea rolled over him once again

The rat lay on its side, its legs still twitching pitifully. The huge knife towering above them had sliced through the body leaving entrails of wiring and fittings hanging out of the huge open wound.

Ayisha stood at his side.

"Are you sure you're all right?" she asked, looking at him worriedly.

Nick smiled weakly.

"Yeah, but now we've got to think of a way to…"

"To what?"

Nick snapped his fingers, the smile becoming a broad grin.

"Got it! The way to get the knife out. Simple of course."

"It is?" replied Ayisha, frowning.

"I'll do it. The shrinkage post's in there. Get everybody out of the boardroom. I'll sort this."

With that, he leapt back up the body and probed through the hatch till he found the shrinkage post. In an instant he'd jumped back off the rat, reverted to his proper size, and was bent down, pulling out the knife.

Church was right. Dave had been furious and the

force with which he'd thrown the weapon made it difficult to pull out of the floor. Finally though, the blade began to give.

With a sickening slurping sound he dragged the knife out of the rat and shivered again at the thought of just how close he'd come to being skewered!

He was so immersed in these thoughts that as he stood up he failed to hear the door swing open, or hear the words, "is it safe? Are they all gone?" whispered hesitantly.

So it came as a huge surprise when he turned to see Mr.Denton and three of his directors standing in the doorway.

By the astonished looks on their faces, it came as an equally huge surprise for them, to see a tousle haired boy with cuts and grazes over his hands and face, rise from behind the central table, a knife in one hand and the remnants of a very large, sliced open rat in the other!!

*

Chapter 8

REMOVALS

For the second time that day Beak Nose screamed and ran out of the room.

Nick grimaced. His head already hurt and the screaming only made it worse. He tried to smile in a re-assuring 'this isn't quite what it seems' type of way, but by the totally bewildered expression on Mr.Denton's face, no amount of re-assurance could explain the bizarre set of circumstances before him.

So with a helpless shrug, Nick gave up with the smile.

"Er…Hello," he muttered in a curiously apologetic manner and slowly began to slide back down behind the table.

His gradual disappearance broke the spell.

"What the devil is happening here?" roared Mr.Denton, bounding towards the table with his two companions following a discreet distance behind.

Nick heard the clamour and knew he had to act fast. He threw the knife aside and leapt for the small opening near the base of the panelling.

He flung the rat through and grabbed the shrinkage post from his pocket, pressing the top hard against the ring on his thumb.

Immediately the screaming roar of shrinking pierced through his mind and body, but the momentum of his leap carried him forward. In that split second he prayed that he'd reduce in size sufficiently to squeeze through.

He did.

Just!

The back of his head and shoulders brushed against the edges of the entrance as he rolled over into the darkened tunnel. By the time he'd reached Elverey size, willing hands were pulling him away from the light of the boardroom.

Out the corner of his eye he glimpsed the enormous, towering figure of Mr.Denton, hands on hips, surveying the scene with an expression somewhere between absolute bewilderment and total fury.

As they edged further into the safety of the tunnel, the booming voices outside drifted through the gloom.

"…He was here wasn't he?" yelled Mr.Denton incredulously. "I wasn't seeing things was I?"

"Oh, no sir," relied the voice of the bald man. "He was certainly here."

"Then where the devil is he now?"

"Er…I…We…Just don't know."

"Boys cannot just vanish into thin air." Mr.Denton's voice was getting higher. "I want …No! I demand that every possible…"

The sound was abruptly cut off as the entrance door crashed back into place. Immediately the lighting in the tunnel came on.

Nick sighed heavily and tried to calm himself down. He was still shaking as he leaned on the shrinkage post. He glanced at his friends as they edged round the battered, smouldering wreckage of the rat.

"I shall make arrangements to get that victim of our great battle sorted," said Hercules pompously, looking very pleased with himself, as though he'd personally overseen the whole operation.

"I'm sure you will," replied Angel, peering unhappily at her broken sunglasses as she limped down the corridor, aided by Church and Ayisha.

"And what a victorious battle it was," continued Hercules, pausing only momentarily as he tripped over something invisible on the floor. "Why, we struck our enemies to the very earth. We…"

"Thank you Hercules," interrupted Varn, looking pained. "All this excitement is really not good for my blood pressure you know."

"Guys," said Nick grinning. "Can we hurry up a bit. I know this sort of doesn't seem very important after what we've just been through, but I've really got to get back to school. Lunchtime's nearly over and I'll be in serious trouble if I don't get back in time!"

*

The atmosphere was surprisingly subdued and nobody seemed to want to talk much as they flew back in the swan towards Nick's school.

Hercules had trapped his hand in one of the doors during boarding and was now sulking in the corner, flexing his bruised fingers.

Varn was trying to sleep after complaining about his headache, stomach-ache, and some sort of stabbing pain in his left leg.

Church and Ayisha were sitting in window seats, staring out at the world passing by far below them.

Nick glanced at his watch and bit on his lip nervously. He really didn't want to be late getting back to school. He'd have enough trouble explaining things as it was. There was a graze on his cheek, a cut on his arm, and his shirt was torn.

He'd managed to clean himself up a bit in one of

the swan's washrooms, but he still looked pretty bad!

He drummed his fingers impatiently on the seat in front of him and stared to his right through the hazy mist of white feathers. Way below, a road wound across a land of fields, dotted by the occasional farm building.

He glanced at his watch again and sighed. Looking towards his left, he could see through a large glass screen which offered a view of the swan's cavernous hold. Down below were numerous crates and containers, varying in size and colour and all neatly stacked one on top of the other.

This was the first consignment bound for Hightower. The Elvereys were starting the move earlier than was originally planned. The swans were great cargo carriers but there was an awful lot of stuff that was going to have to be shifted from Barrowhouse to Hightower.

Again he looked at his watch and sighed.

"Hey Nicky," said Church brightly. "Don't be so nervous. It's me who should be nervous. I might be voted off tonight."

"What?" snapped Nick.

"Voted off. That is, if the public didn't like my performance."

"What is he talking about?" said Nick, appealing to Ayisha.

"It's something he's been watching," replied Ayisha, sounding bored.

"I don't want to be down in the bottom two. It'll go to a judges decision. Then anything can happen."

"Yeah right," said Nick, absently watching as the tiny figures of two Elvereys carefully checked the containers down in the hold.

Suddenly, a young woman in a bright blue uniform tapped him on the shoulder.

"Excuse me," she said politely. "I'm sorry to interrupt

you but we'll be arriving near your school in five minutes. Perhaps you'd like to accompany me to the forward cabin for disembarkation."

"Oh yeah; sure," replied Nick, grabbing the shrinkage post and jumping from his seat. "I'll see you all tomorrow evening to help with the big move then?"

They all nodded in agreement.

"Jed's coming too."

The nodding became less enthusiastic.

"He's not bringing Goldie is he?" asked Ayisha cautiously.

"I hope not."

With a loud snort Varn returned to full consciousness.

"How are you getting there Nicky?" he asked.

"Paul and Laura are taking me. They're helping to bring some of the Barrowhouse stuff back. Apparently Mindi's arranging it."

"Of course," said Ayisha coldly.

The woman in the uniform was trying to catch his eye as she waited patiently by the entrance to the tunnel through the swan's neck.

"Look, I've got to go," said Nick, subconsciously looking at his watch again. "Oh, and Church...Good luck with the voting thing and the judging and all that!"

He strode over to the tunnel and the woman helped him into one of the now familiar snails.

"Travelling along the neck is much easier while the swan is in flight," she said as they rumbled down the tunnel. "It's straight you see during this time. When the swan has landed or is on water, the neck is in a more upright, or more curved position..."

"So these snails have to become more like a lift then," cut in Nick.

"Exactly," replied the woman, beaming.

The snail emerged into the swan's head. The cabin

was quite small, with the usual eyes that were windows, but the control panel seemed much more modern and complex than most birds he'd flown in!

The two pilots, wearing immaculate blue uniforms, glanced round and hurriedly waved to him but it was obvious that all their concentration was required to fly the thing.

"Please stay in the snail and strap yourself in till we've landed," said the pilot on the left. "Landing in one of these can be a bit bumpy sometimes."

Nick did as he was told. It was eerily quiet up here at the front. The engines were a long way away, right near the back. Even the huge wings were strangely absent of the thumping noises that usually occurred as they flapped during flight.

He still felt a little apprehensive though as the bird banked, first to the left, then to the right, wobbling unsteadily as it levelled out.

His ears popped and he knew they were starting to descend. Gradually the horizon appeared in the two round screens. The pilots' hands flashed across the control panel and Nick glanced at the woman strapped into the seat at his side. She smiled at him reassuringly.

As they dropped lower, he began to hear the whine of the engines as they fought to stabilize the flight.

The pilots constantly talked to each other but he couldn't make out what they were saying. He gripped the armrest anxiously, his fingers digging into the soft material.

They began to turn to the right as the descent increased.

Suddenly, the view through the screens changed. Directly in front of them was an enormous figure, and they were flying straight towards its head. Nick could clearly see the look of astonished fear as the head ducked down at the last moment, revealing a second, equally frightened figure.

The pilots desperately dragged their controls to the left and the swan rolled violently as the engines rose to a scream.

The woman gasped.

Nick closed his eyes.

The bird straightened back into level flight and dropped down still lower. The engine level settled back to a whine once more and Nick opened his eyes.

The screens now showed a blur of green that was gradually rising as the bird lowered.

The pilot on the right pulled back on a large central lever and the swan shuddered once, before thudding gently onto the ground.

"There. That wasn't too bad was it?" said the woman, smiling again as she unclipped his belt.

"Er...No..." replied Nick, staring at his shaking hands.

The whole lower, central column between the two pilots began to drop down, revealing steps down to the ground.

"Thanks for flying Swanlines," said the pilot on the left cheerfully.

"Sorry about the bit of turbulence at the end," added the pilot on the right with a grin. "These things take a bit of controlling when they've got a full load."

Without waiting for a reply, both began checking the various dials and gauges.

Nick spluttered his thanks, staggered down the steps and stepped off the beak and onto the ground which, after the swan, felt nice and solid.

He moved quickly over into a clump of scraggy weeds as the swan's wings began to flap once more. He didn't want to get sucked in by the draught from them, or get hit by a huge webbed foot.

The bird took six or seven clumsy steps forward, its wings beating frantically before it wobbled up into the air, the wings making a heavy thumping sound as it fought for height.

He watched it till it was a tiny dot heading in the direction of Hightower, then checked that he wasn't under any overhanging bushes or branches before pressing the ring to the shrinkage post.

As usual, it took him a few moments to regain his senses after returning to his normal size. He was just putting the post back in his pocket when a voice called out.

"Hey Nickers. Did you see that bird? Me and Tommo nearly got killed by it."

Nick stared blankly at the two figures on the bank above him.

"Swan!" said Tommo.

The taller figure frowned.

"What?"

"Swan," repeated Tommo. "That bird Smiffy, it were a swan."

"Don't care worrit was," replied Smiffy sullenly. "It were proper vicious. It were screaming all the time… real loud and angry like."

Tommo scratched his head and peered at Nick.

"Hey Nickers, did it go for you?" he said, his eyes widening. "Looks like it did."

Nick touched the graze on his cheek and glanced at his torn shirt.

"Er…Yeah. I was just coming back up the school field and it…like…flew over the fence and straight at me. I jumped out of its way and landed in those bushes.

Tommo nudged Smiffy's arm.

"See, I told yer. Dangerous them swans."

"Yeah, whatever," replied Smiffy, rapidly losing interest. "Come on, it's time we were getting back."

Nick followed them, feeling quite relieved. Tommo and Smiffy were all right. They weren't exactly his friends and they weren't exactly bright but they'd never done him any harm. They were however, very loud and it wouldn't be long before the whole school knew about his encounter with a swan.

But that was fine with him. It did sort of explain his battered appearance. After all, a strange attack by a swan was always going to be slightly more believable than being trapped inside a rat by a gigantic breadknife!!

*

That night Nick didn't sleep too well, which wasn't surprising considering the type of day he'd had, and when he did finally manage to drift off in the early hours of the morning, he was rudely awakened by the sound of the toilet flushing.

He was now fully awake once more and further sleep was impossible as the thought that he too now needed the toilet gnawed at his brain.

With a heavy sigh he slipped on his dressing gown and slippers and shuffled out into the hallway, rubbing his eyes and shivering in the cold darkness.

As he reached for the handle, the bathroom door swung open and a shadowy figure loomed over him.

The figure gave a muffled scream and leapt back, fumbling for the light cord as it did so.

"What you doing creeping around?" mumbled Dave, his face suddenly illuminated by the bathroom light.

For a fraction of a second Nick glimpsed fear in the man's wide, bulging eyes.

"Er, going to the toilet," he replied defiantly, holding his breath against the smell of stale beer.

"Don't try to be clever," sneered Dave, recovering

his composure, "and turn the light off when you're done. I'm going down to get myself some water."

He stumbled past, staring uneasily around as he lurched downstairs.

By the time Nick returned to his bedroom, he was deep in thought. His dislike for Dave now bordered on hatred. Sure, the success at Barrowhouse gave him immense satisfaction, but the man was still here; still in the cottage, making life unbearable.

Earlier that evening, Dave had staggered back from the pub and slumped into the chair, drinking can after can of beer, his expression so dark and angry that his mum, completely unlike her normal, old self, had merely tiptoed round him.

"What's wrong dear?" and "do you want anything to eat dear?" had just been met with a sullen silence that made Nick want to leap to his feet and announce grandly that he knew exactly what was wrong with the miserable little swine!

But of course he couldn't, no matter how satisfied he felt over the day's proceedings, so he'd slipped quietly off to bed.

Now he could hear Dave clumping back up the stairs.

He slipped silently over to the bedroom door and opened it just a fraction to see the figure staggering past, the eyes still anxiously scanning side to side.

Nick had a sudden idea. He fumbled through a drawer in his desk and found a small plastic pencil sharpener.

He edged the door open a little more and threw the pencil sharpener out into the gloom. It rebounded off the far wall with a resounding crack and settled in a corner.

Dave gave a muted yell and pressed himself up against the wall. With a trembling hand, he fumbled for the bedroom door, thankfully found it and pushed it open and with one final nervous glance, disappeared hurriedly inside.

Nick quietly shut his own door and grinned.

So, Dave was frightened of the dark. Or frightened of what could be out there in the dark.

He slipped back into bed. Sleep would be a long time in coming. He had too much to think about.

Maybe… Just maybe…!!

*

"Look, I don't care what it says on this," said the harassed man, waving Mindi's authentic looking delivery note at the cluttered warehouse behind him. "They're not there!"

Paul, Laura and Nick were huddled round the back of the battered old car, its door open, waiting to accept the four large boxes containing vast quantities of stuff that was to be shipped from the Barrowhouse complex to the Elvereys new home at Hightower.

"I can't understand it," said Paul, drumming his fingers on the car roof. "We were told they'd be ready and waiting when we got here."

"Well they're not," snapped the man irritably. "Quite honestly, I've got enough to do without searching through this lot. It is the Christmas rush you know."

"You don't look that busy to me," said Laura, glancing round the empty loading area.

"Maybe not now," replied the man tapping his watch. "It's getting late. Most people have picked up today's deliveries. But I've got to get all that lot back there ready for tomorrow. I'm all on my own too. Tony left at nine thirty. Honestly, I don't know what…"

Nick stared at the car park behind him. It was

emptying fast. Soon the place would be closing and everyone would be back snug and warm in their own homes.

He envied them. He felt miserable, cold and tired. Paul and Laura had been good enough to bring him down here and to take some things back for the Elvereys, but the whole thing was an enormous operation and he'd promised to help with the removals at the other place; the main one at the island on the lake. It would be a long time before he'd be able to sneak back to his bedroom and get some sleep, which considering how little he'd managed to get the previous night, was something he needed desperately.

Laura's elbow nudged him in the ribs and he spun round. Behind the man, who was still droning on about how busy he was, something was moving.

Nick gasped and his stomach lurched in that 'oh no, how are we going to mange this,' type of way that was becoming so familiar to him.

Four large cardboard boxes were wobbling slowly across the warehouse floor, and they seemed to be moving on hundreds and hundreds of tiny, brown, furry feet!

Nick looked aghast at the spectacle.

The man paused, aware that he was no longer holding the attention of his audience of three with his ramblings. He frowned and slowly began to turn in the direction they were staring.

In desperation, Laura screamed hysterically.

"OH NO," she yelled, grabbing the man's sleeve and waving vaguely in the opposite direction.

"What the...?" he muttered.

"My car!"

"Your what?"

"My car," she repeated, pointing at a large, flashy

German car parked at the edge of the warehouse bay.

"Your car?" mumbled the man, looking totally confused.

"Somebody's hit it. They've scratched it," she moaned, her voice rising still higher.

"But I thought you were with them," said the man, jerking his thumb at Paul and Nick as he was dragged away towards the other car.

"Them? Oh no. I was just er… queuing up behind them."

"Queue? But there's no one else to…"

"Waiting my turn," cut in Laura, pulling on the man's arm and pointing at the car.

"There," she announced triumphantly. "Look at that mark. My car's ruined. RUINED."

The man scratched his head and bent closer to the side of the car.

"And it's all your fault. I'm going to sue this place."

"But I can't see anything; and we take no responsibility for…"

"Look closer. See…? Just there," wailed Laura, pushing the poor man closer to the metalwork whilst peering desperately at Paul and Nick.

Paul and Nick got the message. In a flash the two of them grabbed the boxes and, despite the weight, they began to haul each in turn into the back of the car.

As they strained to lift each one, the rats below, now free of their burden, scampered away and leapt through the open flaps in the top of the fourth box.

Laura was still yelling at the unfortunate man as they lifted the last box. As they took the strain, the final group of rats crawled up their legs and jumped onto the top of the box before disappearing inside.

Despite the fact that they weren't actually real rats, Nick still shivered with revulsion at what had just happened. He glanced at Paul. By the look on his face, he felt exactly the same.

They hauled the final box into the car and slammed the door shut. The back of the poor car was nearly scraping on the ground with the weight.

Paul wiped sweat from his forehead and nodded at a camera in the corner.

"Hope they don't monitor those all the time," he said with a grim smile.

But at that moment they had more to contend with than just cameras.

"Exactly what do you two think you're doing?" called out a loud, authoritative voice.

Nick spun round.

An immaculately dressed, elderly couple stood by the big German car. The man, his hands on his hips, was tall and imposing. The woman, smaller and stockier, had a face like thunder.

The warehouseman looked up. If he'd looked confused before, he was totally bewildered now.

"Just looking for a scratch on this lady's car," he mumbled.

"A scratch?" roared the man.

"This lady's car?" yelled the woman.

Laura began to tiptoe away.

The warehouseman stood up.

The elderly couple stepped forward.

All three began to talk at once, their voices rising higher and higher.

Laura began to run.

Paul and Nick slipped into the car.

Paul started the engine and crunched into first gear. The car lurched forward and stalled. Nick groaned and slipped down in his seat, wishing once again that he was invisible.

The passenger door wrenched open and Laura jumped in. Nick glanced up to see the three figures rushing towards them.

"Come on," said Laura, looking down nervously as Paul fumbled with the key. The car spluttered into life and they jerked forward.

Laura lowered her window as they began to move.

"I think I've decided I prefer this car to that one," she said apologetically to the warehouseman as he slowed and stopped. His expression had gone way beyond bewilderment now. He just stared at them and held the delivery order up in a sort of blank way.

"Oh, and don't bother about that. We've got our boxes thank you."

Both the warehouseman and the elderly couple stood in utterly bemused confusion as the battered old car spluttered away in a haze of acrid smelling, eye watering blue smoke.

*

Paul and Laura dropped Nick off at the far end of the car park, near the lake, where he met Jed and the members of the overseer committee as previously arranged. Once he'd discreetly shrunk down to Elverey size they all travelled over to the island on the lake in order to help with the removal operations.

Nick liked travelling by fish. It was his favourite form of transport as they always seemed to be more modern, quieter and more comfortable than animals and birds.

Now, standing in the vast hall at the centre of the island, staring up at the massive glass dome in the middle of the ceiling, whilst hundreds of Elvereys rushed around, carrying boxes and bags, bits of furniture and crates full of equipment, the enormity of what they were doing was starting to sink in.

"What actually is this place?" he asked, shouting above the constant babble of voices.

Mindi glanced up from her clipboard and adjusted her earpiece.

"What? Oh this? This is the central reception area so to speak. This is floor one, the ground floor. Below us are living quarters, shops, administration and suchlike. The lifts actually go down as far as floor fourteen and…"

She broke off and pointed menacingly at a small, tubby figure dragging a large green sack.

"No, no, no. Put your back into it. Carry it properly, the way you were shown in my 'lift the safe way, not the sorry way' meeting last week."

"But…"

"I hear what your saying," said Mindi, tapping her clipboard, "but we all need to be singing off the same hymn sheet, as it were, with this."

"Now, where was I?" she said, turning back to Nick with a forced smile.

"Er, down as far as floor fourteen I think," replied Nick, noting that the tubby little Elverey, who was still dragging the sack, was now sticking his tongue out behind Mindi's back.

"Oh yes, the first three are…"

"Can I ask," cut in Nick. "The old spaceship. The one you originally arrived in. Is it still here?"

Mindi's smile broadened.

"It is. It's below level fourteen. We built on top of it."

"Wow. Is it used at all? The one at Hightower isn't…..
Well, there are Deebers down there, but nothing else."

"Deebers?"

"They're Elvereys that never left when the craft landed all those hundreds of years ago," replied Nick with a shiver. He still had nightmares about his encounter with them deep down in what the Elvereys called the old home. "They live in almost total darkness down there and are quite mad and terribly dangerous."

"We don't have anything like that," she assured him.

"So your craft is empty?"

"Absolutely," said Mindi brusquely. "It's remained derelict and out of bounds for centuries. When we finally leave, the issue will be addressed and it will be discreetly destroyed. When the big ones move in there will be no trace of it left whatsoever."

Nick stared around him.

"What about all this?"

"The same. Anything that can't be taken will be, what we like to call, finalized."

"What about the big glass dome?" said Nick, pointing to the ceiling.

Mindi shrugged. "That will stay."

"Stay?"

"Absolutely. It's actually something from the big one's world. It's some sort of fruit serving dish. One of the overseers brought it many, many years ago and placed it here upside down. So if it's left, no one will think much about it. Makes a nice, light, central feature don't you think?"

"Well yeah, suppose it does," said Nick, staring through the glass as a swan drifted by overhead. It had obviously not been loaded very well as the tail of some sort of fish was wriggling wildly from its rear end!

Mindi shook her head and consulted her clipboard.

"Really," she tutted. "That's flight LY 236. They should know better. After all, it's not rocket science loading those things."

"Yeah right," agreed Nick absently, still staring up at the night sky. A wasp hovered for a while at the edge of the dome then shot away as another swan flew across.

"There must be a lot of swans out there."

"There's a great deal to be transported," agreed Mindi. "That's TR 431…and it's twenty three seconds late!"

Before Nick could ask anything else one of Mindi's phones started to buzz. She glanced at the screen, sighed heavily and marched away.

"Oh Nicky," she said suddenly, spinning round to face him. "Before you finish tonight, can I just touch base with you? I need to have a word about something. It's a bit confidential. Need to run it up the flagpole so to speak."

"Er, yeah. Sure," replied Nick, not quite understanding what she was talking about.

"Oh, and Nicky. Your next job is to pick up some boxes down on floor six. Use the lift. Mr. Stowlumple is on that floor. He'll show you where they are. And please hurry. We need to push the envelope on this, and you're already four and a half minutes late by my schedule!"

*

Nick caught up with Jed and together they spent the next two hours going up and down in the lifts carrying various items up to the reception area, but to be honest, they spent more time messing about, much to the irritation of the extremely harassed Mr.Stowlumple.

They were kicking a rather deflated ball around in the reception hall when they ran into Church and Hercules who were on their way to the main entrance.

"Evening wing commander Nicky," said Church in a drawling, posh English accent. "On a special ops tonight are we, what?"

"Hi Church. What's up?" said Nick, trying not to

laugh at the little Elverey, who was wearing flying goggles, an enormous white scarf that hung to his knees, and had a big moustache that he constantly twirled at the edges. On the breast pocket of his battered leather jacket it said CHURCHILL – SQUADRON LEADER. Strapped to his back was a bag with bits of old yellow material hanging from it.

Church reached over his shoulder and patted the top of the bag.

"Trusty old parachute. Jolly helpful if the old bird comes down in enemy territory don't you know."

"Right," said Nick. He could hear Jed giggling behind him. "So you're off flying somewhere huh?"

Church tapped his nose and peered round cautiously.

"Top secret. Very hush hush."

"Taking the Barrowhouse engine-heart to Hightower," said Hercules grandly. "I, of course, am guarding it along with twenty of my very best men."

"Yeah, very top secret," muttered Nick under his breath.

Jed's giggling got louder.

Church shot an irritable glare at Hercules who took absolutely no notice.

"The best of all our pilots is taking us," announced Hercules loudly, putting a hefty arm round Church's shoulder, then wincing as he cut his finger on one of the buckles on the parachute bag.

Church softened at the big Elverey's words.

"Biggest mission of the whole campaign," he said happily, "and I'm captain of the swan."

Hercules nodded.

"We're taking it now as it's so important, but it won't stop the power here for a while as the …"

"…power is retained for a while even after the thing has gone," interrupted Nick, "yeah, I know. We've had dealings with these engine-heart things before."

At that moment he was suddenly aware that Mindi had returned and was tapping her clipboard impatiently and scowling at Church.

Church took the hint.

"Well, must be ready for the off and all that," he said, looking at his wrist, despite the fact there was no watch there. "Flying at ninety three hundred hours don't you know."

Mindi passed him the clipboard.

"Sign here please."

Church took the board and scribbled on the paper.

"This is to acknowledge receipt of the aforementioned items," she said importantly.

Church signed.

"Then sign here to confirm."

Church signed.

"And here. Disclaimer."

Church signed.

"And here. Health and safety. Clause five; paragragh B."

"Thank you," she said, grabbing the clipboard and ticking off each signature before marching away.

Church and Hercules rolled their eyes at one another and Nick grinned.

"Well, you two guys mind how you go," he said.

"Roger and out," replied Church with a twirl of his moustache.

"Who's Roger?" asked Hercules with a frown as they disappeared into the crowds.

Out the corner of his eye Nick glimpsed Mindi glaring at them and tapping her feet.

"Come on," he said, nudging Jed, "I think we'd better shift a few more boxes."

"Yeah, before old trout face blows a doozin' fuse!"

So they brought a few more boxes up and Mr Stowlumple relaxed a little.

They were near to finishing when Nick looked up at the dome to see a huge swan wobble past, its wings almost clipping the glass as it struggled to gain height.

That'll be Church, thought Nick, turning back towards the lift for one more collection. Jed, who'd had quite enough work for one day, went to get them a drink of earwig's blood, leaving Nick waiting at the lift doors.

When it arrived, he was surprised to see that he was the only one going back down. Usually, there were so many people around that it was a tight squeeze to fit everyone in. But then, it was getting later and the crowds were starting to thin out.

The doors swished shut and he pressed the button for floor six before leaning back against the wall to savour the quiet isolation.

His stomach did a little jump as the lift began to descend. He felt tired now, but contented. By the look of it, the Elvereys should all be finished soon and the enormous job of moving an entire world would be over.

He glanced at his watch. Soon he'd be flying home. He reckoned he'd be able to sleep a little better tonight. He was physically tired enough to.

The buttons flashed out each floor as the lift went down. Two, three, then four.

The machinery above droned out its soft buzzing noise.

Five.

Nick leaned forward, finger hovering over the 'open door' button.

Six.

He frowned. The lurching sensation in his stomach continued. The buzzing noise appeared to be a little louder.

Seven.

Eight.

"What the...?" he muttered, hurriedly pressing the number six button.

Nine.

Ten.

Eleven.

The lurching sensation in his stomach became a flutter of apprehension.

Twelve.

Thirteen.

He was starting to get really worried now. The buzzing noise was definitely louder. The lift began rocking as though the speed was increasing.

Fourteen.

He jabbed his finger furiously on the number six button and braced himself for the lift to crash into the ground. The flutter of apprehension became a stab of fear. The buzzing sound became a roar as the lift gained speed.

He punched the alarm button.

Nothing!

The lift swayed with the momentum and he closed his eyes, his ears deafened by the noise. His limbs were shaking and he was sweating in the heat of the little room.

He slowly opened his eyes again, sensing a gradual change as the swaying stopped and the lift slowed; and as it slowed, the roar died back to a distant buzzing.

The descent suddenly stopped and there was a little juddering bump, then nothing but silence.

Nick tried to swallow but his mouth was dry. He stepped back till he was pressing up against the back wall.

Very slowly, the lift door slid back.

Nick peered out, his heartbeat crashing against his

chest. At first he could make out nothing but blackness. He blinked and began to see a pale glow way out there in the distance.

The air smelt old and fusty.

"Hello…" he mumbled hoarsely. "Hello. Is anyone there?"

His frightened, timid voice drifted out into the darkness.

"Is anyone there?" he repeated, trying to add some confidence to the tone.

There was a long, eerie silence, broken only by his own, laboured breathing.

Then he heard it, whispered out in that black void, and his blood turned to ice.

"Dominic Oliver Collins," it hissed. "I have been waiting for you…"

*

Chapter 9

SNOWFALL

That night, many of the Barrowhouse Elvereys, along with some from Hightower, worked right through until the early hours. By the time they finally staggered off to bed for a well earned rest, most of the work was done.

Mindi was immensely pleased. They were now ahead of schedule and were well on the way to being integrated into their new home.

A huge amount of cargo and passengers had been shifted from Barrowhouse to the new home of Rixal in Hightower. Over two hundred flights by swan had been made and the whole thing had been achieved with great efficiency and secrecy. Nobody had witnessed what had taken place.

Well, almost nobody…

A report by Mr.Mulholland, vice president of the Barrowhouse and district bird watching society would later say that he'd been dive-bombed by an enormous swan. Worse, rather than making the usual normal call of a swan, this one seemed to be singing out something like the Dambusters theme! The same Mr. Mulholland also swore that earlier in the evening he'd seen a fish waving at him from the rear of a swan flying slowly in the direction of Hightower. Upon receipt of the report, the unfortunate man was apparently relieved of his vice presidency, on grounds of alleged possible drinking problems!

One other figure that observed the evening's operations was Tritus, standing in the darkness, his one good eye fixed intently on the swans circling one by one around Rixal, a grotesque, humourless grin on his distorted face.

But despite these two incidents, that night was a total and complete success.

Yet for one person, one way or another, it was a night they would never quite forget...!!

*

...Nick kept jabbing the buttons but it was pretty obvious that the door was not going to close and the lift was not going back up.

He considered his options. He could stay where he was, shivering nervously in the tiny, brightly lit prison, or investigate the black void beyond.

He knew that there was really no choice, so with a heavy sigh he stepped hesitantly out into the new surroundings.

He felt his way forward into the darkness, carefully probing the walls with his hands and it became immediately clear that he was walking down a narrow corridor.

It was a silent, eerie place. The walls felt slimy and warm under his touch, the ground was soft and spongy, and the air felt thick and uncomfortably warm.

He paused for a moment and concentrated. In the silence there was just the slightest wheezing sigh, over and over again, like soft, distant breathing.

Looking back, the lift, with its comforting lights already seemed a long way away.

Where was he?

Mindi had said earlier that the Barrowhouse craft was still there, way below the ground.

Was that where he was now?

He shivered. If he was, he hoped she was right and there were no Deebers around.

Then another thought struck him. Mindi had said that the craft would eventually be destroyed, along with everything that couldn't be transported. 'Leave no trace whatsoever,' had been her exact words. What if he were trapped down here? What if he couldn't find a way back? Panic bubbled up within him and he forced the thought from his mind, concentrating instead on the faint glow of light ahead.

He walked on towards it, yet despite getting closer, it didn't seem to get any brighter.

His steps faltered. The sound drifting up the corridor was definitely breathing, a harsh, rasping sound now, as though each breath was a desperate struggle.

Once more Nick glanced back at the lift. The light was a mere dot in the distance. He felt a sudden urge to run back, to cower in the corner under the glare of the lights with his head covered by his hands.

He looked back the other way. It was the sheer blackness around him that he feared the most. Anything could be out there. Anything could be next to him, or above him, waiting to pounce and devour him, or rip him to shreds.

He tried to calm down and concentrated on the glow again. The answer, he was sure, was there. He needed to take control, so with a deep breath, he strode purposefully forward, once more.

Incredibly, the blackness seemed to get thicker, as though closing in and the glow remained nothing but a small dot of light.

As he stepped up to it, he realized the light was coming from what looked like a small window in the corridor wall.

He leaned forward and peered in. There was no glass in the misshapen opening and a pungent smell of decay drifted out. It was so strong it made him recoil.

Holding his breath he cautiously leaned forward again.

Inside was a room, but it was far too dim to make out either the size, or what was in there.

He scanned the gloom and his heart seemed to jump. Over to the left something moved in the semi darkness. He squinted but it was difficult to make out much.

There was a strange, pale form that at first glance seemed to roll like water, then flicker like flame, but never quite achieving any form or substance that he could recognize.

With every movement that rasping breathing echoed out into the darkness.

Nick blinked, trying to make some sense of the shape before him, to work out what it was, but any idea seemed frustratingly just out of reach.

He felt terribly afraid, but just a little curious too.

"Dominic …Oliver…Collins," hissed the mass, writhing and contorting with each word. "You are… here. Finally…you are …here."

Each syllable was spoken between sharp intakes of breath as though a mighty effort was required just to communicate.

Nick shook himself from his state of fascinated shock.

"Who? Who are you?" he muttered.

"No…Matter."

For a moment the breathing subsided.

"How do you know me?" Nick asked cautiously.

"I…have… chosen...you," it replied slowly.

"For what?"

"…Chosen."

Nick scratched his head. He didn't seem to be getting very far.

"Look," he said, trying a different line. "All this is going to be destroyed soon. Everything's being moved to a new place. I can tell the others and you can…"

"NO!" it roared, the vague mass writhing with the urgency of the sound.

Nick took a step back.

"I am aware… of this… move. I am…finally dying. After all this …time. My time…is complete…"

Nick couldn't think of anything to say to this. Comforting a dying blob of something wasn't an area he'd much experience in!

"You…must take…"

The voice drained away and the glow dimmed still lower. Out the corner of his eye, Nick glimpsed something on the window ledge, tucked into the corner.

"Take it…and leave."

Nick peered closer. As he did so, the light increased for a moment and he saw a small, strange object. It looked a bit like a small, broken coin or medallion, with one round edge and the other sharp and jagged. It glistened like metal, yet looked gnarled and grained like wood.

"Take it… Keep it…but tell no one of…its existence."

Nick held out a trembling hand.

"But what is it?" he asked anxiously.

"It …is… forever…" came the hoarse reply. "I am dying…but it…is…forever…. It is the Circle…"

Nick frowned, his hand hovering uncertainly. It certainly didn't look much like a circle.

"Take it…" hissed the thing, with a renewed sense of urgency.

Nick paused a moment longer, then hesitantly picked the object up. As he did, a strange spark of energy suddenly tingled through his body and then was gone.

"What was that?" he spluttered.

"Tell no one of me...tell no one of... of what you have...acquired."

"But..."

"Tell no one...To do so...would be...dangerous...for you...for them...understand?"

"Dangerous? Why?"

"NO ONE...! UNDERSTAND?"

"Yeah OK," conceded Nick, trying not to anger the thing. "But what do I do with it."

"Use it...wisely," came the answer, the voice back down to a whispering hiss.

"Use it? When? How?"

"Whenever you...you are in your greatest moment of...peril...of danger...when there is nothing else left to use..."

Nick shook his head.

"What do you mean by that?" he said, looking uncertainly at the object in his hand.

As if in reply the creature's breathing became a series of short, sharp gasps, and Nick wasn't sure if the sound was the thing struggling to breathe, or whether it was actually laughing!

"You will know...It will... know," it finally said, recovering its composure. "Now go...Leave me...to my...destruction."

Nick slipped the broken coin thing in his jeans pocket and just stood there. He didn't know quite what to do.

Run back to the lift?

Stay and chat with his new acquaintance?

Try and find out more?

"Remember... no one must know...any of this..."

"Right," said Nick hesitantly. "Are you sure I can't help..."

"GO…NOW!!!"

Nick's decision was made by the ferocity of the command. He quickly walked back down the corridor in the direction of the tiny speck of light from the lift. He focused on the light, not once looking back, his hurried steps becoming a jog, which gradually turned into a run.

Thankfully, that awful, forced breathing dissolved into the blackness the greater the distance he got from the creature.

As he reached the lift he suddenly heard the hissing voice back down the corridor.

"… Chosen," it said, as he pressed the button, knowing somehow that this time the door would shut.

"I chose…you," it said as the doors closed, though for some weird reason he couldn't really tell if he were now actually hearing the words, or if they were somehow seeping into his mind. It was a strange sensation but then, everything seemed strange in that place.

With a huge sense of relief Nick felt the lift lurch upwards. He slid to the floor, the coin type thing feeling heavy in his pocket.

His mind was churning with questions. The trouble was, they were questions to which he had no answers.

*

"Where have you been?" said Jed irritably as Nick tumbled out of the lift. "I've been waiting with these drinks nearly twenty doozin' minutes."

Nick glanced at his watch. Was it only twenty minutes since he'd gone back down? He tried to compose himself, but he was still trembling.

"Well I'm here now," he muttered dismissively.

"She's been looking for you too."

Jed nodded towards Mindi, who appeared to be

ticking off a couple of bored looking workers in bright orange overalls.

"Great!"

At that moment Mindi noticed his re-appearance and with a tired smile, marched towards them.

"Can't we just go?" said Jed, sighing. "I've had enough today."

"Fraid not. She wants to run up a flagpole or something!"

"Do what?"

"Exactly. I don't know what she's talking about half the time either!"

"Ah Nicky," said Mindi briskly, "so glad we've managed to touch base. Just need to push the needle so to speak, on a one to one basis."

She swung her gaze on Jed, the smile fading.

"I think Mindi means she wants a private word with me," said Nick.

"Just the two of you?" replied Jed frowning.

"Well that's like, usually what private means, yeah."

"Well don't be long then, I'm tired," said Jed, failing to stifle a huge yawn as he sauntered off.

"Now," said Mindi, placing her laptop on a chair. "I need to have an executive, high level, one to one meeting with you."

Her fingers leapt across the keyboard and the screen flashed out a bewildering array of graphs and figures.

"You do?"

"...I suggest Sunday at 9.30 am. Does that synchronize with your schedule?"

"My what? Well, I suppose so, but what's this all about?" replied Nick, feeling totally baffled. As it happened, by the weekend it wouldn't matter what day Mindi wanted. Friday was the last day before the Christmas holidays and his schedule was hardly packed after that!

"Good…good," said Mindi, tapping more keys. "Now, where shall we meet. Thinking outside the box, I suggest somewhere over your way. Hightower way."

"Mindi, what's this all about?" Nick's tone was more annoyed now.

Mindi paused and cautiously looked around before she spoke.

"Look Nicky. This is highly confidential so to speak. Something just between ourselves."

Nick groaned. Just how many secrets was he supposed to keep?

"It's not something unpleasant. In fact, quite the opposite," she continued, noting his look of irritation, "but it's…it's not something to disclose to anyone else. Not yet anyway. Please, believe me, this level of confidentiality will be most worthwhile."

Nick glared at her.

"Please…"

Nick softened.

"OK," he replied, not feeling particularly convinced. "How about we meet at the station then? On the platform."

"The station?"

"The railway. In the spare bedroom at Hightower cottage."

Mindi beamed and tapped the details into her laptop.

"The station it is then."

"Can I ask you about something else?" he said slowly as she started to tuck the laptop back into its case.

"Absolutely."

"Earlier, you said the old craft, the Barrowhouse one, is below these floors."

Mindi looked up, her eyes narrowing suspiciously.

"Yes, that's correct."

"Well, is there… is there anyone, or anything down there in it?"

She looked confused.

"With all due respect Nicky, as I said before, there's nothing down there. Hasn't been for many, many years. It was all, so to speak, sealed off."

It was Nick's turn to be confused.

"Sealed off," he spluttered. "So the lift doesn't go down to…"

"The lift?" interrupted Mindi, throwing him a quizzical look. "No. It stops at floor fourteen. It can't, and doesn't go down any further. Not to my knowledge. At the end of the day, anything below has always remained sealed and derelict. Why do you ask?"

A shiver rippled through Nick. He wanted to ask so much more, but the words 'dangerous to you… and to them,' echoed through his mind.

Before he could say another word however, Mindi's phone began bleeping and with an indifferent wave, she hurried away.

He was suddenly aware of Jed tapping him on the shoulder.

"Troutface gone then?"

"Yeah," replied Nick, grinning.

"What did she want?"

"She wanted to…" he began, then remembered just in time. "Oh, nothing really. You know what's she's like. Come on, let's get back. I'm shattered."

As they trudged through the reception doors, two thoughts struck him. One was how totally and completely shattered he actually was. The other was just how acutely aware he was of the strange, coin-like medallion jangling in his pocket.

*

The snow that fell early Saturday morning, leaving the

ground covered in a thick, white blanket, didn't hamper the Elverey world much. Life pretty much went on as normal. The squirrel buses still scurried from tree to tree and branch to branch, brushing snow to the side as they went, and for those who wanted to travel by foot, special snakes bore large tunnels through the snow. Even the flights were hardly interrupted as the birds were all extremely sure footed.

Nick had arranged to meet up with Jed at Miru and by the time he arrived the clouds had rolled away and a pale, watery sun hung low in the sky, just above the leafless branches of Hightower woods.

He was feeling good. School was over for a while and the Barrowhouse move was pretty much completed. Overhead, the last flock of swans were swooping in low, packed with families of excited Elvereys bound for their new homes up in the Rixal area of Hightower.

It felt great to be away from the slog and the tedium of such a huge operation and Nick was determined to enjoy himself.

First, he and Jed spent some time in the bustling, circular shopping levels inside the trees at Miru. Surprisingly, considering the vast crowds, they bumped into Ayisha, who was doing her usual mountainous amount of shopping then, a couple of floors higher, into Varn who was buying his weekly supply of tablets and potions, creams and medicines.

Nick, still troubled by events earlier in the week, took him quietly on one side and asked him what sort of things could possibly live inside the old home, the old craft at Hightower.

Varn stroked his trim beard and looked at him curiously.

"I think you know the answer to that Nicky," he said soothingly. "After all, you've been down to the craft.

Deebers and more Deebers. Things you really want to keep away from."

"Yes," replied Nick hesitantly, trying carefully not to say too much. "But is there anything… anything else?"

"Like what?"

Nick stood there awkwardly and frowned.

"Oh, I don't know. Something… something weirder. A blob type of thing perhaps?"

"Blob?"

"Yeah. Blobbish. Sort of twisting, squirming sort of thing." He waved his hands around vaguely, trying to describe the indescribable.

It was obvious from Varn's blank expression that he hadn't the faintest idea what Nick was talking about, so Nick gave up and told him to forget about it. When the old Elverey started to talk about his most recent ailments, the two boys made their excuses and left.

"Hey Nicky," said Jed excitedly, later on when they were outside in the bitterly cold fresh air, "ever been sledging?"

"Well yeah, of course," he replied, marvelling at the carpet of snow flakes that crunched softly under his feet. At the size he was, each one was an individual, six pointed star, laid layer upon layer on the ground.

He picked one up and was mesmerized. It was about the size of a plate but quite thin, and the intricate crystal pattern looked so delicate, shimmering in the light. He gripped one of the points and broke it off. The ice was brittle and snapped loudly.

As a gentle breeze ruffled his hair, he threw the crystal up. It floated into the air, sparkling in the sunlight before silently drifting back to the ground and merging into the whiteness.

Nick just stood there, astonished by the brilliant, silent beauty of it all.

The moment didn't last long.

"Er, hello. Anybody there?" said Jed, tapping him impatiently on the arm.

"Sorry," said Nick. "What were we saying?"

Jed rolled his eyes.

"Sledging. Do you want to go doozin' sledging?"

Nick wasn't sure. It wasn't something he'd ever been much into. When he'd lived in the town he and his mates used to go to the local park sometimes, but there never seemed to be that much snow around and it all seemed a bit half-hearted.

But it was pretty obvious that Jed wanted to, so Nick offered a weak smile and said he thought it was a great idea.

The 'sledge' turned out to be a sliced open acorn, turned sideways, and fastened to skis. Harnesses from the acorn were attached to a large spider with long, delicate legs.

"Are you sure about this?" Nick said, anxiously eying up the spider in front of him as he squeezed into the acorn. His experience of spiders in the Elverey world hadn't always been good!

"Course," shouted Jed from the other acorn sledge. "You know the only insects Elverey has are ones that have been trained. Just enjoy it."

"Hmmm," mused Nick, leaning back in his seat and trying to relax. The attendant appeared above the top edge of the acorn and grinned.

"Just cover yourself with this blanket. Keep warm, like. See these two straps? Pull this one and Killer will go to the left."

"Killer?" spluttered Nick nervously.

The grin broadened.

"Just our little joke. Killer wouldn't hurt a fly."

"Hmmm," repeated Nick, thinking that a fly would be exactly what Killer would love to hurt!

"Pull this other strap and you'll go to the right. Shake both straps to go forward, and pull back on both and you'll stop... hopefully! Got it?"

Before Nick could reply, the attendant gave both straps a good shake and leapt back.

Suddenly, Nick's world lurched forward, pinning him back in his seat as the acorn skimmed briskly over the snow. Ahead, the big, furry body of Killer faded behind a blurred haze of snow and ice, kicked up from the spindly legs as they slithered over the ground.

He was swept down tunnels, swung round corners and flung through vast open spaces. Gradually, unease turned to excitement, and Nick began to love it.

Jed constantly tried to overtake but Killer was the faster spider. They yelled and cheered, catching their breath in the bitter, biting wind as they hissed over the ice.

The harnesses didn't seem to control much but both spiders appeared to know exactly what they were doing. The speeds got faster, the corners sharper, and the world outside became a blur of white, but the longer the ride went on the more confident Nick became. If one of Killers legs slipped in the snow, there were another seven to take control!

When at last they started to slow down, Nick felt disappointed. He wanted the ride to go on and on. When they finally came to a stop and the attendant let them out, he still felt giddy with excitement.

"That was so cool," he enthused as they walked through one of the snow-snake tunnels.

"Yeah," agreed Jed, before bursting out laughing.

"What?"

"Your face," he spluttered. "It's bright red."

Nick started laughing too.

"So's yours. It must have been the cold. You look like a beetroot!"

"A ...what?"

Both boys collapsed into convulsions of laughter.

Suddenly Nick was aware that Jed's mirth had trailed away and he was just standing there, staring around with wide, anxious eyes.

He glanced round. Others in the tunnel had paused, all with equally concerned expressions on their faces.

"Jed? What's up?" he said.

Jed grabbed his arm.

"Can't you hear it?" he whispered.

"Hear what?"

"The hornets. Mr'S's hornets."

At that moment Nick detected a vague, low buzzing sound, muffled by the walls of snow around them. As it got louder, the buzzing broke into vague, distorted words.

'...ning...warning...big...the...ity...warning...big people in the vicinity...ing...'

Gradually it faded back to muted buzzing, then silence as the hornets moved on.

For a moment everyone seemed to hesitate.

"Come on," snapped Jed urgently. "We've got to get out of here. This tunnel's right under the main path."

"Yeah," agreed Nick in a much calmer tone than he felt, "but most of Mr.S's warnings are false alarms."

"Maybe, but we can't stay here. If it isn't a doozin' false..." Jed's voice trailed away as a thudding noise above rocked the tunnel.

The boys looked questioningly at each other. Someone further down the tunnel screamed.

Nick pointed towards an entrance in the roots of one of the trees at the edge of the covered path.

"Come on Jed, this way," he yelled, and together

they ran while above the thudding footsteps grew and bits of snow and ice began to drop from the ceiling.

They ran in what felt to Nick like slow motion, their feet slipping on the icy surface. The entrance didn't seem to be getting any bigger yet the crashing roar of giant footsteps was getting louder with every second.

Slowly; gradually, they struggled on. Slipping and sliding, going as fast as they could till finally, with a massive sense of relief, Jed and Nick reached the safety of the tree entrance.

Nick glanced back. The last Elvereys rushed past, fear etched onto their faces.

Just then, a thunderous footstep crushed the tunnel and for a moment the whole world behind them became one mass of falling white before becoming a solid black wall.

"Phew! That was doozin' close," muttered Jed with a weak smile.

"Yeah," agreed Nick. "But what's anyone doing here? Hardly anyone knows about this path into the woods."

"Dunno," said Jed, brushing splinters of ice off his old jacket.

"Well let's go and see shall we? I'd like to know who's just tried to crush me into the snow!"

So they took one of the lifts up the main tree in Miru, then travelled through one of the overhanging branches. As they walked along, from the height they were, Nick could just make out Hightower cottage. Parked down the side was a big, flash four by four.

Nick frowned. He didn't like the look of that. When they were over the centre of the path he looked the other way. Below, and a little further down the path, toward the stream and the land of Glug, two men were standing. One was Dave, the other was an important looking man in an expensive coat and big hiking boots that looked weirdly out of place with the equally expensive looking suit.

"Come on," said Nick, dragging Jed by the arm, "I want to hear what they're saying."

He pushed open a tiny door and the two of them slipped out onto a small balcony, disguised by the thick bark of the tree.

The sudden coldness of the air took their breath away.

"Oh yes," Dave was saying grandly. "All this land belongs to the estate. Pretty much as far as the eye can see. Of course, the actual boundaries are in the plans I've shown you back at the cottage."

"Very impressive," agreed Mr.Expensive suit. "Very impressive indeed. I'm sure we'll be able assist you with your project for this property and its lands."

Dave rubbed his hands together. He was almost jumping up and down with excitement.

"Excellent. And just how quickly do you think we'll be able to proceed?"

Mr.Expensive suit rubbed his chin and looked around thoughtfully.

"Pretty quickly I would say. With something of this size and quality there won't be any problems. No problems at all."

Nick leaned back against the wall with his mouth wide open. He felt aghast at the conversation he'd just heard. Though he didn't know exactly what Dave and the guy below had in mind for Hightower, he knew enough to realize it was bad.

Whatever it was, the Elvereys world was in danger.

He had to do something and he had to do it fast.

Memories from the incident with Dave the other evening drifted back into his mind.

He turned to Jed.

"I think it's time I had a little chat with Mr.S," he said, smiling grimly. "This afternoon would be good. I've a bit of an idea that he might be able to help me with!"

*

Chapter 10

SURPRISES

Oh, it was all coming together so well, so beautifully, just like he'd planned. Of course it had taken a long, long time, but in the end it would all be worth it.

Just one more day and the plan would swing into action.

The Deeber standing respectfully at his shoulder moved forward to offer a re-fill but he covered the glass with a scrawny hand and shook his head. What he needed was a steady nerve and a sharp mind.

The figure slipped back into the shadows, leaving him alone with his thoughts once more.

He leaned back in the chair and sighed contentedly.

One more day!

Mindi Pankhurst would be the first to play her part, the part that would set it all in motion. The part that would begin the ultimate downfall of Dominic Oliver Collins…And as the boy fell, he would rise.

The wait was over.

Tritus was back!!

*

Jed had lived a sad life. His parents had died when he was very young and Napoleon, his uncle, had considered himself too important and too busy to look after the lad, so had sent him as far away as possible.

The place decided upon couldn't have been further away or more remote. That place was with Mr.and Mrs. Scoggins.

Jed's guardians lived high up inside a tree, well away from the main residential areas of Hightower. This, along with the fact that they were a most peculiar couple, had made Jed's life lonely, as well as sad.

That was, until Nick had come along.

For some strange reason, Mr.and Mrs.S. quite liked Nick. For some even stranger reason, one he really couldn't explain, Nick actually quite liked the Scoggins'.

OK, their accommodation (if it could be called that) wasn't too great. In fact, it was appalling. The rooms were dirty and smelly. Mr.and Mrs.S. were dirty and smelly. The 'food' Mrs.S. tried to force on Nick was usually pretty much inedible...and always smelly!

But a visit to the Scoggins' house was always an experience that could be described, at the very least, as interesting!

As Nick sat there in Mr.S's cramped office, looking out into the branch that held row upon row of hornets, he felt a twinge of anxiety as the scruffy Elverey read through the ideas he'd hastily scribbled down, with Jed peering casually over his shoulder.

With the paper held close to his nose and a frowning squint on his ugly face, Nick couldn't tell whether Mr.S. had trouble with his eyesight or couldn't actually read too well.

Finally, with a chuckle he threw the paper onto the cluttered desk and leaned back in his chair.

"You really don't like this Dave bloke much do yer?"

"No Mr.Scoggins, I don't. But this isn't just about me. If he has his way I reckon Hightower would be in great danger. What's happened to Barrowhouse could happen here."

Mr.S. picked up part of a fly's wing from the desk and stared at it.

"An what yer want to do is frighten 'im like. 'Aunt 'im out 'o the 'ouse. You reckon that'll work huh?"

"I don't see why not. He was pretty wound up by the dark the other night."

"Might be able ter cum up wiv somethin'," mused Mr.S. rubbing his chin, the coarse bristles making a harsh, scratching noise.

"We could get a sheet and cut two holes in it for eyes," said Jed excitedly, "and…and let it float around in the dark, supported underneath by hornets and stuff."

"I think we need something a bit more subtle than that," said Nick.

"…and we could light it up from the inside somehow, so the eyes glow, and…"

Mr.S. threw him a dark look.

"Shut up," he growled and Jed slumped against the wall, a subdued expression on his face.

"I'm sure with your knowledge and skills we could find a way," said Nick carefully, trying to flatter Mr.S. as best he could.

It worked.

The little Elverey bristled with pleasure at such compliments.

"O' course I could," he said grandly. "Not sure if I'd use them 'ornets out there o' course. They're far too important like, what wiv bein on constant call against the big uns an' all…"

Nick nodded, playing to the importance of Mr.S's role. Not that he could see why the hornets couldn't be used. After all, they'd been used for various strange purposes in the past, even to help decorate his room once, but there was no way he was going to argue that point now.

"… maybe I could use them bats I 'ave upstairs. Maybe get a few o' them flies an' stuff…"

Footsteps clattered on the stairs below.

"Ello up there," came Mrs.S's screeching voice. "You want some refreshments?"

Nick's heart sank.

"No thanks," he said politely.

"Yes, bring 'em up," said Mr.S. eagerly.

"Great," muttered Nick.

The footsteps got louder and a new smell filtered up. Well, two actually, both of which easily overcame the aroma of musty staleness in the office. One was Mrs.S's awful perfume, the other was a rancid scent coming from the cracked and dirty jar she was carrying.

Mr.S.dragged open a drawer in his desk and grabbed three equally cracked and dirty glasses. With his arm he swept the top of the desk clear, sending numerous objects including bits of insects legs, half a mouse eye and Nick's paper scattering onto the dusty floor.

"So what we got 'ere then Dorothinia?" he said, eying the jar.

"Your favourite drink."

Mr.S. rubbed his hands.

"Not…?" he said excitedly.

"Oh yes," replied Mrs.S. spitting out generous amounts of saliva on the word 'yes.'

"What actually is it?" asked Nick without much enthusiasm.

Mrs.S. grinned through blackened, rotting teeth.

"Rat snot."

Nick's stomach lurched.

"Ow much you want?" she said as she poured some of the grey liquid into a glass. It wasn't easy as the stuff came out in lumps and as she pushed it out of the jar, bits stuck to her grimy fingers in long, thin strands.

"Er, none for me thanks Mrs.Scoggins," he replied politely as a queasy feeling rolled over him.

"Suit yerself. Yer can 'ave it warmed up if yer want."

Nick shook his head and covered his mouth.

"Not the same, rat snot if it's 'ot," said Mr.S. "Not the same at all. Needs to be cold. Keeps all them strands nice an' lumpy."

With that he picked up a glass and threw the contents down his throat. The stuff stuck to his lips and dribbled down his chin.

"You goin' to the ceremony tomorrer?" he said suddenly.

"The what?" replied Nick, looking at him blankly.

"The ceremony. The one at Tarey arena. Official transfer o' Barrowhouse engin-'art to Rixal or sumfin."

Nick remembered now. Varn had mentioned something about it the other day.

"Yeah, I might be," he said without much enthusiasm. He wasn't particularly keen. The Elvereys loved these big, official things but they were usually long on boring speeches and short on entertainment! Still, as overseer he was usually expected to attend, despite the fact that very few in the crowd would actually know, or care, who he was.

"I'll be there," said Mr.S. pompously. "Got ter make sure no big-'uns are in the area. Be thousands there, an' all o' them got ter be protected like."

"Yeah," agreed Nick. I expect there'll be loads of security there too."

With a shudder his thoughts drifted back to Tritus and Napoleon and all that had happened with Rixal's original engine-heart.

"Bound ter be. Guards are there night 'an day."

"What time does it start?" asked Nick, dragging his thoughts away from Tritus.

"Two thirty."

Well, at least that means it might not go on too long, he thought. After all, it would be pretty cold out in the open. Maybe he would go, at least for an hour or so.

He was suddenly aware of Mrs.S. looking at him intently and it was most unnerving.

"Everything all right Mrs.Scoggins?" he said, looking at the jar hovering in front of him and trying to keep the sickly feeling down.

"That spot," she said, pointing to his face. "That big spot wiv the big white top on it."

"Oh, er yes," Nick replied, his face reddening. Without thinking he covered the blemish with his hand.

"Nice stuff that. When you're like, your normal, big un type size, squeeze it fer us an' keep that yellowy pus. That stuff's really nice. 'Specially warm!"

Nick breathed slowly and deeply in an effort not to throw up.

"So," he said, changing the subject, "getting back to Dave then Mr. Scoggins, when do you think we might be able to come up with something?"

Mr.S. scrabbled round on the floor with one hand and twined a long thread of rat snot off his chin and into his mouth with the other. He picked up Nick's crumpled note and stared at it.

"Not long I reckon."

"Good. When it's worked out I'll take the details to Varn and the overseer committee. I think it'll need a lot of us working together on this one."

Mr.S. nodded but remained silent.

"I'll tell them I spoke to you, that you're really the best…no, the only person that can make this possible."

The flattery worked again.

"Yeah. I am. But yer know what I fink o' those bunch o' pompous windbags wiv their rules an' regulations…"

"I know," replied Nick thinking that he hadn't even met the worst two yet. When it came to pompous windbags, Mindi and Hercules took some beating!

"…But I'll do it. Do it fer you…an' fer 'Ightower."

"Thanks," replied Nick, feeling mighty relieved. He smiled weakly and concentrated on settling his stomach down. It was working too, until Mrs.S. leaned towards him.

"You want ter stay fer somethin' ter eat later?" she snapped, the stench of her breath blowing full into his face. "We're avin' mouse entrails on a bed o' vole droppin's."

Nick groaned. This time his poor stomach did a triple lurch as the nausea welled up once more!!

*

The answer to what Dave was up to with Hightower came the following morning. Nick really couldn't miss it. The plans were out on the kitchen table and Dave and his mum were talking loudly as he entered.

"Course, the work will take some time," Dave was saying, sitting at the table, a mug of tea held out for Marion to spoon sugar into. "Taking down all those trees and flattening the land is a pretty big job."

"Taking down what trees?" said Nick, staring first at his mother, then at Dave.

"Morning Dominic," replied Marion, stirring Dave's tea. "So glad you could join us at last. Want some breakfast?"

"No. What's this about the trees?" he repeated coldly.

"Dave's got an idea."

"Dave has?" Nick could hardly speak for the anger welling up. "What's it to do with him?"

Dave said nothing. He just sat there with a smug grin on his face.

"You just be careful what you're saying young man," warned Marion, her tone turning icy.

"But it's my inheritance," he snarled, thumping his chest and pointing accusingly towards the table. "He can't touch my inheritance."

"He's making it better. He's trying to get the most out of it. For your future."

"My future? I'm happy as I am thank you very much."

"You weren't a few month's ago. All you were bleating about then was how much you missed our old house back in the town and how you hated the countryside."

"That was before."

"Before what?"

"Just... before," snapped Nick. "I like it now. I want to stay here."

There was a long, awkward silence. When Marion spoke again, her voice had softened a little.

"Look Dominic. We know it's your inheritance, and we know you like it here now. We're not leaving the cottage. Not for very long anyway. The clause in the contract wouldn't let us sell in any case. We're just trying to improve things for you."

Nick noted the sudden 'we' in the argument but knew full well this was all Dave's doing.

He paused a moment, thinking over what had just been said.

"Wait a sec. What do you mean, not leaving the cottage for very long?"

Marion glanced at Dave. The gloating grin broadened.

"Well, Dave's idea is to have a hotel with a big car park on the Hightower land..."

"Hotel?" interrupted Nick, "and how much would that cost?"

Dave carefully placed his mug on the table.

"A big hotel chain would do all that side," he said slowly, as though explaining something extremely complicated to someone extremely thick! "I…we wouldn't have anything to do with that. We'd merely rent the land to the hotel group. You see, that wouldn't affect the inheritance. The land would still be in trust to you, but with a nice big income coming in."

"And with so much work to be done," added Marion cautiously, "we'd probably move out of the cottage for a while. We could rent a place nearby till everything was completed and settled once more."

Nick stared at them, open mouthed.

"But…but… I don't want a hotel here. I like this place as it is."

"It's progress," said Dave with a look of maddening superiority.

"It's for your future," insisted Marion soothingly.

"No it isn't. It's for him," yelled Nick through a mist of fury.

"Watch what your saying," warned Marion, pointing her finger at him.

"He's just out for himself…"

"Dominic!" The voice was louder, more ominous.

"He doesn't care about…"

"DOMINIC! OUT…TO YOUR ROOM…NOW!!"

There was a long, awkward silence. Over Marion's shoulder Dave gave a sly, triumphant grin.

Without another word Nick turned and walked out, slamming the kitchen door as hard as he could as he went.

He stormed into his room and retrieved the shrinkage post. He was still visibly shaking with anger as he slipped into the spare bedroom and quietly shut the door.

How could Dave do this? How could his mother let him?

But for now he had to push all that from his mind and concentrate on his meeting with Mindi.

He stared at the model railway taking up almost the entire dimensions of the room and tried to compose himself. The old, American style train and its two carriages stood at the station. There were numerous plastic figures on the platform and Nick peered closer to see if he could see Mindi amidst the little groups.

She didn't seem to be there so he scanned further over the model. It really was quite impressive. The railway line curved past a row of cardboard shops and a plastic church, cutting through the rolling hills dotted with plastic cows, before plunging into the black hole of a tunnel on the right. On the left was an identical tunnel where the track re-emerged and wound back to the station.

Everything seemed in place, if a little run down. There was a thin film of dust over everything and one or two of the figures had fallen over. Nick didn't spend a great deal of time in here. It wasn't a toy after all, merely another way of gaining access to the Elverey world in Hightower. But he supposed he really ought to dust it down occasionally. His mum was always moaning at him to look after it.

"It's your problem Dominic," she was so fond of saying. "If you want it, you look after it. I've got enough to take care of in this house."

He pushed his mum's whining voice from his mind and concentrated on the task in hand. With a careful check on just where the table was at its strongest, he hopped up onto the layout, balancing on one of the hills between a bungalow and a cardboard road with a lorry on it.

Two more figures on the platform fell over as the layout rocked and he steadied himself before fumbling for the shrinkage post.

With gritted teeth he pressed ring and post together and the world dissolved into the usual flashing, screaming turmoil of indistinct images and sudden, searing pain.

When it cleared, he was leaning heavily on the shrinkage post, looking at the somewhat abandoned looking bungalow and the road that wound down to the station.

Everything seemed eerily quiet and not quite right. Nick always felt this sensation whenever he visited the model railway. Nothing seemed to be quite the correct size and the angles all appeared to be a little off centre. The lorry was larger than the bungalow and up close its paint looked rough and heavy. The cardboard shops down the hill seemed to lean more than a proper shop would. Even the chickens in the yard by the farm didn't look right at this size, with their thin legs wedged in a pool of white plastic to keep them standing up.

There was no sound and nothing moved.

Nick glanced at his watch. It was time he moved, otherwise Mindi would be behind schedule and, as Jed would say, 'We don't want old Troutface blowing a fuse do we?'

He smiled as he sauntered down the hill towards the station, using the shrinkage post as support over the rough ground.

He felt calmer now, but intrigued as to what she actually wanted. All this secrecy stuff was getting a bit out of hand. He reckoned the best thing Mindi could do was chill out a bit more.

He leapt up onto the platform and dodged round the expressionless figures. There was no one in either carriage and no one up on the train.

Strange, he thought with a frown as he scanned the platform.

Nothing.

He strode over to the waiting room and peered in. There were only two small windows and it was almost black inside. An overwhelming, and not surprising, smell of plastic enveloped him.

"You're four and a half minutes late," snapped an accusing voice and Nick jumped as Mindi emerged from the shadows.

She was wearing her dark business suit as usual and carrying the lap top in its case, but in her other hand was a brightly coloured gift bag with handles made of shiny blue ribbon.

"What's that then?" asked Nick, nodding at the bag.

"Never you mind," replied Mindi in her usual businesslike manner. "We're behind schedule. Please, if you'd like to follow me we really must hit the ground running so to speak."

With that, she marched off towards the train. Nick followed, wondering who on earth was going to drive the thing, but instead of scrambling up into one of the carriages, she marched on past and kept walking along the track towards the tunnel.

"Where exactly are we going?" said Nick, catching up to her.

Mindi fumbled in her jacket pocket and pulled out a small torch.

"Bear with me," she replied with an authoritative wave of her hand.

Nick sighed and shook his head as they strode into the darkness of the tunnel.

"Now, where's the…ah, there we go," observed Mindi, her voice echoing as the thin beam of light flashed over the walls.

She steadied the light onto the track in front of them as they walked. Nick glanced back. The tunnel entrance was getting smaller, the train standing at the station smaller still.

"Should be somewhere around here," muttered Mindi, more to herself.

"What should?"

There was no reply.

"Mindi, can you please tell me…"

Nick's voice trailed away when he heard a rustling noise up ahead. There was a sudden blinding flash, then darkness once more.

Nick's heart missed a beat.

"What the?" he spluttered.

"Sorry Nicky. Didn't mean to startle you," said a cheerful voice that he instantly recognized.

"Church? Whatever is going on?"

The beam of Mindi's torch swept forward to reveal a familiar little figure standing on the track, his body shrouded in some sort of material that covered right up to his nose. Only the eyes and the top of his head were visible. In his hand was a bulky, old fashioned camera.

"Another shot please. One for tomorrow's paper.

There was another flash.

"CHURCH!" yelled Mindi and Nick in unison.

"Sorry. So Nicky, can we have a few quotes. Something for our readers."

"Church," repeated Mindi. "With all due respect, can we please get out of here."

"Sorry."

The figure moved out of the beam and shuffled around in the darkness to the right of them for a moment.

A shaft of light emerged, broadening slowly as a small door opened.

"This way," said Church, beckoning them.

They walked through the door into a tiny cupboard like room. Church shut the door and pressed a button.

"Going up," he said happily as he fumbled with the camera once more.

Nick frowned again, wondering just how many lifts and passageways there were in Hightower cottage.

"Church, why exactly are you dressed like that?"

The camera clicked but thankfully there was no flash this time. Suddenly he whipped out a microphone and thrust it under Nick's nose.

"I'm on a shoot. Big report to be put in tomorrow. Do you want to say a few words?"

The microphone inched closer. Nick pushed it away irritably.

"Reporter? You're a reporter?"

Church glanced around confidentially.

"Shhh," he whispered.

Then it clicked with Nick.

"Ah, you're an undercover reporter?"

Church gave the faintest of nods.

Nick grinned, wondering just where he'd got this latest fad from.

"But being undercover doesn't mean you have to wear a cover!"

"Doesn't it?" muttered the voice through the sheet.

Nick slapped his palm on his forehead and Mindi sighed heavily.

At that moment the lift stopped and the door swung open. Immediately a blast of cold air engulfed them.

"Where are we?" enquired Nick.

"Top of one of the chimneys," answered Church. "We're inside the bottom part of one of the chimney pots."

"Right," said Nick dubiously, "and where exactly are we going?"

"Up there. There's a magpie waiting on the chimney pot."

"To go where?" repeated Nick, turning to Mindi.

Mindi shook her head.

"I'm afraid it's…"

"…a secret," cut in Nick irritably. "Yeah, I reckoned as much."

"Before we go," said Mindi, unzipping the lap top case and pulling out the now familiar clipboard. "Church, would you please read and sign the flight disclaimer form RY 436 on the four lines as marked?"

"Sure," muttered Church, grabbing the clipboard and signing each part with a flourish without bothering to read anything.

Mindi added her own signature on pages two, three and six before placing the document back in the case.

"Must keep the paperwork up to date," she said.

"Oh we certainly must," agreed Nick sarcastically. Some thought flashed through his mind; something not quite right. He tried to figure out what it was but it slipped away as quickly as it came.

"Come on then," piped up Church. "We've got a bit of climbing to do. Mindi, I'll carry your things if you like. You'll need your hands to climb the ladders."

"Ladders?" mumbled Nick as they walked out onto a round balcony. He stepped cautiously up to the rail and looked down into the circular shaft but could see nothing but blackness. He looked up. There was a large, round hole above, with the clouds scudding by beyond. It wasn't far to the top where a large magpie perched on the rim, blocking out some of the light, but Nick still didn't fancy climbing the precarious looking ladder much. What was worse, there was another ladder attached to one of the legs of the magpie.

"Right, let's push the needle on this so to speak," said Mindi, handing the gift bag to Church and strapping the lap top case across her shoulder. "After you Church."

Church grabbed the ladder and hauled himself up towards the light.

Mindi, in her usual brisk manner, followed leaving Nick on the balcony watching them struggle upward. His annoyance was gone, replaced by apprehension.

With a deep breath he gripped the rungs of the ladder and carefully crawled up.

It was a difficult climb. He hated heights and struggling with the shrinkage post made it worse still. He was worried about dropping it, for if it fell, it would be almost impossible to find again, and he'd be stuck at Elverey size forever.

He was also worried about falling off himself, and his hands were sweating and slippy as he crawled slowly upwards, staring at each rung of the ladder rather than looking at the long drop below.

Only the fact that it was getting lighter and the air was getting fresher told him that he was nearing the top. Suddenly Church's hand pulled him up and in an instant he was standing on the top of the pot, looking down over the sloping roof of the cottage to the gardens and the trees so far below. There was no rail here and the edge they were standing on wasn't very wide.

His heart thudded and he felt dizzy as he leaned against the leg of the magpie for support and safety. He glanced at Mindi. Her wide eyes and pale face told him she was feeling pretty much the same.

"Come on," said Church as he cheerfully climbed up the magpie's leg, the camera swinging round his neck. In an instant he was up and disappearing through a hole in the feathers.

With steely determination in her eyes, Mindi

struggled to the ladder and crawled up.

Nick followed grabbing the rungs so tightly that his knuckles turned white.

A sudden breeze swirled around, ruffling his hair and grabbing at his coat and for a heart stopping moment he thought it would drag him away and send him tumbling down over the roof.

He forced himself to calm down and crawled slowly up, the world below a mere dizzy haze that gradually disappeared when he finally climbed through the entrance and hopped shakily out onto the safety of firm ground.

Church snapped the door shut and escorted his passengers to their seats. He checked they were strapped in then produced his camera and took a series of shots before scrambling into the cockpit.

Not that Nick cared much. He was trying to get his heartbeat back to something like normal and even as the bird began its gentle take-off he was still trembling. One glance at Mindi's hands confirmed that she was too.

They spoke little during the short flight. Nick was too immersed in his own thoughts. Where were they going? Why all the secrecy? He was glad Church was with him though. They'd been through so much together before.

The only words spoken were as they were coming in to land.

Mindi turned to him, a slightly nervous look on her face.

"You didn't tell anyone about this did you?" she asked hesitantly.

He shrugged. "I didn't have time. But no, I didn't tell the overseer committee anything, or anybody else for that matter. It's our little secret."

"Good, good," she muttered absently, leaving Nick more curious than ever.

As they thudded to a standstill, Nick stared out the window but with the blur of feathers and the gloominess of their new surroundings it was impossible to make out much.

"We're here," yelled Church, leaping down from the cockpit. He snapped off another photo and re-opened the hatch.

"Any comments for our readers on how fantastic your pilot was before you leave?"

"No," snapped Nick, stepping onto the ladder. He felt a little less nervous with the ground so much nearer this time.

"I'll write in something suitable on your behalf then shall I?"

"Do what you like," Nick replied, jumping off the final rung and looking uncertainly around.

It was a dismal, large cavern of a place. Way above was the distant opening that the magpie had travelled through, but down here it was difficult to make out anything. Not that there seemed to be much, just bare walls and floor made of stone or some type of metal. It was comfortably warm but eerily quiet.

"Where are we?" The words echoed softly off the walls.

"You'll see," replied Mindi brightly. "You'll find out very soon. Come on, we need to follow Church."

She grabbed the gift bag from Church, who was now striding off down a long corridor, constantly snapping off shots that momentarily lit their surroundings with a blinding light but unfortunately revealed nothing.

Nick shrugged and followed the two figures. He felt resigned to go along with it. After all, his curiosity was nearly bursting. He needed answers.

The journey seemed to go on and on, along corridors, up flights of stairs, through rooms, each one as gloomy and dismal as the last.

Finally, on one particularly long and low corridor Church pointed to a heavy door with a small metal window in it.

"In here," he said, his eyes gleaming as he beckoned first Mindi, then Nick inside.

Nick frowned and followed Mindi through the door and into another gloomy room.

It was then that everything seemed to happen at once.

He was vaguely aware of rough hands from behind pushing him into the centre of the room. Inside were people, distant shadows in the corners. Mindi was turning to him, holding up the gift bag and smiling.

"Happy birthday Nicky," she was yelling excitedly and the figures were moving forward, emerging from the shadows.

At that moment, two sudden questions flashed through him.

One was, why was Mindi wishing him a happy birthday when his actual birthday was still some five months away?

The second was, what was Napoleon, his men, and the fearsome, disfigured Tritus doing there, standing before him with self satisfied, smug grins on their faces?

*

Chapter 11

CAPTIVITY

"Why, Master Collins. Welcome my dear friend," said Tritus coldly. "It's so good to see you again."

The sarcasm in his tone wasn't lost on Nick.

"Just what is this all about?" demanded Mindi. "Where's the others? And who are these people?"

Tritus's one good eye glanced at her for a second then fixed back on Nick.

"Happy birthday," he hissed, the cracked voice breaking into a chuckle that froze Nick's blood. Behind, the other figures laughed respectfully in the shadows. Only Napoleon, his arms folded, his eyes like fire, stood motionless.

"With all due respect," insisted Mindi, "could somebody please tell me what's going on."

Nick dragged himself out of his shocked trance.

"I think," he muttered slowly, "you've been used to get me here."

"But...but, I was told to keep your birthday a secret."

"Mindi. It's not my birthday."

There was a long, empty silence while the thought sank in. As it did, Nick had his own moment of realization.

"Who told you it was," he asked, hardly daring to hear the answer. Tritus was staring at him intently, a lop-sided sneer on his face.

"Church," came the whispered reply. "He told me

not to say anything. He said there was a surprise party for you and all your friends would be there."

"And here we are," roared Tritus as laughter again filled the room. Only Napoleon remained silent.

Tritus held up a long, thin hand and the laughter stopped. His eye never flickered and the deep loathing reflecting from it made Nick's heart miss a beat.

"Come in my friend," he said, beckoning with a long, taloned finger. "Don't be shy."

Nick heard shuffling footsteps behind him. He could still feel the pressure on his back where he'd been roughly pushed into the room.

"Church...? Why?" he muttered as the little figure calmly walked in and stood beside Tritus. Tritus gave him a withering look and Church took a couple of steps respectfully back.

Nick just stared at him open mouthed and shook his head. He searched the eyes that were staring defiantly back but saw no clue; no answers. Was it the engine-hearts? Had the power corrupted him like it had done Tritus? He didn't think so. One engine-heart alone couldn't do that; only two or more, and to Nick's knowledge Church had never been subject to two engine-hearts in close proximity.

"Why Church?" he repeated sadly.

The little Elverey shrugged his shoulders. For the first time he couldn't hold Nick's gaze.

"I have my reasons," he snarled in a harsh voice that was so un-Church like it made Nick jump. "Big reasons. Things you'd never understand."

There was so much anger and hatred in that voice.

"I knew none of this," wailed Mindi. "I'm sorry Nicky. So sorry."

Nick glanced at her. It was a relief to look away from Church.

"I know," he said kindly. "How could you? You've never met these...these..." He searched for the word that would do justice to his feelings of shock, surprise, and now anger.

"But what will become of us?" said Mindi, her voice getting higher and higher till it was almost a shriek. "What is the bottom line here, so to speak?"

Tritus had obviously had enough. He raised a hand to his forehead as though he were getting a headache.

"Get her out of here," he growled.

Two of Napoleon's men emerged from the shadows.

"Don't you hurt her," warned Nick, gripping the shrinkage post as though it were a weapon.

Tritus seemed surprised in an amused sort of way.

"She's not going to be hurt, only locked up for quite a while, as you are too," he said, nodding at the shrinkage post. "And I wouldn't think of using that. These walls are strong and thick. You'd end up rather crushed I'm afraid."

There was a murmur of agreement and Nick lessened his grip.

"Take that thing from him Napoleon," he hissed.

For a moment Nick thought Napoleon was going to ignore the order. He glared at Tritus with an expression that was difficult to make out in the gloom. Finally, he unfolded his arms and stepped forward.

Nick stepped back. To his left he could hear scuffling noises and Mindi's whining voice protesting.

"Give it to him," growled Tritus, the tone becoming deep and threatening. "Give it to Napoleon or your friend may get hurt."

For a moment Nick paused, but he knew it was hopeless. Napoleon was a big brute, he was outnumbered, and Mindi was being threatened.

Napoleon snatched the post from his hand and with

the faintest of nods to the men holding Mindi, returned to the shadows.

The scuffling sounds increased as Mindi was pushed roughly out the door, her protests still echoing as she was led away down the corridor.

Slowly, the voices trailed away into the distance.

"Ah, that's better," sighed Tritus. "I do like tranquillity don't you?"

"So what now," said Nick, eying the shrinkage post in Napoleon's hand. He felt utterly lost without it.

"Now?" replied Tritus almost pleasantly. "Now you get locked up too."

"But why," asked Nick, sweeping the hair back from his face. "What's all this about?"

Tritus considered the question.

"Well, first it's about getting you out of the way for a while," he said at length. "You need to be, confined if you like, so you can't ruin my plans like you did before."

"What plans?"

Tritus smiled, sort of, and tapped the side of his nose with his finger as though about to share a big secret.

"What plans?" repeated Nick, his voice getting higher and more unsteady.

"The ceremony."

"Ceremony?"

The smile became darker.

"The ceremony at Tary arena," said Tritus, patting Church on the shoulder. "Our friend here has installed a bomb in the engine-heart. When it goes off, the arena, and everyone in it will be no more."

Nick was horror stricken.

"What...? Why...?" he spluttered, glancing from Tritus to Church.

The smile vanished.

"To teach the Elvereys a lesson. To show them. To

164

show you. To show you all what happens when you cross me and try and leave me for dead…"

Nick took a step back. Tritus was shouting now, his one good eye gleaming with a wild madness.

Napoleon placed a hand on his arm. Instantly the yelling stopped. Tritus stood there, breathing heavily, trying to compose himself.

"I don't understand," said Nick, his mind working overtime. You've always wanted to get two or more engine-hearts together. You've always wanted the power to feed and grow till it took us all over. Why destroy one of them now?"

"I have no desire to take this engine-heart," he replied, smiling weakly. "My victory is in revenge. Over them and over you."

Nick stared at the figure before him and realized that Tritus was quite mad. But he had to play for time. He had to save the Elvereys.

"So why not let me be one of the victims at the ceremony? Why go to all this trouble to bring me here?"

Tritus shook his head as though frustrated by Nick's lack of understanding.

"Because I want you to know it's happened. I want you to know it's your fault. It's all going to happen because of what you did to me. All this time I've been watching you and waiting till the right time. All this time my wasps have been flying into every corner, watching, reporting. I know everything that's going on. The right time has arrived."

Yet again Nick felt that hammer blow of shock. The wasps! All those wasps were from Tritus. No wonder Dave couldn't destroy them at the cottage!

He glanced at Church. Were they made by him? He felt so sad and so angry that he couldn't even bring himself to ask the question.

"Take him away," said Tritus in a weary manner.

Nick felt hands grabbing his arms and propelling him out of the door. As he went he glared one last time at Church but there was no response. It was impossible to make out what the little Elverey was thinking.

He was half dragged, half pushed down the corridor and then down some stairs to another heavy door.

He heard the rattle of keys and the squeal of the door opening. He heard Mindi's voice in the next cell asking questions. He felt hands push him into the tiny cell. He smelt the damp of his new surroundings. But it was all distant and vague. His mind was too overloaded by recent events.

Tritus?

Napoleon?

Church? …Not Church…

Sadness engulfed him as he sat down on the stone bench and put his head in his hands.

"Nicky? Nicky? Is that you?" came Mindi's voice.

"Yeah," he replied softly.

He had to think. He had to take control of his shattered thoughts and come up with an idea. So many lives were dependent on it.

But ideas wouldn't come.

It wasn't helped by Mindi's constant voice. Part of the time she was asking questions, the remainder she was asking for his forgiveness for getting him into this mess. When he could get a word in edgeways and tell her about the ceremony her input to helping included so many comments like 'optimising blue sky thinking' and 'run it up the flagpole' that he felt like telling her what she could do with the flagpole!

When she said that they ought to 'systemize a tailored workshop to achieve key objectives' he was about to angrily snap back when a key rattled in the lock and his door squeaked open.

"Anybody in?" said a cheerful voice as a head appeared around the door. "Oh, bit of a daft question that. Course you're in. Can't be anywhere else can you?"

Nick stared at the head. The face was very round, with big eyes and a buck-toothed grin. Perched above shaggy brown hair was a baseball cap turned back to front.

The newcomer strutted into the cell, a round, bulky sort of figure wearing baggy dark clothes that sort of merged into Nick's gloomy surroundings.

"Hi. I'm Leroy. I've brought you some food."

Nick eyed the open door.

"Now don't you go getting any ideas of escaping. My boss wouldn't like it.

"And who's your boss?" said Nick coldly, "Tritus or Napoleon?"

Leroy shuffled back to the door and produced a tray with a drink and some rather unappetizing food on it. He slammed the door shut and placed the tray on the bench next to Nick.

"Napoleon of course. Don't have much to do with that weirdo Tritus."

"Who is it?" came Mindi's voice from next door. "Who's there? Are you all right Nicky?"

"You don't like Tritus much then?" said Nick, relaxing a little.

Leroy shook his head and slumped to the floor facing Nick, his considerable back up against the cold stone wall.

"Nah. Napoleon doesn't like him much either. They're having a right old argument right now back up there."

Interesting, thought Nick.

"Nicky, are you sure you're all right?"

"Fine thanks Mindi."

"Are we singing off the same hymn sheet so to speak?"

"What? Oh er, yes," replied Nick irritably, rolling his eyes at Leroy.

"What's up with her?" Leroy whispered, waving a chubby finger at Mindi's cell.

"She's OK I suppose. Just a bit bossy at times."

"Yeah, Church said that."

Nick felt a pain of sadness cut through him. He tried to shake it off. There'd be time for that later.

"She does my head in a bit sometimes."

"Well maybe I could put something in her food to knock her out," replied Leroy with a grin, his teeth standing out in the gloom. "If I sent her off to sleep for a while maybe you'd get a bit of a break!"

Nick wondered if he were kidding. The grin had grown even bigger and he knew that he was. He was starting to like Leroy.

"That'd be good. Just knock her out for a while huh?"

"Let her curl up and sleep like a baby," said Leroy, warming to the theme.

"Yeah," whispered Nick, returning the grin, "to be able to say Mindi's dead to the world for a while would be music to my poor ears!"

"Nicky, can we touch base on a few items?"

Nick rolled his eyes again and Leroy giggled.

"Can you hear me Nicky?"

He sighed as the voice got higher.

"Nicky, I'd appreciate some sort of response from you, so to speak."

Nick leaned towards Leroy. "I'll sort her out myself if she doesn't shut up soon," he said, still with a grin, before leaning back and shouting, "I'm fine Mindi, just give me a couple of secs huh?"

Leroy's giggling increased and he covered his mouth with his hand.

"Very well. At the end of the day we must prioritise as one unit, as it were."

"Oh yeah. Sure."

"Right on," agreed Leroy, standing up. "I'll leave you with your dinner and your irritating friend."

With that he left, locking the door carefully behind him.

Nick left the food but drank the cold, refreshing liquid. Next door the lock rattled and he heard Leroy and Mindi's muffled voices. It was obviously Mindi's turn for food.

The voices didn't last very long and the door was soon re-locked. He smiled to himself. Leroy was on his way much quicker this time.

Time dragged on. Nick kept checking his watch but the fingers didn't seem to move with much speed. They never did when he had nothing to do.

He felt so helpless. There was a bomb set to explode and he could do nothing about it. He clenched and unclenched his fists and paced slowly round the tiny cell.

Even Mindi seemed more subdued. Her pointless questions and even more pointless statements were getting less and less, but then there was little more either of them could say, and even less that they could actually do.

Nick stopped pacing and tilted his head slightly to one side.

Footsteps!

Someone was coming.

He listened carefully. There seemed to be more than one set of steps creeping stealthily down the stairs and onto the corridor.

He held his breath and leaned back against the far wall, staring at the door. The key rattled in the lock, followed by whispered voices, then silence.

Slowly, very slowly, the door began to open, the screeching noise of the hinges nothing more than a thin squeal that set his teeth on edge.

A broad figure stood in the doorway, the features nothing more than a black silhouette.

"Hello?" whispered Nick nervously. "Who is it?"

The figure stepped into the room. Others behind him, stayed outside, patiently waiting. For a moment a hint of light swept across the big, bushy face and Nick's heart missed a beat as he stood there, frozen to the spot, staring into those brilliantly fierce, hypnotic eyes.

"Well, well, well kid," said Napoleon, whispering in an almost affable manner. "Here, take this."

Something flew through the air. Instinctively Nick reached out in the gloom and caught the shrinkage post.

"Why...? What...?" he spluttered.

Napoleon gripped him by the shoulder, but not roughly.

"Come on kid," he hissed, "we're getting you out of here. We need your help, and there's not a moment to lose!"

*

Chapter 12

BREAK OUT

…Decisions!

Looking back over how quickly events unfurled that afternoon, in the end, it all really came down to the decisions Nick made.

The first one came up as he was being hurriedly bundled out of the cell door, his mind a confused blur of questions.

"Just wait a second here," he said, grabbing Napoleon's arm. "Why are you helping me?"

Napoleon whirled round, his eyes blazing at the thought that someone would have the nerve to touch him. With an effort the anger softened and he forced a smile.

"Think about it kid," he said, tapping his forehead. "Do you really think I want to spend my life with that lunatic, stuck in the old home, hiding away in the cold and the dark?"

"Well…no," muttered Nick with a frown.

"And do you really think I want to kill a load of my own people? Why should I want to? What would be in it for me?"

Nick shrugged.

"Mr.Weirdo just wants revenge," Napoleon growled, pointing back up the stairs. "What good's revenge to me?"

Nick gave the argument some thought.

"OK, I'll go along with that," he said slowly, making his first decision, though in truth he realized he had little choice. "So what now?"

Napoleon smiled, the white teeth shining in stark contrast to the thick, bushy beard.

"We go and stop that bomb, and in doing so we save a lot of people. Me? I'm one of the good guys from now on kid."

Nick doubted that but he returned the smile, a weak, unsure one, but still a smile.

As soon as they were out in the gloomy corridor the confusion grew. The indistinct shadows of three figures were huddled round Mindi's cell door.

Napoleon strode over to them and Nick waited as they muttered and whispered together. He could see the conversation was getting heated. There was much shaking of heads and waving of arms, particularly Napoleon's. Finally, Napoleon sighed and sauntered back, shaking his head even more vigorously, his ponytail swinging from side to side.

"What's wrong?" whispered Nick.

"Leroy there's only got the key to your cell. He's gone and left your friend's key back up there."

"So?" replied Nick, looking over Napoleon's shoulder at a very subdued Leroy. "Can't he go and get it?"

"Not if we want to deactivate that bomb. We're on a tight schedule here. Besides, it's a long way back to get the thing and the Deebers will be back by now guarding it."

"But we can't just leave Mindi here," said Nick realizing now, with the mentioning of the Deebers, that he was actually inside the old home at Hightower.

"We've no choice," snapped Napoleon impatiently.

"We haven't time. It's her release, or the death of thousands at the ceremony. Your call kid."

Nick looked uncertainly from the cell door to Napoleon, to his men, and back to the cell door.

"Leave me Nicky," called out Mindi. "At the end of the day, the bottom line is that those people need saving. Come back for me after."

"But what about Tritus?" said Nick, appealing to Napoleon. "What will he do to her when he finds out I'm gone?"

"He won't do anything. Tritus used her to get you. He's no interest in her now. She'll be fine."

"I'll be fine," agreed Mindi. "You have to prioritize. You know there's no choice."

Nick had never heard Mindi's voice sounding less confident, but he knew she was right.

"Er, I hate to push you," said Napolean, casually flicking dirt from his fingernails with a large, gleaming knife, "but we are like, running out of time here."

Nick gave the faintest of nods.

"Forget the key. Leave Mindi in her cell," he said with a sudden burst of authority that he didn't really feel.

Napoleon slipped the dagger back in his belt and clicked his fingers to his men as Nick rushed up to the cell door.

"I'm sorry Mindi," he whispered miserably, "but I'll be back as soon as I can with Varn and the rest of them. We'll get you out of there."

"Don't you worry Nicky. I know it wasn't an easy decision, but leadership is via mentoring so to speak. You've had to think outside the box and push…"

But Mindi's voice was trailing away into the distance as the hands of Napoleon's men softly escorted him down the corridor towards freedom.

"I really hope she shuts up before Tritus and the Deebers hear," muttered Napoleon under his breath as they climbed up a circular staircase. The further they climbed, the brighter the light got and the fresher the air.

Nick paused near the top of the steps and pointed at the smallest figure in the group, a surge of anger welling up inside him.

"What's he doing here?"

"Who? Oh, Church. He's coming with us," replied Napoleon calmly.

Nick, who was anything but calm, froze on the stairs and Napoleon grabbed him by the arm.

"Come on kid," he snarled. "We haven't time for this. Who do you think's going to deactivate the bomb? He set it. He's the only one that can stop it."

Nick reluctantly started moving again, his gaze fixed on the little figure.

"What makes you think he will stop it?" he said, feeling a strange, empty sensation. They'd been through so many things in the past together; funny things; dangerous things; exciting things. It was as though his senses couldn't accept anything else.

"Oh, he'll do it all right. He'll do it, or..." replied Napoleon ominously, leaving the rest of the answer unfinished.

By the time they reached the entrance the sun was sliding towards the horizon. Nick blew on his hands, his breath drifting away in a grey mist on the bitterly cold air. He stood there with the rest of the group on some sort of raised wooden platform, surveying their means of transport. All that was visible was a large ear. It was the only thing on the same level as them. The rest of the bulky body was below, leaning against the struts of the platform.

"A rabbit...?" he muttered unhappily.

"A hare," corrected Napoleon.

"My hare," insisted Leroy. "Pretty good huh? Lot faster than a rabbit is a hare."

"But rabbit's hop!"

"And...?" said Leroy, looking confused.

Nick felt that exasperated feeling again.

"Well how can we travel in one of those things without getting bounced to death?"

Leroy took off his baseball cap, scratched his head, and thought for a while.

"We all sit at the front," he said finally, "well away from those big back legs."

Nick wasn't much convinced by this but before he had time to answer a voice suddenly whispered in his ear.

"Hares? Magpies? Cats? You really do get around don't you Nicky. Really think you're Mr Big round here don't you?"

Nick swung round and peered into Church's sneering face. This wasn't the Church he knew. This was Church with hatred and contempt in his eyes. A surging anger exploded and he grabbed the little Elverey by the shoulders and crashed him back into the entrance wall.

"You shut your mouth," he bellowed.

Church offered no resistance. He just stood there, pinned against the wall with a self satisfied, sneering expression that only served to increase Nick's fury.

Napoleon's two men dragged Nick back and Church calmly brushed himself down.

"Don't kill him kid," yelled Napoleon. Then, almost as an afterthought and in a much softer tone he added, "well, not until our little friend here has made the bomb safe at least!"

The men laughed. Nick just glared.

"Come on kid, time's running out."

The others all walked to the end of the platform and disappeared into the long, quivering ear. Nick kept a wary eye on Church. He tried to calm himself down, taking long, deep breaths. When his hands had stopped shaking, he followed, cautiously peering into the huge dark opening of the ear, before hesitantly stepping forward.

"Just jump," called somebody from inside and below, so he did.

The sensation was like going down a narrow, twisting slide. It was enough to put a grin on his face as he slid downwards. It wasn't a long ride but it was fun. As he swirled round one bend he glimpsed the usual type of control area with the usual type of eyes for windows. One of the controllers seats was empty, the other occupied by a plump figure with long, flowing white hair. Then the view was gone, replaced by nothing but the blurred dark images of the walls.

He emerged into a cramped seating area which was extremely small considering the size of the hare. There was only one seat left, next to a happy looking Leroy. On the back bench sat Church, looking far less happy, bordered on one side by Napoleon, and on the other by a brutally vicious looking thug with an eye patch.

Nick sat down next to Leroy and glanced round nervously. Without any windows, the room had a compact, almost squashed in feel. It was hot and the air smelt of sweat. Clearly Napoleon's men weren't in the forefront when it came to bathing!

"I thought this was your rabb...er, hare?" he said, turning to Leroy.

"It is."

"But you're not driving, or piloting, or whatever you do."

"Oh no," replied Leroy. "Isruttis."

"What's isruttis?"

Leroy chuckled.

"Not isruttis. …Isrutt is! Isrutt controls the hare. Does it all by himself too. You probably saw him. Tubby old bloke. Long white hair."

"Oh, yeah," Nick said absently.

"Make sure those buckles are tight. You want to be sure you're well strapped in."

This made Nick more nervous.

"I thought you said we'd be a long way from those back legs."

"Oh we are," said Leroy, waving his hand in a confident, no problem sort of way. "This hare's got them gyro-sponder things. Helps stop any bouncing. This ride will be as smooth as a snake."

Nick thought of the frog he'd travelled in the last time he'd been to the Tary arena and didn't feel at all convinced.

He was right.

Whatever 'them gyro-sponder things' were, they didn't help much and the ride was anything but 'smooth as a snake!'

By the time they arrived at the Tary arena Nick's body felt like it had been through a spin dryer! He had bruises where the straps had cut into him, his hair was sticking out in all directions, and he had a throbbing headache.

Considering the dark glares his fellow travellers were giving Leroy it seemed everyone felt the same!

Exit from the hare was via the mouth, with the hare's head resting between its paws. Nick squeezed through the narrow passage between the teeth, glancing up to give a sarcastic 'thank you' for the ride to the weirdly named guy with the white hair. Predictably, there was no response.

He jumped down into the loud, bustling crowds making their way towards the Tary arena and pulled his collar up against the cold wind.

Napoleon and his men looked somewhat out of place in the jovial multitude but no one seemed to take any notice. What was noticeable was that as time passed the group seemed to be getting more tense. Eye Patch was gripping a sombre looking Church, Napoleon kept glancing anxiously at his watch. Even Leroy looked apprehensive.

"How long have we got?" asked Nick to Napoleon.

"Not long. Ten minutes."

"And how long," he said, nodding fiercely at Church, "will it take him to deactivate the bomb once he's got the engine-heart?"

"Only a few seconds. Half a minute at the most."

"Come on then," he urged, pushing his way into the crowds, "we've no time to lose."

But by the time they arrived at the edge of the arena and looked down over the vast scene it became pretty obvious that they were not going to make it.

The place was huge and the crowd was enormous. Clearly the hand over of the Barrowhouse engine-heart to Rixal was a most important and popular occasion. Most of the people were already seated, waiting patiently for the ceremony to begin, but many were still blocking the aisles, checking their tickets for the right row or right seat, or edging their way along to buy drinks and food.

Way, way below, in an open area where the plug used to be in the days when the Tary arena was a bath, he could just make out the tiny round sphere of the engine-heart, surrounded by a large group of people, many of them guards.

He tried to squeeze forward but it was almost impossible to get through the mass of bodies.

"There's no way through," he yelled to Napoleon, throwing his hands up in frustration. "We'll never get there in time."

"We have to warn them somehow," replied Napoleon, shouting into Nick's ear.

"Even if we do get close, will they believe us?"

"Not me, no." Napoleon smiled at him, but with a look of uncertainty on his face. "You, perhaps. You are the overseer after all kid."

"Can't we get the hare any nearer?"

"No. The arena's sunk into the ground."

Nick stared around him, panic welling up in his stomach. Just a few rows away to the right he could see the overseer committee settling down into their seats. Hercules was trying to sit next to Ayisha, who as usual didn't seem too pleased with the attention. Varn was wrapping a scarf tightly round his neck and sniffing some sort of inhaler.

They were so close yet when he shouted to them his voice was drowned out by the noise of the crowd.

"Leave them," yelled Napoleon impatiently, tugging his sleeve. "We've got to stop the bomb."

"But how?"

"We've got to get that engine-heart out of the arena."

Nick glared at the spectacle before him. All those happy, smiling faces. He felt so useless, so frustratingly powerless. He gritted his teeth and clenched his hands, his fingers gripping tighter on the shrinkage post.

…The shrinkage post!

…Get the engine-heart out of the arena!

…Decisions!

"Napoleon," he yelled, "how long now?"

Napoleon rubbed his beard thoughtfully and glanced at his watch.

"Five minutes at the most."

"Right. Take Church away from the crowd and put him near the hare where it's quieter…"

Napoleon frowned but nodded.

"…and get Leroy to bring Varn, Hercules and Ayisha."

Napoleon said nothing but nodded again. Nick wasn't sure if the Elverey had worked out what was about to happen but he hadn't got time to explain. He leapt away from the edge of the arena and ran back through the crowds still making their way in, squeezing through till there was sufficient space around him.

He paused a moment, staring at the shrinkage post. Everything and everyone depended on him. His senses suddenly became finely tuned. Somewhere the cheerful music of a band drifted above the sound of the crowd. The delicious smell of frying food hung in the air. The wind tugged playfully at his coat.

…Decisions!

He had to do it. There really was no other choice.

With a deep breath and trembling hands, he closed his eyes and pressed ring and post together.

Everything changed in the usual, painful roar. When he opened his eyes, he was swaying over a sunken bath with thousands of ant like figures scurrying in every direction. The noise of the crowd was now much softer and more distant. The band had stopped playing, replaced by yelling and screaming.

He placed the tiny shrinkage post in his left hand and leaned forward, reaching down towards the plug hole with his right.

The tiny figures scattered as he gripped the little sphere in finger and thumb. Carefully lifting it up, he withdrew it from the arena, turned, and held it above the ground, near the hare, where he could just make out the figure of Napoleon and the others.

He paused. Beads of sweat were breaking out on his forehead, despite the cold.

What should he do now? Take the engine-heart and throw it as far away as possible? Plunge it into the stream, well away from any Elvereys? If he did either of those, how big would the explosion be? How could he be sure he wouldn't kill someone? ...And then, if the engine-heart was destroyed, Rixal would still have no power.

How long was left to go? Could the bomb be deactivated?

All these thoughts flashed through his mind in an instant.

...Decisions.

Below, the crowd was starting to panic. Above, the sound of hornets sending out their belated warning was starting to grow.

He looked from engine-heart to shrinkage post and with renewed conviction, placed the engine-heart on the ground by the hare and pressed post and ring together again.

By the time he'd shrunk back down and recovered his senses everything seemed to be happening at once. He tried to clear his head but there was so much noise.

Church and Eye Patch were standing over the engine-heart. They seemed to be shouting at each other. Nick staggered to his feet. Church turned and began yelling and beckoning to him, his expression frightened and desperate.

For a second Nick's befuddled mind couldn't take it in. He squinted his eyes and concentrated, trying to hear Church's words above the melee of screams and yells from the crowd behind.

He stumbled forward. The sound of the hornets above faded as they broadcast their 'all clear' message and zipped away.

"Help…" Church bellowed. "Help him lift the thing. The deactivation plate's underneath. I can't get to it!"

Nick stared at the engine-heart. Eye Patch was struggling to lift it up.

"Help him," screamed Church. "There's less than a minute left!"

Nick ran forward and grabbed the sphere. Somewhere in his mind he vaguely hoped that being so close to the thing didn't affect him the way that the power had affected Tritus, but he knew deep down it took more than one engine-heart in close proximity to do any harm.

Besides, he reckoned, gritting his teeth as he took the strain, if Church didn't manage to do his thing, being taken over by the power would be the least of his problems!

"You hold it," said Eye Patch's gruff voice, "while I help Church get to the deactivation plate.

Nick took the full weight of the purple sphere, trying to work out how many seconds were left and wishing that Church would hurry up, for it seemed to be taking an eternity, when another thought flashed through his brain. The engine-heart was heavy, but not that heavy. He could just about hold it by himself, and he was a twelve year old kid. So why did Church want him to help Eye Patch, a fully grown thug of a man, to help him hold it?

Even as he was trying to come up with an answer a familiar voice roared out above the noise of the crowd.

"Put that engine-heart down and stay where you are."

Nick was very pleased to put the engine-heart down. It was starting to hurt his back. He straightened up and turned round and as he did so a horrible sinking feeling welled up in the pit of his stomach.

Napoleon stood in front of his men, shaking his head sadly. Varn and Ayisha were just staring, astonishment on their faces. Hercules stood dramatically, spear in hand, his expression one of utter rage. By his side stood Church, with just the tiniest smile at the corner of his lips, one that only Nick could see.

"Nicky...Why?" Church said with a most convincing sob.

"Why what?" asked Nick, feeling totally bewildered.

"Why?" repeated Church, wiping a tear away and shaking his head. "You and Tritus, working together. Till I saw it for myself I never thought it possible."

"I can't believe it. I simply can't believe it," said Varn, closing his eyes and shaking his head.

"What?" muttered Nick, thinking this shaking the head thing must be catching!

"But tis obviously true," yelled Hercules pompously, "for here he is, caught putting the precious engine-heart into this rabbit..."

"Hare," corrected Leroy.

"What?" repeated Nick, glancing round at the hare just a few steps from where he stood. "Putting it into...? ...Oh no, it was the bomb. I was getting it away from the crowd because of the bomb."

"The what?" said Church.

"What bomb?" asked Napoleon.

Nick stared at their puzzled, innocent expressions. The acting was really quite excellent.

"I can't believe it," said Varn again.

"Oh, Nicky," sighed Ayisha sadly.

"Thank goodness Napoleon saved me," said Church, the puzzled look being replaced by one of gratitude.

"Napoleon?" hissed Varn, coldly.

Church nodded with a heavy sigh.

"Tritus and Nick had me imprisoned when I

overheard their plans. I must say I never thought I'd come to be thanking Napoleon but…" he gave him a sickly 'thanks pal' expression that Napoleon most humbly acknowledged.

"Now hang on a minute…" cut in Nick, his anger starting to rise.

"NO!" roared Hercules, raising his spear (but unfortunately catching it in the sleeve of his robe). "We must meet at a later date to discuss these awful events. We must strike to the very earth in our endeavour to uncover the truth."

"Yes," agreed Varn without much conviction.

"But surely you don't believe any of this rubbish?" pleaded Nick, appealing to Varn.

"That is what we must find out Nicky," he replied sadly. "We'll all meet tomorrow, at the cave, nine o'clock. For now though, there is a ceremony to complete. But I must say my heart is no longer in it. "

With that he turned away with tears in his eyes.

"Why Nicky?" said Ayisha, following Varn without even waiting for an answer.

It was a question Nick was going to be asked many times over the next few days but never with the intensity that Ayisha gave, and her look of sadness and betrayal hurt him more than he thought imaginable.

"Tomorrow then; nine o'clock at the cave," muttered Hercules, still trying to extract the spear from the robe. "I expect Mindi will be there to oversee the arrangements?"

"I'm afraid not," said Church sadly.

"No," snapped Napoleon, glaring icily at Nick. "Not after what he's done."

Perhaps Hercules was too tired, or he'd had enough surprises for one day. Whatever the reason he didn't pursue it.

"Whatever," he said with a sigh. "But before you leave today, please put the shrinkage post somewhere where we can see it if you don't mind."

"Why?" Nick spluttered.

"Security."

"Security? You mean you believe all this?"

"The safety of the Elvereys is the most important thing here."

"So that's it then," he snapped angrily. "I'm looked upon as a threat then am I?"

When there was no answer, he realized that was exactly how they looked upon him.

"OK," he said miserably. "I'll leave it in the cave like I used to."

Hercules picked up the engine-heart and marched back through the crowd. For a second the onlookers stared at Nick curiously, their expressions a mixture of confusion and anger. Then they turned and went back to the arena. The ceremony was to continue, a little more subdued perhaps, and a little late, but for Rixal it was still a time of celebration.

As Church and Napoleon followed they exchanged satisfied glances.

Only Leroy spoke to Nick. With that beaming smile, he raised his hand to his head, forming the forefinger and thumb into a letter L on his forehead.

"Loser," he drawled as he walked past.

Nick just stood there, drained, shocked, bemused.

Now he knew. He'd made the wrong decisions and he'd been set up.

But it was an impressive set up, and one that he really wasn't sure he'd be able to get out of!

*

Chapter 13

LIES

Marion Collins watched her son trudge slowly up the stairs to his room, a worried frown creasing her brow.

She was used to his sullen silences but this seemed somehow different. He'd hardly eaten anything and spoken even less. There was no spark in him and no fire in his eyes.

Usually, when Dave spoke to him he'd answer with some sarcastic comment. Tonight though, there'd been nothing but a sigh and a shrug of the shoulders.

The bedroom door quietly clicked shut and she returned to the kitchen. Dave was sitting with his feet resting on the table, his big toe sticking out of a large hole in one of the socks.

"What's up with him then?" he growled, taking a long swig from his beer can.

"Don't know," said Marion absently. "I asked him if he was feeling unwell."

"And?" The word merged into a large belch.

"He said he was all right."

"Maybe he's tired, though heaven knows why. The kid hardly does anything."

"He could be tired," she replied, glaring at him with an air of disapproval, which was unusual. Marion rarely glared at Dave. "It's a good job school's finished for

Christmas. I suppose he can sleep in a bit if he wants."

"Suppose so."

He threw the empty can at the bin. It missed and bounced off the wall, causing Marion to glare again.

"We're still OK for tomorrow though aren't we?"

"I don't know. Maybe we should see how Dominic is first."

"But we're going for my Christmas present," he moaned. "You're buying it for me."

"I know," she said as she washed the dishes. "I'm sure he'll be all right."

"Nothing but trouble that kid," muttered Dave under his breath as he got to his feet and strode to the door.

"What did you say?"

"Nothing," he replied, slamming the door behind him with a sulky air.

Marion gave a mournful sigh and stacked the wet pots on the drainer. She could hear Dave's footsteps upstairs, followed by the toilet flushing. The footsteps began down the stairs again, then suddenly stopped.

She wiped her hands on her apron and listened. There was no sound at first. She cocked her head to one side and concentrated. A strange wailing noise drifted from the hall. It made her shiver.

Suddenly she heard a little shriek from Dave. Hurried steps rushed down the stairs, the door banged open and he darted in, eyes wide, face deathly pale.

"Whatever's the matter?" she asked worriedly.

He hid behind the door and peered up the stairs, his whole body shaking.

"David? What is it?"

She walked towards him, her own nerves tensing.

"David, whatever…"

He slammed the door shut and pushed past her to get back to the seat.

"Nothing," he snapped. "Just… just the water in the tank or something."

"But you look so pale."

"Just leave it," he yelled, his hands trembling. "Get me another beer."

For a moment Marion paused before opening the fridge, but when she passed him the can, she gave him the strongest look of disapproval she was capable of.

*

If Nick thought things couldn't get any worse than the previous day, he was sadly mistaken.

He'd slept well enough; at first anyway. He couldn't even remember his head touching the pillow, but then troubled memories dragged him back awake in the early hours and for the rest of the time he just lay there thinking.

At least he didn't have to make any excuses to Dave or his mum. They'd set out early to go Christmas shopping; again! His mum had fussed around him for a while but he'd persuaded her that he was feeling better.

Only he wasn't, and that sinking, nervous feeling just got worse as he stood there in the cave, staring down at the tiny shrinkage post.

The arrangements had obviously changed as none of his friends were there to greet him, only Hercules with a couple of guards.

He hesitantly picked up the shrinkage post, thinking that he just wanted to get the whole thing over with. It was the first time ever that he really didn't want to go to Elverey.

By the time he'd shrunk and was leaning over, supported by the post, the two guards were standing to attention at either side.

"Morning Hercules," he said, trying to sound calm.

Hercules held a hand aloft, as if to tell him to be quiet.

"Ready?" he called to the guards, and with the briefest of nods the group marched off towards the waiting train in the corner.

"Nicky…Nicky…" called a voice from behind them.

The four stopped and swung round.

"Jed!" cried Nick. He'd never been so pleased to see his friend, but he was apprehensive as to what the reaction might be. He needn't have worried. Jed's grin was as broad as it always was.

"Keep back," yelled Hercules grandly, "we've an important meeting to attend."

"Yeah right," said Jed dismissively. "You all right? I heard they've set you up."

"Glad someone thinks so," replied Nick as they started walking at a brisk pace once more.

"The others will too when you explain, you'll see…"

Nick wasn't so sure.

"…and Mr.S. says he'll help however he can. He did a mean job on your pal Dave last night by the way."

Nick managed a weak smile, but there was a lump in his throat. Mr.S. and Jed seemed to be the only ones left on his side!

They reached the train and Hercules started fussing around, ordering them all to their seats.

"Look, I'll see you later," said Jed, peering through the glassless window as Nick settled down onto the hard, uncomfortable bench. "You can tell me about how you sorted them all out."

"OK," replied Nick without much enthusiasm. He couldn't even manage another smile when Hercules tripped up into the carriage. By the time they'd rounded the bend and the waving figure of Jed had disappeared from sight, his mood had sunk to an all time low!

*

The meeting was held inside what looked like one of the stones on the top level of the bridge spanning the stream at Glug, and as soon as Nick walked in he knew things were going to go badly.

The room was small, dominated by a large wooden table, around which sat four figures. Two chairs were vacant. Hercules sat down in one, propping his spear against the table, (though not securely enough as it promptly fell over with a resounding crash) and gestured to Nick to sit in the other.

He looked round. The room was spartan in the extreme. The only object other than the table and chairs was a huge flat screen television fastened to the wall. A large window looked down over the river. Despite the cold and the snow, two small twig boats were bobbing up and down on the water. Further upstream, a fish was lying on the bank, its tail submerged. Its mouth was open and tiny figures were emerging, carrying boxes and stacking them on the bank side.

Nick turned back to face the group.

"What's he doing here?" he snapped, pointing at Napoleon.

"Me?" said Napoleon, looking at him in a gentle, innocent manner. "Why, I'm just here to help sort out this little… misunderstanding."

Nick clenched his hands tightly together and scrutinized the others. Church, his face bruised and battered, had the same 'butter wouldn't melt in the mouth' expression as Napoleon. Varn looked tired and worn out. Ayisha was staring down at the table as though absorbed in something intensely interesting on the sheet of paper before her.

"Please Nicky, sit down," said Varn with a weak sigh.

Nick sat on the edge of the seat, his hands on his lap, his fingers fidgeting nervously.

"Let us commence," yelled Hercules, making everybody jump. "Remember, everyone must tell the whole truth. I shall strike to the very earth anyone who lies and…"

"Please," cut in Varn, massaging his forehead. "I am the one in charge of proceedings here."

"Just trying to help," muttered Hercules sulkily as he bent down to pick up the spear. It came as no surprise to anyone that he banged his head on the table on the way back up!

Varn glared at him before turning to Nick.

"We'll start with you Nicky," he said kindly. "Just tell us about yesterdays events."

Nick cleared his throat and stared at the table. It was easier to talk not looking at the eyes watching him. He told them everything, from Mindi's request to see him in secret, right through to when he was left holding the engine-heart. There was silence as he spoke apart from the occasional derisive snort from Church.

By the time he'd finished there was a great deal of hastily scribbled notes on the papers before them.

"Thank you," said Varn thoughtfully. He popped a tablet in his mouth and noisily gulped down some water before rummaging through the papers. "Now, I think we'll move on to Church next."

From that point, and from Nick's point of view, everything went rapidly downhill!

With a humble smile of thanks to Varn, Church proceeded to tell his story, backed up by the occasional quiet nod of agreement from Napoleon at his wise words.

He told how he had been watching a programme about undercover reporting and had, as usual, got into the part. He'd followed Nicky innocently enough in order to do a small feature on him, but was surprised to find Nicky going to the old home and even more surprised to see him talking happily with Tritus. What was even worse was that they seemed to be making plans to steal the engine-heart.

Unfortunately, Nicky and Tritus caught him and threw him in prison but not, Church sighed with a sad shake of the head, before Nicky had beaten him up on the way to the cell.

"That's ridiculous," yelled Nick, leaping to his feet. "It's all just complete lies! All of it!"

"That's enough," snarled Hercules, pushing him back into his chair.

"Please Nicky," said Varn unhappily, "you must not interrupt."

Nick slumped back in the seat. Napoleon gave a sad shake of the head. For good measure Church touched one of the bruises on his face and winced before carrying on.

He told them how he was placed in a cell next to poor Mindi who had apparently stumbled on the place in error, not knowing Hightower of course.

"Oh, very convenient," muttered Nick, drawing angry glares from the others and just the faintest of triumphant smiles from Church, who then went on to tell how Napoleon had managed to save him. This was followed by a graphic description of how they'd rushed to the ceremony to warn the committee about Nicky and Tritus's evil plans to steal the engine-heart.

When he'd finished there was a long silence.

"So what about Mindi?" asked Nick angrily,

sweeping the hair back out of his eyes. "Why didn't you take her with you?"

Church looked at him with tears in his eyes.

"I think you know very well why we didn't... couldn't, take her," he said dramatically.

All eyes turned on Nick. He had a very bad feeling about this.

"Which is?" he said slowly.

Church made a sobbing noise and looked down, pausing just long enough to heighten the tension.

"Because," he muttered, "she's dead! You had her killed."

The room erupted. Everyone spoke at once, their faces reflecting the shock and outrage they all felt.

Varn held his arms aloft. Gradually silence returned.

Nick leaned forward in his chair and banged his fist down angrily on the table.

"None of this is true," he yelled, looking from one to the other. "Mindi's alive. I was with her. There's no truth in any of this. There's no proof of any of this rubbish."

"I only wish there weren't," replied Church, placing a small, slim box on the table. "But I was reporting don't forget." He fixed Nick with a cold stare, full of angry hate that looked very impressive.

"You thought you'd managed to destroy all my recordings but you didn't. I managed to retrieve some. Not much I'm afraid, but hopefully enough to ensure you'll be convicted for you crimes."

He pressed a button on the box with slow deliberation. Suddenly Nick's voice bellowed around the room. There was just a series of sentences, distorted and difficult to make out, but they were definitely his voice.

'...Leave Mindi in her cell...'

'...I'll sort her out myself...'

'...Knock her out for a while...'

'...Mindi's dead!....'

"But they were just bits of conversations with Leroy," Nick spluttered. "That wasn't the whole..."

His voice trailed away as suddenly the huge screen flickered and an image of a snarling Nick pushing Church back against a wall grabbed everyone's attention. From the angle Church's face couldn't be seen, but Nick's could, and the fury was very clear.

For good measure Napoleon's voice blasted out of the speakers...

"Don't kill him kid..."

Then the picture went off.

In the shocked silence Church coughed politely.

"That was just before he banged my face into the wall. It didn't feel too bad yesterday I suppose," he said apologetically, gently touching his battered cheek, "but the bruises have come out so much more this morning."

"It was a vicious attack and it all happened so fast," agreed Napoleon.

Church nodded. Napoleon placed a consoling hand on his arm.

Everyone just sat there in stunned silence.

At that moment, Nick knew he was in real trouble.

*

Nick was lying on his bed, legs crossed at the ankles, head propped on folded arms, feeling thoroughly miserable, when the lap top on his desk made a most peculiar chirping sound.

He rolled off the bed and stretched. It was late. His mum had gone to bed as usual. Dave was downstairs, drinking as usual.

He frowned as he clicked the lap top open. For one thing, the noise was unlike anything he'd heard from it before. For another, it wasn't even switched on.

He dragged his chair over and sat down, the frown deepening as the screen shimmered into life. At first there was nothing but a series of flashing, diagonal stripes that made his head hurt, then the picture cleared and Jed's infuriatingly happy face appeared.

"Hi mate," he said. His voice was high and squeaky, as though he'd been inhaling on a helium balloon.

"Oh, hang on a sec."

The face disappeared, leaving Nick staring at Mr.Scoggin's scruffy little office. There was a lot of clicking noises and whispered conversation before Jed appeared again.

"That's better," he said in his normal Jed voice. "Now, can you see me?"

"Er... yes," replied Nick. "How did you manage that?"

"Nothing to it. Just simple stuff really."

"Really?"

"Well, OK. Mr.S. did it. How did today go?"

"It didn't," Nick said, shaking his head sadly.

For the next fifteen minutes he told his friend exactly what had gone off in the room. Jed remained silent throughout but his jaw dropped and his mouth hung open in astonishment with every revelation.

"What a load of doozin' idiots," he said when Nick had finished. "What's up with Church? Has he gone as loopy as Tritus or what?"

"Dunno," said Nick miserably. "That's exactly what they're trying to say has happened to me. But whatever is up with him, he's certainly got it in for me."

"So has Napoleon, but that's not so surprising. He's always felt he had a score to settle with you. Surely everyone can see it's my dear uncle who's in league with Tritus, not you?"

Nick shrugged. "Napoleon says although he's lived in the old home for months, it's a big place and he's never been in contact with Tritus."

"But he just happens to turn up to save Church?"

"Yeah."

"And they believe him?"

"Dunno yet. The overseer committee are going to reach a decision in three days time."

"Three days? That'll be the 22nd. That's nearly Christmas."

"Yeah," replied Nick bitterly, "merry Christmas huh!"

"And what happens if the decision goes against you?"

The question hung in the air. Nick just shook his head and sighed.

Jed leaned forward till his head nearly filled the screen.

"So what are we going to do then Nicky?"

"Dunno," replied Nick sadly. He really didn't want to think about it anymore. He'd had enough for one day.

"We could try and find Mindi. She could prove what you're saying is true."

"I've already thought of that." He felt a stab of conscience at the mention of Mindi's name. Before the meeting he'd been so swept up in his own problems that he'd almost forgotten about the promise he'd made to go back and get her. After the meeting he'd tried to do something about it.

"I went looking for the wooden platform at the old home," he explained, "but it's impossible to get through all those prickly bushes…"

"Yeah," agreed Jed. "That's why they're there; to keep nosey giants like you out."

"Besides, the fresh snow's covered up everything. From that height I wouldn't have been able to see anything even if I could have got through."

"Well, maybe we can try again tomorrow."

"Maybe," Nick replied, without much enthusiasm.

Jed leaned back again. There was a long, uncomfortable silence.

From downstairs came a strange, eerie wailing noise followed by a squeal from Dave.

Suddenly footsteps rushed up the stairs. They paused for a second on the landing. There was another squeal, followed by a bedroom door banging shut.

Then silence once more.

"What was that all about?" asked Nick.

"That my friend," replied Jed, the smile returning to its fullest, "was Dave getting his usual nightly scare, courtesy of Mr.S."

Nick tried to return the smile. It was good of Jed and Mr.Scoggins to be doing this, and in the long term it might just work and frighten Dave out. At least it would save Hightower from being buried under a hotel.

But if it didn't work, sooner or later they would all be in big trouble. At the moment though it was the short term that really mattered and he couldn't help but feel that if everything went wrong on the 22nd, the chances for any of them would be gone forever.

*

Chapter 14

INSPIRATION

Jed was growing increasingly concerned about his friend.

He sort of expected him to be pretty shocked and depressed on that first night, but usually Nicky seemed to be able to bounce back from things with renewed vigour.

This though, was different.

When Jed contacted him via the screen the next morning his mood, if anything, seemed even more dejected.

"Come on mate," he pleaded, trying to cajole him into action. "Let's go and see if we can find Mindi. She's your best chance. What do you say?"

"Yeah, I suppose," Nick muttered with a shrug. "What about the shrinkage post though?"

"What about it?"

"It's guarded. I'm not supposed to use it except to meet the overseer committee."

"Yeah? And who do you think's guarding it?"

"Dunno," muttered Nick with yet another infuriating shrug.

"Hercules! So it won't be a problem!"

…And it wasn't.

Jed simply slipped into the cave, crept past the loudly snoring Hercules cuddled up in a very comfortable looking chair, and replaced the shrinkage post with a stick he'd found in Mr.S's workshop!

They spent the first day, and the second wandering around the area of the old home looking for the platform without success. It was a big area and they were plodding round it on foot.

It was hard going. Nick's heart obviously wasn't in it and conversation was little, and sometimes none at all.

Jed tried his best. On the way out that first afternoon, squashed in the hot and uncomfortable rat bus with all the noisy passengers he tried to raise his friend's spirits.

"Have you thought of telling Varn about what we're doing?" he asked cheerfully.

"I already have," came the clipped reply.

"And?"

"And what?"

Jed sighed. "What did he say? Are they going to help find Mindi?"

Nick stared out the hazy window at the bleak, white landscape.

"No. They think she's dead."

"But you did explain?"

"Varn said I shouldn't contact him, not while they're investigating what happened."

"But did you argue your case? After all, how could a twelve year old boy beat up someone like Church? And how could Napoleon be there to pull you off if they were supposed to be rushing to stop you stealing the engine-heart? It's not right. It doesn't make doozin' sense. You can win this."

But it was no use. Since losing the trust of the overseer committee it was as if Nick had lost all interest in saving himself. Jed pleaded with him, shouted at him, reasoned with him, but nothing worked. All he got back was that infuriating shrug!

More than once, when Jed did try to say anything, Nick would cut him off.

"I'm thinking about something," he'd say with an intense look of concentration on his face.

"Thinking about what?"

"Something," would come the reply. "Something that's not quite right."

Jed gave up. Two days and no sign of the entrance to Mindi's prison.

It was hardly surprising that he was getting so worried about his friend.

*

On the morning of the 22nd, Nick was still wearing his pyjamas when he shuffled into the kitchen, blinking and yawning, to be confronted by a huge plate of bacon, sausage, eggs, beans and fried bread that his mum had put out in the forlorn hope of enticing him into eating something.

It didn't work. Nick chewed on a piece of bacon for a few seconds, stared blankly at the plate, and put his knife and fork down.

"Dominic, for heaven's sake, you've got to eat something," she pleaded, "you'll waste away if you don't."

"Leave him Marion," said Dave's voice from behind a newspaper. "He'll eat when he wants to. Here, pass it over; I'll have it."

Nick heard no more. He drifted back into his own thoughts. Something was gnawing at his brain, something he'd seen that wasn't quite right. The answer felt desperately close, yet frustratingly just out of reach.

Dave skewered one of the sausages with a fork and disappeared back behind the paper. Nick glanced vaguely at the writing.

Marion was in the process of burning a slice of toast.

'Dog saves man from drowning,' said one of the headlines.

The smoke alarm screeched and Marion wafted it with her towel.

"Can't get a moment's peace," grumbled Dave from behind the paper.

'Collision at notorious blackspot,' read Nick, paying little attention to the words. The smoke alarm stopped but the smell of burnt toast hung in the air.

Near the bottom of the page it said;

'Second set of twins born to local family.'

Something stirred in Nick's mind. He sat up and scanned the words again. Memories of Matthew and Emily, the Slater twins came back. They were in Australia now, too far to be of any help.

But that wasn't it.

Twins!

The woman at the house…Number 216 …What had she said about the kids?

He stood up. The chair screeched back.

Clipboards!!

"Dominic?" said Marion, concern in her voice.

Nick held his hand up. "I'm OK Mum," he muttered, hardly daring to break his train of thought.

He charged out of the room and rushed up to his bedroom. In his mind the woman was talking about twins, telling him how common it was to have one left handed and one right handed.

A sudden shiver rolled through him.

He dragged his thoughts back to when Mindi had got Church to sign that ridiculous document before Church flew off from Barrowhouse to take the engine-heart to Hightower. He closed his eyes and concentrated.

Clipboard in left hand…pen in right.

Now he fast forwarded to memories of them climbing up to the magpie and another of Mindi's daft forms for Church to sign.

Clipboard in right hand…pen in left! He was sure of it!

His eyes sprang open and he leapt over to the parrot.

"Who's a pretty boy then?" he snapped.

For a few moment's there was silence.

"Come on…come on…" he muttered, hopping from foot to foot.

"Nicky?" a worried voice finally said.

"Varn," he cried, forcing himself to stand still.

"What is it?" The voice sounded even more drained. "You know I'm not supposed to talk to you while the investigation is in progress."

"Varn. When I first came to Hightower, Church told me he had a brother."

"Yes, Chamberlain. Poor Church hasn't spoken to him for many months. They don't get on anymore."

"Right," said Nick, holding his breath. "Just answer me this…are they twins?"

There was a long pause.

"Why yes. They're almost identical. Slight differences but most people can't tell."

"YESSS," hissed Nick, balling his hand into a fist. "Thanks Varn."

"I really have to go. I've got such a migraine. Terrible headache. Really terrible."

The communication went dead and Nick hurriedly got dressed, his thoughts tumbling over themselves, only now they were positive thoughts.

Suddenly his laptop made that strange chirping sound and the worried face of Jed appeared on the screen.

"Hi Jed," Nick beamed. "What time shall we meet

today? Better make it early. I don't want to be late for the overseer committee."

The question caught Jed off guard.

"Er, whenever," he stammered. "We still going to the old home then?"

"Sure. I've got a good feeling about today."

Jed stared at him with a quizzical frown.

"Why the sudden change?"

Nick tapped his nose and the grin broadened. Downstairs, the kitchen door opened and someone started to climb the stairs.

"You know I said something wasn't quite right?"

Leaning forward, Jed nodded faintly.

"Well, I worked it out." He lowered his voice to a whisper. "I'll tell you when I see you. If I'm right... let's just say, things are going to get interesting. Look, I've got to go. Make it same time as yesterday. Same place."

He clicked off the screen just as Marion bustled into the room and sat down on his bed. Her hand hovered sort of close to his and for one awful moment Nick thought she was going to squeeze it tenderly. Nick always hated shows of affection from his mum. Fortunately they were quite rare. What he did like was the slightly unsure look in her eyes when she talked about Dave, as this was something new.

"Is it this hotel thing Dominic?" she asked softly. "Is that what's worrying you?"

Nick leaned back and pretended to give the question a lot of thought.

"Well..." he said at length, "You know I don't like the idea. I don't want to leave this place. Not even for a short time."

"But Dave only wants to do this for your own good."

Yeah right, thought Nick.

"But I like my school, and my home. I don't want to move again."

"Well how about we all sit down and talk it through together like adults?"

Or Dave shout it through like a kid, thought Nick, his mind working overtime.

"Maybe," he replied.

"Good," said Marion happily, patting his hand.

Nick shivered at the touch.

"We'll all have a little chat soon. Get Christmas over first. How does that suit you?"

"Great," he said without much enthusiasm.

Marion relaxed and peered round the bedroom, looking immensely pleased that she'd solved all her son's problems. Now that was done it looked like she wanted to spend a bit of quality time with him.

Nick, on the other hand, was anxious to get out and rescue at least one prisoner, clear his name, and save an entire world!

"How's your parrot these days?" she suddenly asked, raising her considerable frame from the bed and strolling over to Polly's cage in the corner.

Nick's heart sank. Keeping his mum away from the Elverey's first line of communication had always been something high on his list of priorities!

"Oh.... fine," he spluttered. "Just fine."

"Mrs.Bailey in the village has one. It seems a bit more active than yours though." She leaned forward, looking intently through the bars. At that moment Polly made one of her programmed, but infrequent steps across the perch. With an odd, wheezing sigh, she stopped and wobbled precariously.

"She's old," Nick said anxiously.

Marion looked back at him with a huge smile.

"Do you know? I much prefer Polly here to

Mrs.Bailey's parrot. That thing never shuts up. It'd drive me mad to have to listen to it all day. She goes up to it and says 'who's a pretty boy then' and off it goes. Never shuts up."

Nick leapt from the bed in horror as Polly stirred.

From somewhere inside the cage came a cough as though someone was clearing their throat.

Marion's smile melted. As she turned to look at the parrot Nick grabbed his left leg and wailed as loud as he could. Even so, he could just about hear the deep voice of Hercules as it called out his name. He yelled even louder.

"Dominic? Whatever's the matter?" cried Marion in alarm.

"Cramp," he screamed, hopping towards her, trying to push her away from the cage.

"Nicky…" said the voice.

"I'VE GOT CRAMP," he desperately yelled, trying to drown out the sound.

"Well quieten down," said Marion in a soothing voice as she guided him to the bed. "It's only cramp. Just bend your toes back."

But Hercules' voice wouldn't stop.

"Nicky…"

Marion turned with a confused look on her face.

"Owwww," he bellowed. "It hurts. MUM, CAN YOU HELP ME WHILE YOU'RE IN MY BEDROOM?"

From the cage came, "Are you…"

"I SAID, WHILE YOU'RE HERE IN MY BEDROOM MUM!"

"…Ooops," came the voice from the cage.

Marion looked from cage to boy, boy to cage.

Nick started writhing dramatically on the bed.

"For heaven's sake," she said, grabbing his toes and bending them back. It's only cramp Dominic. It won't kill you."

There was silence in the corner.

Nick moaned a couple more times and rubbed the back of his leg for good measure.

"Thanks Mum," he said apologetically.

"What was that voice?" she muttered, turning back to the cage.

"Oh...nothing. Just...just my radio alarm coming on."

He leapt to the bedside table and slammed a hand down on the top button.

"There," he said with a forced and incredibly insincere smile.

Marion's frown deepened. She stared at the cage, then at Nick before leaning towards him and putting her hand on his forehead.

"No. No temperature," she confirmed.

"I'm fine Mum, honest!"

The frown gradually dissolved. With a final glance at the cage and a slow shake of the head, she slowly shuffled out of the bedroom.

Only when the door clicked shut did Nick start to relax.

*

Despite the incident with his mum, Nick still managed to meet Jed on time and from the start it was obvious they were going to have more success than on the previous two days.

As they travelled on the rat bus Nick explained to an amazed and incredulous Jed that he'd not been set up by Church, but by his twin brother Chamberlain. Suddenly the boy grabbed him by the arm.

"Look," he shouted, pointing out the window as they bounced down a path towards the old home.

Nick squinted through the dirt and the fur of the window. In the distance, hopping through the snow was the hare.

"It's going towards the old home," he said excitedly.

"Must be Napoleon," Jed hissed.

"Must be. Are we close?"

Jed thought for a moment. "Close enough. Come on, let's go."

He grabbed Nick's arm and they staggered down the central aisle of the hot, sweaty bus. The passengers grumbled as they squeezed past.

"You gerrin' off 'ere?" said the driver with a casual glance in their direction.

"No, just stretching our doozin' legs," muttered Jed sarcastically.

"Yes," corrected Nick with a glare at his friend.

"Well there's nuthin' much 'ere. Nuthin' much till we get round ter Yada. Don' know why these routes 'ave ter come all the way round this way. Nobody ever wants ter come 'ere. Adds 'alf an hour onto the journey this does."

"We've got off round here for the last two days," said Nick amiably.

The rat wheezed to a stop.

"Well you're the only ones. Waste o' time if you ask me…"

He was still moaning as Nick and Jed slipped through the ear and jumped down into the snow.

It was bitterly cold outside and Nick pulled his coat tight around him as the rat scampered away into the distance.

Jed tried to tighten his old black coat too, but with three of the five buttons missing it was a pretty hopeless task.

They both stood there shivering.

"Which way?" Nick asked, blowing onto his hands.

"Over there," replied Jed with a grin. "We just follow the hare's tracks.

It seemed weird to Nick that the hare's footprints in the snow were so large they could have jumped into them. Even after all this time the various scales of things sometimes confused him.

Their progress was slow, hampered by fallen twigs that formed awkward barriers and small stones that became boulders. By the time they'd found the hare Nick was getting concerned as to whether he'd get back in time for the meeting.

"Look! Over there," whispered Jed as they hid behind the stem of an enormous prickly weed. Its thin branches were bent over by the weight of snow and Nick was worried about some falling off and burying them in an avalanche!

He tried to concentrate on what Jed was pointing at. The hare sat crouched against the supporting pillars of the platform, its long ears resting on the platform itself.

His spirits soared. They'd found it!

He focused on two figures struggling towards the ears.

"There's Napoleon," he said triumphantly.

"Yeah," replied Jed, his voice taking on a bitter edge at the sight of his uncle. "Who's the other guy?"

"That's Leroy, one of Napoleon's henchmen; and that…" he said pointing at a white haired figure standing just inside the top of the ear, "…is another. He seems to control the hare."

The two figures carried something to the ear. Leroy jumped in and Napoleon threw it down before jumping in himself.

"What do you reckon that was?" asked Jed.

"Dunno, but I hope they leave soon. My hands feel as if they're going to fall off in this cold."

"Mine too. Plus my nose and my ears!"

After a few moments the hare began to stir. The ears twitched away from the platform and the enormously strong back legs suddenly flicked, propelling the body forward in a shower of snow. Within three or four hops the thing had jumped over a ridge and disappeared.

Jed and Nick cautiously stepped forward, anxious not to meet up with any more of Napoleon's men or worse, any Deebers. Not that they were likely to meet Deebers out in the light. But once inside, well that was a different matter.

They climbed a ladder attached to one of the wooden pillars and hauled themselves up onto the platform.

There was a strange, eerie silence. The snow seemed to muffle any sound. Nick half expected to see one of Tritus's wasps come flying over but since his 'birthday party,' the wasps seemed to have disappeared.

"Come on, this way," he whispered to Jed, who hesitantly followed him into a gloomy tunnel.

The journey was easier than Nick expected. He hadn't been taking much notice on the way out, but there was only one way to go. As they crept down stairs and round corners they paused cautiously, their hearts in their mouths, anxious to make sure they didn't bump into anyone.

As they proceeded their limbs began to thaw out as the temperature rose to something approaching comfortable.

Finally, they emerged into a long, low and rather familiar corridor.

"I think this is it," whispered Nick, increasing his pace as he approached the stairs at the end.

Just before the stairs were two thick doors. He tapped on the first and peered through the tiny window.

"Mindi? Are you there?"

In the silence he heard a rustle.

"Nicky, is that you?"

Nick could have yelled with delight.

"Yes it's me," he said with a broad grin. "I said I'd come back. Sorry it took so long."

"Nicky, we've got to think outside the box on this one so to speak. We've got to…"

"Nicky…Nicky…" cried a distinctly familiar voice from the cell next door.

Nick's feelings became all confused. Relief, mixed with pleasure and sadness, and just a twinge of irrational anger.

"Church? Are you all right?"

"I am," came the reply, but from the tone it was difficult to tell. "Nicky, be careful of the Deebers. Have you a plan?"

Even as he spoke they could hear footsteps in the distance.

Nick's heart stopped. He looked at Jed who held his hands out in a gesture that suggested 'what now?' He looked up. The corridor, though warm carried a cool draught and the air smelt fresher than earlier.

Above them was a grill with thick, sturdy bars, but it was what was beyond those bars that excited him. He could see the branches of a holly bush wavering in the wind and beyond that, grey clouds scudding across the sky.

The footsteps grew in intensity. Jed looked at him, his face pale and scared.

"Stay here Jed," Nick said, his smile as confident as he could make it. "If they come down just hide round the corner up there. They're guarding these two. They don't know about us; I hope!"

Jed tried to return the smile without much success.

With the faintest of nods he backed slowly down the corridor. Nick rushed past him, running as fast as he could, back the way they'd come.

When he emerged into the daylight and stopped on the platform, his lungs were nearly bursting and he paused a moment to catch his breath.

The coldness didn't bother him now. He was on a mission and he had to concentrate.

He threw himself onto the ladder, leaping down the rungs two at a time, then ran across the snow in the direction that the buried prison was most likely to be in, stopping every so often to check the surroundings.

He kept looking up, desperately searching for the holly bush. He ran up over a small ridge and there it was! His heart leapt at the sight. Almost hidden behind the vicious looking thorn bushes towering above, the branches looked small, almost delicate, but this was the one, he was sure.

He ran into a clearing, hoping there was enough room, and pressed ring and shrinkage post together. The pain was even worse than usual, only this time it seemed to sear up his right arm. When his senses began to recover he saw a tear in the sleeve of his jacket and blood seeping through. The thorns had ripped into his arm as he'd grown, but he had no time to dwell on that now.

He carefully surveyed the ground from his new perspective. As usual everything seemed so different. The branches of the holly bush were way below him now. He bent down and examined the ground. After much searching he thought he could see a couple of tiny holes. They had to be the grates. They seemed to be sunk into a long, thin area that could only be the underground corridor.

He carefully brushed the snow away. The ground

underneath seemed to be made of some sort of weird metal. The dull brown surface was pitted and flaking. He probed the long plate containing the grates with his fingers and felt a lip at the edges. If he could get his fingers under it perhaps he could prise the roof off. He bent down and with all his strength, tried to lift the top, his face contorting with such exertion, his right arm stinging with pain.

It was no use. He looked round for something to use; something to lever the top off with. There were bits of wood and a few branches but nothing strong enough. He couldn't move far because the vicious branches held him prisoner.

Scanning round on the floor he noticed a long, thin piece of metal sticking out of the snow, buried under a particularly large thorn bush. He bent down, his fingers snagging on razor sharp spikes as he carefully leant forward. He stretched as far as he could and for a moment the thing seemed tantalisingly just out of reach. Gradually though, inching further and further forward, he edged his finger round the top and dragged. It moved just enough to allow him to get his hand round and pull. As it came up he knew it was just the right size, but was it strong enough? It was a bit rusty, but pretty sturdy. He didn't know what it was, probably some part of the old craft, but he didn't really care, it was only needed for one thing.

He pressed one end under the lip and pushed down. Almost immediately there was a groan and the metal plate moved slightly. He clenched his teeth together, sweat trickling down his forehead despite the cold, and pushed harder. A small gap appeared. He threw the bar down and put his fingers into the gap. With all his might he dragged the heavy plate up. It lifted, slowly at first, but then more and more till it was standing on edge.

With a final heave he threw it over and bent down to look at what was revealed.

The two prisons were clearly visible. The corridor was a long, thin line covered in figures rushing in all directions, desperately trying to get out of the light. It reminded him of the insects that scurried away when you lifted stones in the garden, but in this case he could vaguely hear the screams of the Deebers as they gradually melted away into the shadows.

At the far end of the corridor Jed emerged from the corner. Nick gave him an enormous thumbs up sign. He couldn't tell if Jed did the same or just waved.

He turned his attention back to the two prisons. The occupants were staring up.

"Well, what are we waiting for?" he said cheerfully. "We've all got a meeting to attend; and I really don't want to be late!!"

*

Chapter 15

THE TWEEDLE THEATRE

As far as dramatic last minute rescues were concerned, trundling to Glug on a bus filled with screaming babies and passengers moaning about the weather, wasn't that impressive. But the last minute part was certainly true. Nick arrived to clear his name with just seconds to spare.

"You three wait out here," he whispered, finger to his lips, as they stood outside the door. "Let's see if we can find out just what this is all about first."

Jed looked excited, Mindi full of businesslike eagerness while Church just looked lost.

He turned and knocked timidly on the door.

"Enter," roared the voice of Hercules.

Nick stepped hesitantly into the room, leaving the door just a fraction open.

"Hello Nicky," said Varn, his face pale and drawn. "Sit down please."

Nick meekly sat at the table. He fidgeted with his hands and bit on his lower lip. 'Church' watched him with a cool, self-satisfied expression on his face. Clearly he was enjoying the boy's discomfort.

"Where's Napoleon?" Nick stammered.

"He can't be here," said Varn, shuffling the papers set before him. "He's not on the Hightower overseer committee."

"Not yet," muttered Church.

"Neither is he," said Nick, nodding at Hercules.

"Yes he is Nicky," replied Varn, looking uncomfortable. "We voted him on yesterday. We need more on the committee since the inclusion of the Barrowhouse Elvereys; and…since the death of poor Mindi."

They all respectfully bowed their heads.

"Poor Mindi," wailed Hercules.

Before Nick could say anything 'Church' gave a polite cough.

"And soon there will be another," he said, casually leaning back in his chair.

"Another?" snapped Nick, trying to mask his concern.

"Oh yes. Napoleon is up at Rixal at this very moment waiting for us all."

Nick glared at the others, waiting for a full explanation.

"We voted just before you came in," said Varn.

"On whether to accept Napoleon onto the committee," added Hercules.

"And we're going over to tell him the outcome after… after…" muttered Ayisha.

"…After we've informed you of your fate," concluded 'Church.'

"Will he be voted onto the committee?" asked Nick incredulously.

"That cannot be disclosed," replied Varn. "Not until we meet with Napoleon."

"But it will be a foregone conclusion," piped up 'Church,' not very subtly nodding at Hercules and Varn before tapping his own chest to indicate who had voted in favour.

"After all the trouble he caused, especially at Rixal," said Nick, shaking his head.

"Times change," said 'Church.'

"People change," agreed Hercules.

"Now, I really think we must get to the matter in hand," proclaimed Varn, hurriedly changing the subject. He began shuffling the papers again as he added, "Ayisha, would you please pass these copies of the findings out."

Ayisha silently slipped a paper to each in turn. She avoided Nick's gaze as she did so. Nick tried to see what was written on the single sheet but upside down reading had never been his strong point.

"We all know what the conclusion's are," continued Varn unhappily. "Can we all please sign this copy in turn and we'll then give it, and the verdict, to Nicky."

He took the pen, paused for a moment before signing, and passed the pen and paper to Ayisha who just scribbled her signature without looking. She wiped a tear from her eye as she passed the details to Hercules who read each line slowly and dramatically before writing with a flourish, only to stop with a frown, turn the pen the right way up, and commence again.

Finally 'Church,' with a long, sad sigh, solemnly added his signature.

Silence hung in the air.

"Thank you," Varn said at length, taking the document from 'Church' and handing it to Nick. "You may take as long as you wish reading it through."

Nick didn't look down. Instead he slowly and deliberately stared at each of the Elvereys sat around the table, one at a time. His heart was beating fast but he felt no nerves. It was like he was playing a game of cards knowing the hand he was holding couldn't be beaten.

Only 'Church' managed to hold his gaze, with that almost invisible sly smile on his face.

"Nicky I…"

Nick held a hand up to silence Varn, his eyes still fixed firmly on 'Church.'

"Tell me," he said slowly, "when you signed this document, why did you sign with your left hand?"

For a fraction of a second a flicker of concern crept across the little Elverey's face.

"Well I...I couldn't use my right. Not after you attacked me." He flexed his right wrist and winced. "It's too painful to write."

Nick nodded as though this answer was the most reasonable in the world. Outside, the distant noise of a duck quacking broke the long silence. 'Church' tried to hold Nick's gaze but finally cracked and stared down at the table.

Nick was enjoying himself now.

For the first time he very slowly and deliberately looked down at the document in his hands, then tore it, first in half, then again, and threw the pieces on the table.

There were gasps of disbelief.

"Nicky?" yelled Ayisha.

"What the...?" muttered Hercules, stumbling to his feet.

Nick swung round in his chair and stared at the door.

"I think it's time you came in."

The door banged open and Mindi and Church stepped in, Jed standing discreetly behind them. For a long moment there was silence. Mindi just stood there surveying the scene, Church at her side, with tears rolling down his cheeks as he stared miserably at his brother.

"Hello Chamberlain," he muttered.

"What the...?" spluttered Hercules again.

"I hope," demanded Mindi in her most officious tone, "that the primary key objective here so to speak, will be to make me a member of this overseer committee."

For a moment there was another shocked, surreal silence then suddenly, everyone began talking and shouting at once!

*

"Of course, I never doubted your innocence for a moment," said Hercules with great importance as the snake they were travelling to Rixal in slid effortlessly over the snow. "I saw through that Napoleon straight away. I was just biding my time before I struck him to the very earth; and as for that Tritus, of course I knew you'd never be in league with the likes of him."

"Of course," replied Nick with a wry smile to Varn and Ayisha. "I'm just sorry I had to string you along a bit back there. I thought I might be able to get some more information out of Chamberlain."

That wasn't entirely true, for two reasons. The main one for not inviting Mindi and Church in immediately was because he wanted the satisfaction of seeing Chamberlain squirm, and that satisfaction grew as he watched the little weasel being bustled away to prison by three burly guards. The second reason though, was deeper than that. He felt that his friends had somehow turned against him when he needed their trust the most, and however strong the evidence, he found that betrayal difficult to accept.

Now though, looking at poor Church sitting up at the front with his head in his hands, he felt rather guilty about dragging the whole thing out.

"Why do you think Chamberlain did it?" whispered Ayisha, looking worriedly at the hunched little figure who just wanted to be left alone. Not that he was likely to get his wish as Jed was sitting with him giving a graphic and highly exaggerated account of how he and Nick had stumbled upon the prison at the old home.

"Church and Chamberlain have never really got on," piped up Varn, rubbing his shoulder gently. "They've always been like chalk and cheese. But Chamberlain spent a lot of time up at Rixal. I reckon it must have been in the days when Tritus and the two engine hearts were up there."

"So you think the combined power got to him?" Ayisha asked.

Varn nodded.

"…And corrupted him like it did Tritus?"

Varn nodded again.

"…And turned him evil, like Tritus?"

Varn nodded and winced.

"When Chamberlain had Church captured and made the switch," he said, rubbing the now aching neck, "we never saw the subtle changes between the two brothers because at first he was wearing that ridiculous sheet…"

"Pretending to be an undercover reporter," cut in Ayisha.

"Precisely. Then he started wearing some make-up, saying that it was bruising, which of course implicated poor Nicky here."

But Nick wasn't listening. He was more concerned with what was going to happen now, and the same question kept rolling around in his head…'Where's Tritus?'

"Hercules," he said finally, "are you sure these guards of yours will be there at…" he turned to Varn; "…what's the name of this place again? The one you're supposed to meet Napoleon at?"

"The Tweedle theatre," answered Varn, still rubbing his neck. "It's a big old place. Typical meeting place for someone with a big ego like Napoleon."

Nick thought how quickly people's opinions changed. It wasn't long ago that Varn was voting him onto the overseer committee!

But he didn't say anything. Instead he turned back to Hercules.

"You sure these guards will be at the Tweedle theatre ready to arrest Napoleon?"

"Of course," replied Hercules with a confident wave of his hand. "The elite guard is the best; the very best. Troy, their leader is the fiercest Elverey I have ever known. He commands with an iron fist, the finest, bravest, most experienced guard ever. They will strike to the very earth anything and anyone who is crazy enough to get in their way."

He banged his spear on the floor to emphasize the point, making everyone except Church jump.

"Please," muttered Mindi with a harsh stare, "I'm trying, so to speak, to establish some key performance criteria here."

She waved her phone irritably. Hercules ignored her.

"These brave guards will fight to the very death. They have valiantly fought many battles. Never have they been beaten. Their motto is, 'Death with honour; not death and you're a goner!'"

"Very nice," muttered Nick.

"I have ordered them to be there, therefore they will be there…"

*

"…I wonder where they are?" mumbled Hercules, peering around the foyer of the Tweedle theatre. Despite

220

the imposing double doors being shut, they could hear stirring music drifting out from the auditorium.

"So what do we do now?" asked Ayisha, glaring at Hercules.

"Well we can't arrest him yet," hissed Nick angrily. "Not on our own."

"I will take that honour," replied Hercules, standing tall.

"What if his men are with him?"

"Good point," said Hercules, not standing quite so tall!

Suddenly, above the noise of the music came the sound of a strong, commanding voice approaching the doors. They all looked at each other questioningly.

"You're going to have to go in," whispered Nick. "Play for time. He mustn't see us or the game's up. We'll hide and hope this elite guard of yours turns up soon."

Before anyone could answer one of the door handles flicked down and Nick, Mindi and Jed slipped behind one of the ornately decorated pillars bordering the foyer.

The door creaked open.

"Ah, hello my soon to be fellow members of the overseer committee," said Napoleon's good natured voice. "Let's get this little show on the road shall we?"

There was much shuffling of feet.

"Can we please turn that music off? Can't hear myself think with that dirge."

The sound abruptly died.

"Thank you. Church, Varn, Hercules and the beautiful Ayisha. May I introduce you to my little group."

It could have been Nick's imagination, but he felt there was just a slight emphasis when Napoleon mentioned the name of Church. He hoped the little Elverey could pull off the deception. In his present state, he really wasn't too sure.

"Now, this is Leroy…"

"Hi," came Leroy's voice and Nick clenched his fists in anger.

"This is Isrutt…"

"Hi…" Mumbled the white haired guy.

"And this is Rupert."

"Hello," growled the voice of Eye Patch.

'Rupert?' mused Nick with a wry smile.

Then the door clicked shut and the voices faded into vague mutterings.

The three of them stepped forward.

"Now what?" whispered Jed.

"We wait I suppose," replied Nick with a shrug, "for Hercules's men."

"But there's only four of them, and one's a doozin' old bloke. There's seven of us."

"Yeah I know," Nick replied, ticking off with his fingers, "but two of us are kids, we've one bloke who's even older than theirs, and Church, who really doesn't look much up for it. I say we wait for this elite guard."

"Assuming that Hercules told them the correct meeting point," piped up Mindi, shuffling in her bag and taking out the latest copy of The Elverey Times, neatly folded open at the 'Management Today' page. "I for one shall sit over there and wait, without much confidence I might add, for these guards."

She sauntered over to a comfortable looking couch in the corner, muttering something about others being made members of the committee before her and the indignity of having to wait outside whilst meetings of such magnitude were taking place.

"What's up with her?" Nick asked, nodding at the figure now immersed behind the paper.

"Dunno. Come on," replied Jed excitedly.

"Where?"

"Up onto the balcony. Let's go and listen."

He disappeared round a corner, leaving Nick standing there perplexed. Jed had been brought up in Rixal before he'd been sent to live with Mr.and Mrs.S. so he knew the area well. With a shrug he followed, just in time to see Jed slip through a side door.

They crept up the curved, shallow staircase two steps at a time and emerged onto the balcony. Hiding behind the last row of seats, Nick looked up at the high domed roof above. It was difficult to make out much in the gloomy darkness but a huge, unlit chandelier hung from the centre, its crystal droplets shimmering in the weak light from below. The whole place smelt of wood and polish but the seats were tatty and the carpet threadbare, giving the impression that the place had seen better days.

He crept down past the rows of seats till he reached the front of the balcony and cautiously peered over. The theatre was vast, with row upon row of empty seats. Deep red curtains were swept back to reveal the stage, which was empty; just bare floorboards and stark, white-washed walls. It was all very plush and old fashioned, all very gloomy and dark.

The voices were much more distinct now, echoing through the huge auditorium. They were coming from right below, so Nick surmised that everyone had to be sat in the back rows, near the double doors.

"Yes, by all means," Napoleon was saying in that same good humoured voice. "Please Varn, read out the official committee acceptance form. Church, perhaps you'd like to sit over here, next to me."

Church muttered something inaudible and there was more shuffling before Varn began reading in a trembling, hesitant voice that started to gain in confidence as he continued.

It was the most boring of forms, filled with the sort of meaningless jargon that Mindi would have been proud of, but as for playing for time, it was quite impressive.

There was nothing more Nick could really do so he crept quietly back to the rear of the balcony but Jed had already gone, obviously bored to death by Varn's ramblings.

Nick slipped back down the stairs and out into the foyer.

Mindi was still sitting in the corner, the Times in her hand. Jed was sitting next to her, looking fed up. When she saw Nick she picked up her phone and waved it at him.

"Just touched base with Hercules's troops. They said their E.T.A. would be four minutes."

"E.T.A?" asked Jed.

"Estimated time of arrival," whispered Mindi and Nick in unison.

Nick felt relieved. At least then they'd be able to storm in and arrest Napoleon and his men. Tritus would just have to be dealt with later.

He sat down in an old leather chair and drummed his fingers on the arm impatiently, checking his watch every ten seconds or so.

"What are you reading?" muttered Jed to Mindi without much enthusiasm.

"I'm not reading," she replied without looking up, "I'm optimising my thought process with the quiz on page seven."

"Oh. Can I help?"

"I doubt it."

"I might be able to answer some questions."

"I'm not doing any questions," sighed Mindi. "I'm doing an anagram."

"Anagram? What's an anagram?"

She glared at him with a superior, 'that just proves my point' expression.

"An anagram is where letters have to be re-arranged to make another word."

"Oh," replied Jed, looking as confused as ever.

A sort of light blinked on in Nick's brain, like it had when the idea of twins and Church and Chamberlain had first come to him.

He stopped drumming.

"Isrutt...!!" he muttered.

Mindi and Jed exchanged glances.

"Isrutt...! The white haired guy" he repeated. "He's Tritus!"

"Oh, I see; an anagram," said Jed with a smile that immediately disappeared as this new information sank in.

Before anyone could respond, angry raised voices erupted from the theatre.

Nick's heart missed a beat as he leapt to the double doors and pressed his ear against them.

"...But enough of this," Napoleon was bellowing, his voice very far from the good humoured, easy going nature of earlier. "Now that we have told you the truth, you three cannot remain free. We shall escort you to your new captivity."

"And then what?" demanded Ayisha coldly, "are you going to kill us?"

"You cannot stay alive," came the calmly menacing voice of Tritus. "The overseer committee is no more. The overseer is disgraced, and we will take control of Hightower."

"Not if I have anything to do with it," roared Hercules.

"But you won't have anything to do with it you big, bumbling fool."

"What do you mean by 'can't stay alive?' said Napoleon, a trace of uncertainty creeping into his voice. "Just imprison them you said. You never said anything about killing them all."

"Didn't I?" replied Tritus with a raucous laugh that froze Nick's blood.

"But...maybe, for now..." stuttered a new voice. Nick pressed closer to the door and frowned.

Church? What was he doing?

"...For now we should keep these...these fools alive," said Church, his voice gaining in strength as his confidence grew. "They might be more useful to our plans if they're alive Tritus. The question is, is Napoleon starting to lose his nerve?"

There was a long, drawn out silence, broken by an awful mocking laugh from Tritus once more.

"You see Napoleon," he cackled, "only Chamberlain here understands. Only Chamberlain has soaked in the glories of the power like I have; and he is right. They may be more useful to us alive; for now. Take them away."

Good old Church thought Nick. It was a good job that the light was so dismal in the theatre. The little differences, such as absence of any bruising, wouldn't be quite so apparent!

"I have not lost my nerve," snapped Napoleon angrily.

"Then prove it," hissed Tritus, "take these creatures away."

"Perhaps," cut in Church, "I might just be permitted a moment to savour this victory."

"Huh?" muttered someone.

"Now that we have told these poor fools the truth, I'd like to explain just how I tricked them..."

"Huh?"

"...How I tricked Church, my stupid brother and took his place."

"Oh, Chamberlain," gasped Varn, trying to sound convincing, "how could you?"

"Oh, Chamberlain," repeated Ayisha with a sob.

"Who?" bellowed Hercules, sounding confused.

There was a long, ominous silence.

"Very well Chamberlain," sighed Tritus finally, "you have earned your few moments my friend."

"Thank you. Napoleon's men captured my brother and I switched..."

Nick smiled grimly. Church, bless him, was playing for time.

Suddenly, from the outer door of the foyer came the sound of footsteps. Nick swung round as the door swung open.

"At last," he muttered, relief flooding through him as he peered expectantly at Hercules's elite force.

They staggered forward and stood in a line in the centre of the foyer, all four of them! It took a while because two walked with the aid of walking sticks and one was so fat that he could only just shuffle along.

None of them appeared under the age of eighty and three of them were so skinny it looked as though a breeze would blow them away.

Nick surveyed Hercules' elite fighting force open mouthed and his heart sank. They were all wearing a sort of rusty, clanking armour and carried (or rather leaned on) ancient, warped spears.

One stumbled forward and smiled, revealing a row of grimy false teeth before bending double in a bout of coughing.

"Troy?" muttered Nick when the old Elverey had straightened up once more.

"Oh no," he wheezed. "I'm Herbert. Troy couldn't

227

come. Got a bit of a cold I'm afraid."

"Oh, heaven help us," he sighed, cursing Hercules under his breath.

"What now," asked Jed, looking totally bemused, but before anyone could answer, a loud yell erupted from Ayisha back in the theatre.

*

Chapter 16

CONFLICT

Jed, who'd always had a bit of a soft spot for Ayisha, grabbed one of the elite guards spears and ran towards the theatre doors. The guard, who had been leaning on it for support, tumbled to the floor, his rusty armour making a resounding crash that stunned Nick back into action.

"Jed no," he cried, rushing after his friend, but already Jed was through the doors, yelling out Ayisha's name.

Nick followed, holding the shrinkage post like a spear but knowing he'd have little chance against Napoleon, Leroy or Eye-Patch. (He still couldn't think of the thug as a Rupert!)

As he ran into the theatre his eyes had to adjust to the dismal surroundings. When they did, he just stood there, staring in amazement.

Leroy was writhing on the ground, Ayisha standing over him with hands on hips and a satisfied smile on her face.

Hercules was also on the floor, his robes up over his tousled head in a most undignified fashion displaying, not for the first time, those oversized and old fashioned underpants.

Eye-Patch, who was circling round him, ready to go in for the kill suddenly staggered forward as the little figure of Church leapt onto his back, arms around his neck, legs thrashing wildly, and together they tumbled to the floor.

Varn stood defiantly in front of a grinning Napoleon, but the grin abruptly vanished when Ayisha's fist suddenly connected with his cheek, sending him reeling back into one of the seats.

In the aisle, a little further down from all the chaos, stood Tritus, his face registering first surprise, then shock at Church's apparent change of sides, then amusement at the way events were turning out. He dragged the white wig from his head and pulled the obviously uncomfortable packing from his waist before standing motionless, leaning heavily on his cane. His one good eye scanned every detail, and what that detail was showing was that Napoleon and his men were rapidly losing control.

A swift follow up kick from Ayesha's leather boot left Napoleon slumped groggily across the row of seats.

"I told you to watch your back," she yelled, rubbing her fist and turning to Hercules, who was now struggling to his feet and seemed more interested in straightening his robes and grooming his hair back into place.

Not that there was much left to be done. The elite guard had finally shuffled into the auditorium and were busy getting in each other's way as they dragged the battered Leroy to his feet. It wasn't easy though, because two of them couldn't bend very well as their back joints weren't what they used to be! Meanwhile, Church, Ayisha and Jed were restraining the wildly thrashing Eye-Patch, his face contorted with rage.

Nick watched them all and grinned triumphantly, keeping a cautious eye on Tritus, who had apparently given up and was still just standing there looking old and tired.

"Well?" he said happily, "what are we waiting for? Let's take them away."

There was a lot of shuffling and a few groans of pain, not least from Varn who was complaining about that cramp type pain in his stomach again, something to do with bad digestion or too much excitement or something!

"You heard our overseer," roared Hercules with great self importance. "Take these creatures away. We have struck a great blow today. We have struck our enemies to the very earth and…"

"Thanks," said Nick hastily, cutting the big Elverey off before he really got into his stride.

"What's he say?" asked the fat guard.

"Dunno," replied Herbert, trying to keep his false teeth in. "Something about, 'we took our pennies to merry Perth!' Something like that."

"Doesn't make sense."

"Never does," agreed Herbert with a sad shake of the head.

As they started escorting their prisoners to the door, Nick couldn't resist going over to the whimpering Leroy. Standing in front of him, he put his finger and thumb to his forehead.

"Loser!" he growled and Leroy's gaze dropped to the floor.

"Can we perhaps inaugurate me into the overseer committee now, so to speak," said Mindi, leaning on the back row of seats.

There was a moment's pause.

"We're a little busy at the moment," exclaimed Varn politely, "but when we get time, I'm sure we'll be able to arrange a meeting."

"I'll do that," replied Mindi, brightening up. "After all, it's not rocket science."

Jed came over and draped an arm round Nick's shoulder.

"Pretty good huh?" he said with a grin that faded a fraction as he nodded in the direction of Tritus, "but what about him?"

"He's going with the rest of them," replied Nick, squinting into the gloom. There was something though, that was not quite right. Tritus didn't look like someone who was beaten. He just stood there, his tall figure almost on the same level as them, despite the slope down towards the stage. On his face was still that half amused expression.

The atmosphere seemed to change. It was nothing that Nick could put a finger on but it was obviously felt by the others. They all stopped and fell silent, turning to look back at Tritus as though half expecting something awful to happen.

A chill rippled through the silent air and a smell of decay began to seep through the odour of polish. Nick shivered, trying to blame his nerves on an over active imagination.

But deep down he knew that wasn't the case.

The grin on Tritus's grotesque face was growing. The gleam in his one good eye was intensifying.

Something was happening…and fast!

From the corners of the vast theatre and from the blackness of the deepest recesses, shadows stirred.

Nick's blood turned to ice as he glanced at the others. Their frightened faces confirmed that this was not merely an over active imagination.

"Get out of here," he yelled, turning for the exit, but it was already too late.

With a resounding crack that echoed right up to the top of the domed roof, the double doors locked.

They were trapped!

Nick stared in horror at the long bony hand that had snapped the lock shut.

Out of the gloom and the darkness, from every edge, every corner, looming shadows began to emerge.

Silently they swept forward, some with heads shrouded, all wearing long, flowing black robes. The white eyes, with no visible eyeball, almost glowed out in the blackness, as did the razor sharp teeth. Some had their arms raised, as though reaching out to their prey, displaying scraggy, bony hands, with nails that were cracked but viciously sharp.

"Deebers!" someone hissed.

Mindi screamed.

Nick swung back to face Tritus, who was now no longer alone. A line of Deebers waited patiently behind him in the aisle. Only one stood by him, and this one was even taller than Tritus himself. It was wearing robes that seemed to be more dark red than black. Its face was shrouded in a hood but Nick was sure that the eyes had a distinctly red tinge to them. It stood, with shoulders slightly stooped, as though paying respect to its master.

For some reason this one frightened Nick even more than the others.

Tritus raised a weary arm and the advancing army of Deebers stopped.

There was a long, heavy silence.

"Things haven't worked out as I wanted," said Tritus finally. "I have been misinformed and I have been tricked."

The eye swung toward Church who shrank back with a whimper.

"But," he continued with a sigh, "the ending is the same."

Nick glanced round, hurriedly searching for

something on the walls. He was hoping and expecting that Tritus would embark on a long victory speech.

But he didn't!

"Kill them all," said Tritus with a casual wave of his hand.

The circle of Deebers prepared to close in.

"No wait!" roared Napoleon, shrugging off his captors and striding down the aisle to face Tritus. "You can't do this. We worked together."

"You failed," came the coldly menacing answer.

"But you never said anything about killing them." Napoleon turned angrily and surveyed the little group. His gaze went to Jed, his nephew and just for the briefest of moments his expression mellowed.

He swung back to confront Tritus.

"I won't let you do this," he roared.

In the gloom it was difficult to tell what was happening. There was a sudden swishing sound, a grunt, then silence.

For what seemed an eternity, Napoleon stood there, swaying slightly, his back to them.

Then slowly, very slowly, he turned.

Someone screamed; others gasped.

Napoleon, an expression of surprise on his wide eyed face, stumbled back up the aisle, blood dripping from a gash in his stomach.

"Jed…" he whispered faintly and Jed ran forward, crouching down to grab his uncle just as the Elverey slipped to the floor.

"I'm…sorry Jed…so sorry," were his last words as blood dribbled from the corner of his mouth.

Jed held the lifeless body, cradling Napoleon's head. His own body was trembling but from what emotion it was impossible to tell.

Nick stared horror stricken at Tritus, who was looking

down at the body with a coldly satisfied smile on his face. In his right hand he held the blood stained sword which had, until a few moments ago, been sheathed inside the cane he was leaning so heavily on with his left hand.

"Now kill them all," he hissed and turned back down the aisle.

But Napoleon's death had not been in vain. The added time had allowed Nick the opportunity to glimpse what he'd been searching for. As the Deebers began to close in once more, he leapt out of the aisle, using the backs of the seats as stepping stones, till he reached the final row and propelled himself up and into the single line of Deebers guarding the back wall. The momentum of his jump sent them reeling and he crashed into the wall, a sharp pain searing up his shoulder. Dazed but desperate, he struggled to his feet, frantically searching along the wall.

The Deebers struggled back to their feet, grabbing at his arms and legs, but it was too late. With a triumphant cry Nick slammed his hand down on a row of old fashioned light switches and the theatre suddenly erupted into blazing light.

There was a huge, unified wail as the Deebers shrank back, desperately covering their eyes and clawing at their faces as they went.

"Quick. Unlock the door," yelled Nick, but Mindi didn't need telling. In a flash she'd turned the key and pushed the doors open.

The group began to surge forward. Nick watched, taking in every detail as though it were all happening in slow motion. Deebers, wailing and shrinking back. Hercules, picking up the body of Napoleon. Church and Varn, hurriedly dragging a shocked and deathly pale Jed.

"We have to go back," screamed Leroy. "We have to get that murderer."

Eye-Patch grabbed him and hauled him through the door.

"Later," he hissed. "We have to save ourselves first. He'll have slipped into the shadows and be guarded by his friends again by now. We'll get him later."

"We have to regroup first," announced Hercules, tripping over his spear. "We'll return with my full body of men and flush him out."

Yeah; like that's going to happen, thought Nick as he watched them in their panic stricken haste, all struggling to squeeze through the doors at the same time.

The sounds around him were deafening; screaming, wailing, shouting. He was amazed at how calm he felt in all the chaos.

He would be the last out. He would lock the doors behind him and they would race back to safety. He paused and watched as the others shuffled across the foyer and disappeared through the outer doors.

What exactly would they do when they got back to safety? They'd argue and have meetings, and argue some more…and Tritus would escape justice… again!

No!

He stopped, hands on the door handles, and turned to look at the theatre.

Tritus was a small figure, up on the stage, just disappearing into the shadows behind the curtain at the far side, assisted by the Deeber in red who didn't seem as affected by the light as the others. Neither seemed aware that there was anyone left in the auditorium, such was their haste to escape.

"No," Nick whispered, staring down at the blood slowly spreading and soaking into the carpet, and as he did, anger welled up inside him till it burst out like a flood.

He ran down the aisle, blinded by rage. By the time he reached the steps to the stage there was no sign of Tritus or the Deeber with the red eyes.

He paused, trying to calm himself down and think of a plan. He'd follow Tritus and find out where he was hiding, then he'd go and tell the others. He peered cautiously up onto the stage, his heart pounding. There was no one there. He crept up the steps and onto the stage, feeling open and vulnerable up there. Out in the hall the Deebers had gone. Now there was just row upon row of empty seats. Even the sound of their frantic wailing had gone.

He stopped, listening carefully, but there was nothing. The doubts were coming now. This didn't seem such a good idea. He'd been carried away by the emotion of it all. What if the lights went out? What if he was stuck here, in the dark, alone?

Maybe they were right. Maybe it would be better to go back to the others and sort out Tritus later.

But he never got the chance to make that decision.

There, at the edge of the stage, was Tritus, with that same look of grim amusement on his face.

His long, thin fingers were wrapped around what looked like a lever. Nick frowned at it, then down at his feet, but even as realization dawned, Tritus pulled the lever and it was too late.

The floor collapsed below him as the trapdoor opened and with arms whirling uselessly, the stage disappeared as he fell into blackness, the shrinkage post slipping from his hand.

He braced himself for impact, which came almost immediately.

He crashed to the floor, grazing his knee and his elbow caught something that had him wincing with pain.

Struggling to his feet and breathing heavily, he flexed his limbs carefully to make sure nothing was broken. Nothing was, but his body felt a mass of bruises.

Above, the trapdoor crunched back into place. The surroundings were now pitch black and heavy with that smell of decay.

He tried to force down the panic that was welling up inside. He knew that he was not alone; that they were down here.

"Hello," he croaked, his voice sounding ridiculously faint.

Suddenly, hands grabbed his arms and twisted them behind his back. The pain was intense and the panic surged to a new level. He tried to scream but nothing came out.

Then, in that all encompassing silent blackness, footsteps slowly began to thud down a staircase, each step accompanied by the soft click of a walking cane!

*

Chapter 17

THARLL

Thump…click.

Thump…click.

Thump…click.

With each slow, ponderous step the pitch blackness released its grip just the tiniest fraction.

By the time Tritus stood facing Nick there was sufficient light to make out his silhouette, though mercifully not enough to reveal any great detail in that horribly disfigured face. Nick had seen it before of course, but not this close; not so close as to smell the stale breath.

Nick's heart was pounding. Behind Tritus he could just make out the black shadows of the Deebers. He glanced round fearfully. He was trapped within a circle of them, the orbs of their eyes glowing white in the darkness.

One pair of eyes though glowed red. The tall figure standing one pace behind Tritus had his hooded head bent slightly, though whether this was in respect to his master, or simply because the wooden roof was so low it was impossible to tell.

Tritus just stood there, leaning on his cane, his wheezing breath the only sound in the oppressive gloom. He gave the merest of nods and the Deebers behind relaxed their grip, leaving Nick swaying slightly and rubbing his arms.

"So my friend," whispered Tritus with a sigh, "you wish to confront me yet again?"

Nick tried to speak but no words would form.

"…And this time you have the audacity to do so alone."

"I'm…I'm not alone," Nick stammered. "The others will come looking as soon as they realize I'm not with them."

Tritus gave it some thought.

"Maybe," he said finally, staring round him at the circle of shadows, "but they have no idea where you are, or just how outnumbered you are."

Nick tried to swallow but his mouth was too dry.

"I'd say you're outnumbered about sixty to one, wouldn't you?"

"They'll still find you Tritus. You're wanted for murder. You can't hide forever."

Tritus laughed softly. The sound made Nick feel more fearful than ever.

"Why would I want to hide? Rixal is my home. Soon all Hightower will be."

"But you're wanted for murder," insisted Nick, desperately trying to see the direction the conversation was going. "You can't escape forever."

Without answering Tritus lurched to his right. The light increased a little as he moved and the Deebers moaned and covered their eyes as he barged through them.

"Quiet," he commanded, pointing a thin, pale hand to the corner.

Nick squinted at the wall. The room was bigger than he'd thought, with a very low ceiling. Obviously, they were under the stage. He concentrated on where the finger was pointing and began to make out a familiar, sphere shape nestled in the shadows.

"An engine-heart," he gasped.

"Precisely," agreed Tritus. "The one I have had at the old home all this time."

"It was being loaded into that hare when we came back for Mindi and Church."

"Oh yes," replied Tritus, hobbling back. Behind him the circle of Deebers silently closed up once more. "You really are slow on the uptake sometimes. My friends here have been filtering back into Rixal under darkness for some days now. They are my army.

My old engine-heart over there and the Barrowhouse one will be placed together."

He leaned so close their noses almost touched. Nick closed his eyes rather than look at that pitted, horrible face.

"I'm sure you know what that means, Mr.Overseer," he hissed.

"The power will start to effect people," replied Nick, opening his eyes with great effort.

Mercifully, Tritus leaned back.

"Correct," he snarled triumphantly. "When that happens chaos will ensue. I, with the help of my army, will take control. One by one I will get the engine-hearts together, Yada's, Glug's and Miru's, till they all combine and the power, and myself, become all powerful."

"But it's not all gone to plan has it?"

"Don't flatter yourself. Your part in this was just an elaborate diversion. I wanted you to feel an outcast; to know what it's like to be alone. I still have to destroy the overseer committee, but I have the two engine-hearts and that is the important thing."

Nick knew that was true and his heart sank.

"It was over here, I'm sure of it," said a muffled

voice as footsteps thudded across the stage above. "It sounded like someone talking. Didn't you hear it Hercules?"

An indistinct and distant reply, a crash, and a yell was followed by more footsteps.

Nick opened his mouth to shout but quick as a flash, Tritus grasped the top of the cane and the glinting blade of the sword suddenly pierced the gloom, the vicious tip almost touching his neck.

"One sound," whispered Tritus, his eye glistening madly, "just one sound, and it's your last."

Nick reckoned he hardly needed to make a sound as his heart was pounding so loudly he thought they'd be able to hear it on the stage!

"There's nothing there now," came the distinct tones of Church's voice.

"Might have been insects or something," cut in Ayisha.

"Don't think so," replied Church. "I'm sure it was voices."

The footsteps drifted to the corner. Nick held his breath, desperately trying to hold that feeling of panic down.

"Well there doesn't seem to be anyone round here," said Ayisha. "Nicky…NICKY…Can you hear me?"

"NICKY," bellowed Church.

Three was another loud crash.

"Hercules," cried Ayisha, "are you all right?"

From further away came muted mutterings. The footsteps above plodded to the other side and faded.

As silence took over once more the tip of the sword wavered, then lowered and Nick exhaled a long, shaky breath.

"So what now?" he stammered.

The reply when it came didn't register for a moment

as it was said so calmly. He churned the three words round in his brain, trying to get them to make some reasonable sense.

"Now, you die!!"

He shook his head, his mouth hanging open in horror.

"Why?" he mumbled, but it seemed an empty, pointless question. He really didn't want to know. All he did know was that this was the end. Tritus was muttering something about how he'd disfigured him and destroyed his life, but it was as though the words were being spoken from a great distance. It was as if he were witnessing it all down the wrong end of some telescope. Everything seemed distorted and far away. He suddenly felt strangely calm and even had time to glance at his watch. Four thirty it said on the luminous dial. Strange, he thought in a detached sort of way; four thirty is his time of death.

The only other feeling was a vague heat radiating from his leg. What was that all about?

Tritus had stopped talking, the sword rising once more.

The heat was getting stronger. It wasn't his leg, it was his pocket. Something in his pocket was hot, and getting hotter.

The sword continued to rise, Napoleon's dried blood standing out on the gleaming metal.

Nick fumbled in his pocket and his hand gripped the broken coin type thing he'd been given at Barrowhouse.

'When you are in your greatest moment of peril,...' the strange blob creature had said. 'When there is nothing left to use...'

He pulled it out and stared at it blankly. The blade swished...and suddenly stopped.

"What the...?" bellowed Tritus angrily.

Nick glanced up. The red eyed Deeber was standing

forward, a long, claw like hand gripping the arm of Tritus, forcing the sword to lower.

The circle of Deebers moved in still closer.

"Tharll? What is the meaning of this?" demanded Tritus, a hint of concern in his voice.

Very slowly, Tharll's red eyes scanned round the circle of Deebers. With just the faintest of nods, he turned back to face Nick.

"What is happening?" said Tritus anxiously as two Deebers grabbed his arms and held him. The sword clattered to the floor.

Tharll raised a hand to his neck and withdrew a chain from beneath the folds of his robe.

Nick stood there mesmerized. In the Deeber's long, pale hand was a broken disc, identical to the one he was holding. Tharll held it out and Nick hesitantly took it, shuddering at the cold clamminess of the Deeber's skin as he did so.

He stared at the two discs. Where they were broken, the jagged edges matched. It was obvious that the two belonged together.

"What is that?" Tritus cried out. There was real fear in his voice now.

But Nick wasn't listening. Fascinated, he pressed the two pieces together. They fitted perfectly, but they only made two parts of a circle. There was still a smaller part missing.

The pieces gripped together as though they were magnets. As soon as they touched it was impossible to split them again, and as they touched Nick's whole body trembled. It was like the feeling he'd experienced the very first time he'd touched the disc but this was much stronger. A pulsating pain and a screeching noise flashed through him, similar to that when he used the shrinkage post. It was there and then it was gone, but in that instant he knew that the Deebers had felt it too. They trembled just a fraction and the white glow from their eyes intensified... then it was gone, and they all stood, silent and still once more.

Tritus had obviously felt nothing. He stood there looking totally bemused.

Nick too, just stood there, watching the Deebers warily. In the eerie silence Tharll stared at him, the red eyes glowing with renewed intensity.

Slowly, very slowly, he turned round.

"No," Tritus muttered miserably. "No Tharll, I command you. I command you all.

Tharll started advancing on Tritus. The circle of Deebers did the same, their vicious teeth making strange clicking noises in unison as they closed in on their quarry. It was a noise Nick had heard once before, down in the deep confines of the old home and it brought him out in a cold, terrified sweat. The Deebers behind him pushed their way past, their sightless eyes staring forward.

"NO..." bellowed a panic stricken Tritus.

"Leave him," screamed Nick, dreading what was going to happen, but it was no use. If the Deebers could hear him they weren't listening. He staggered backwards till he bumped into the wall, then slid down and sat on the floor.

"NO..." screamed Tritus as the Deebers converged on him. For a fraction of a second Nick saw his scrawny hand above the mass of black shadows, then it was gone, engulfed below the writhing crowd that was dragging him helplessly toward a door at the far end.

Nick looked at the ground and covered his ears with his hands but it was impossible to shut out the pitiful screams of pain and fear from Tritus, or the rhythmic click of the Deebers gnashing teeth.

He closed his eyes tight shut and the noises gradually faded till there was nothing but silence once more.

After what seemed an eternity, he hesitantly opened his eyes, took his hands from his ears, and looked up. The room was empty, save for the towering figure of Tharll, those eyes staring intensely down on him.

"What's happened to Tritus?" he stammered. "Is he dead?"

The Deeber bent down and carefully placed the shrinkage post at Nick's side. He reached out a long, gnarled finger and cautiously touched the combined disc held loosely in Nick's trembling hand before standing up and walking back to the open door.

"Wait," said Nick, scrambling to his feet and waving the disc. "What about this? What is it?"

Tharll reached the door and paused.

"Where did it come from?"

"The...Guardian gave it you," whispered Tharll.

Nick stared open mouthed as the Deeber spoke. The soft voice seemed to seep into his mind rather than through his ears and with each word the figure shimmered, as though seen through water or intense fire.

"Who...who's the guardian?"

The shimmering intensified as though Tharll was agitated by the question.

"The Guardian knows everything... You were saved... by the Guardian... of Barrowhouse."

Nick felt a stab of guilt.

"But I let him die. I didn't tell anyone."

"He was near death...You could tell no one...When a Guardian is dying they choose someone to pass their part of the circle to... As overseer you were the obvious choice."

"The circle," said Nick, holding out the disc. "But what actually is it?"

"It is an emblem...It is their sign...Whoever is chosen

to receive it must be kept safe... That dying wish had to be honoured...Therefore Tritus could not be allowed to succeed in his task."

"Hang on. You had a part of this, this circle thing. Were you given it by a Guardian at Hightower?"

There was a long silence, finally broken by the distant sound of footsteps.

"It came to me many years ago...It is now yours."

"And what do I do with it?"

"Nothing... It has done its job... It has saved you... Keep it as a memory of this day."

As the footsteps got closer, the figure of Tharll started to solidify once more. With the merest nod of his head he slowly walked out of the room and silently closed the door, leaving Nick standing there, holding the disc in his trembling hand.

Suddenly, muffled voices re-emerged upstairs.

"...It came from over here I'm sure."

"...Screaming...Yelling..."

"...Definitely down here..."

"Look! What's that...?"

A series of thuds and bangs echoed from the ceiling and suddenly the trapdoor swung down, bathing Nick in a thin shaft of light.

He squinted and looked up.

"Oh, Nicky. Thank goodness," cried Church, sounding distinctly relieved, "whatever are you doing down there?"

*

Chapter 18

THE HAUNTING

"...*Further heavy snow brought more chaos to Britain today*," said the stern faced newsreader. "*In the south, many roads have been blocked and airports suffered major delays as...*"

Nick sat in the chair and stared at the enormous screen, his legs tucked under him, his arms folded. He could see the woman's lips moving but wasn't really taking much in.

His whole body hurt from the numerous bumps and scrapes he'd received the previous day and his mind was still in turmoil from seeing Napoleon die, then coming so close to death himself.

"...*And in Yorkshire, snow's been blamed for the derailment of a goods train close to...*"

He tried not to think too much about yesterday, but it kept coming back in a series of blurred images. Napoleon's ashen face when he swung round to face them; Tritus's hand hovering above the mass of Deebers; Tharll's piercing red eyes; the weird disc!

"...*A power black out in part of Scotland has plunged communities in the...*"

His thoughts drifted back to Varn on the way back from the theatre.

"I don't know what to think," the old Elverey had

said with a shake of the head. "The Guardians were always considered a bit of a myth. Legend has it that they looked after the Elvereys and kept them safe. From what you've just told me, this Barrowhouse blob thing certainly did that!"

Nick couldn't help but agree.

"By giving you the circle, he gave you the means to save yourself."

"But what is it?"

"I'm not too sure. It's something from Elverey folklore. All I know is, ancient stories say that when all parts of the circle are joined together, it holds great power."

"Great power huh," said Nick, thoughts of becoming invisible or having the ability to fly whirling around in his mind.

"Great rubbish more like," replied Varn. "It is interesting though. Can I take it to have a look in the archives? I might be able to find out more about it."

"Sure. I'll let you have it sometime."

"*...The black out occurred around four thirty yesterday. A spokesperson for the power company said no cause could yet be...*"

The screen suddenly switched to a desert with a group of Roman soldiers in the foreground.

"That's better," snarled Dave, rising from the couch with remote in hand. "I'm sick of all those news programmes. Boring; that's what they are. All boring. What time's your mother coming home?"

"Dunno," said Nick with a shrug, "just said she'd be late."

"Where's she gone anyway?"

"Taking some Christmas presents to someone in the village. Mrs Bailey I think."

"Huh. Won't be back till late then," Dave replied

indifferently, "not the way your mother talks. What's she left me for supper?"

The question pretty much summed up Dave, thought Nick. The guy was only ever interested in himself. He wasn't bothered about his mum. All he wanted was someone to be constantly at his beck and call.

To be fair, his mum had been in two minds whether to go out for the evening. She'd stared anxiously at Nick all day, watching as he'd picked at his food at lunchtime and asking him time and time again if he was feeling unwell.

He'd convinced her he was just tired and she'd reluctantly gone out. He was glad that she had as he just wanted to be left alone.

"Well?"

"Well what?"

"Hello?" said Dave, rolling his eyes. "Anybody in that brain of yours? I said, what's she left me for supper?"

"Dunno," replied Nick, turning back to the screen as the Roman soldiers marched across the desert.

For a second Dave's eyes flared with anger.

"Do I have to do everything in this house?" he muttered, storming out the door. Duke looked up and with a reproachful glare at Nick, followed his master.

Nick sighed and tried to concentrate on the programme. The Romans had grown in number, although some of them didn't look very Roman. In fact some of them looked rather familiar and distinctly Elverey!

He leapt from his seat and cautiously shut the door before kneeling in front of the television.

Hercules, Varn and Ayisha were standing in the forefront, Hercules looking back, nodding appreciatively at the Roman soldiers.

"What are you doing here?" Nick stammered.

"Nicky," said Varn brightly, "have you got the shrinkage post with you?"

"Well yeah. It's in my pocket."

"Good."

"Fine troop of men," mused Hercules, stroking his beard. "Bit like my men."

Varn nudged him irritably and Hercules spun round, catching him on the arm with his spear. Varn howled.

"Oh good evening Nicky," Hercules said, ignoring the wailing Varn. "Are you ready to strike your enemy to the very earth?"

"Well er,…" muttered Nick.

"You see," said Ayisha solemnly, "we all felt really bad about what happened; how we all believed those lies about you…"

"All except me," interrupted Hercules pompously. Ayisha threw him a dark look.

"…so we decided that we had to help you. Mr.Scoggins…"

"Oh, that man," muttered Varn distastefully, rubbing his arm.

"…Mr.Scoggins told us your idea about getting that Dave person removed…"

"…so we're here to help finish the job," said Hercules, "we will strike your enemy to…"

"Yes.Yes," hissed Varn. "Nicky, quick. There isn't much time. Shrink down near the television and wait by the plug socket. You'll be met there." He leaned forward and pointed vaguely toward the bottom right hand corner of the screen.

From the kitchen came the gruff voice of Dave calling to Duke.

"OK," said Nick, grabbing the shrinkage post from his pocket. He'd learned long ago not to bother asking too many questions. It generally just complicated matters!

"We'll see you as soon as we can," said Varn as the three figures trudged to the corner of the screen. "Honestly Hercules, please be careful with that spear. That bruise could lead to a blood clot and I may need my arm amputating if I don't get…"

The voice trailed away, drowned out by the booming voices of the Roman soldiers once more.

Nick shuffled towards the side of the television and peered at the plug socket. There was nothing unusual there, just a socket, plugs, and masses of wires.

From the kitchen came the smell of something slightly burnt and not very appetizing, then Dave's voice, only louder now.

Nick plunged stick and ring together and plummeted down just as the door opened. He'd barely regained his senses as Duke bounded across the carpet, growling ferociously. Behind him, Dave was yelling angrily.

Nick struggled toward the socket. It hadn't seemed far before but at his new size it now appeared an awfully long way away. The carpet wasn't particularly thick but the threads came up to his knees and he had to push them aside as he ran. It was like struggling through a cornfield and the closer he got to the wall the more obstacles he encountered. There were bits of dust, like twine, ready to trip him, crumbs of bread that looked like huge white boulders, and a couple of dubious looking green pebbles that could possibly have been flicked out of somebody's nose! At one point he had to dodge round a long metal bar that he reckoned must be a pin.

The vacuum cleaner really doesn't get into the corners too well, he thought vaguely as he leapt forward. Behind, the deafening growl of Duke was getting louder and louder.

He stared at the huge white plug socket rising up

above. Suddenly a small door opened below it and the willing hands of Church and Jed hung out.

Nick leapt, just as Duke's fangs began to close. He felt the hot breath as hands grabbed him and hauled him in, the fangs snapping shut on nothing.

"Back Duke," Dave's voice boomed out, "whatever's got into you?"

The dog gave a frustrated whimper as Church slammed the door of the tiny room shut and the outside sounds faded.

Nick bent double, trying to catch his breath.

"I am sick of seeing that dog's tonsils!" he said when he finally managed to stand upright again.

Jed and Church grinned. It was good to see, as both had been through so much.

Church was dressed in a long black cloak. His face was very pale; almost white; and when he grinned he revealed two sharp, vicious looking fangs.

"Doing a bit of haunting tonight," he said. "Fright night is bite night."

"So I see," replied Nick, returning the grin. "But how are you Church? What with the Chamberlain thing and everything."

The smile faded.

"Oh, I'm all right I suppose. I still can't believe my brother would do all that."

"It was the power. It got to him."

"Yeah, I suppose," sighed Church. He brightened a little and touched the teeth. "Let's concentrate on tonight huh? I reckon fangs are going to get pretty interesting, don't you?"

"Yeah," replied Nick, turning to Jed as Church pressed a button and they shot upwards. "...And what about you Jed?"

"Me?"

"After…after what happened to Napoleon."

Jed took off his battered hat and scratched his head.

"Dunno. He was my uncle and all that, but he never did anything for me. He never wanted me."

"I know. But he turned to you in his last moments… and he did give us a bit of time. Maybe he did do something for you in the end. Maybe he saved your life."

"Maybe," replied Jed softly, but it was impossible to read the boy's expression.

"We're here," beamed Church, pushing the door open. "Better get a move on. There's a lot at stake!"

"Church," said Nick, grabbing his arm, "if that's another of what is going to be a long line of vampire jokes, can we just stop them right now please?"

"Of course," replied Church. "After all, I really wouldn't want to be a pain in the neck!"

The three of them were still laughing as they emerged onto one of the three shelves wedged into the alcove above the television. They were hidden from view by a large framed photo of Nick and his mother taken in Majorca two years ago.

Nick peered round the edge. Dave was staring at the television, vacantly shovelling lumps of unpleasant looking meat into his mouth with Duke sitting at his feet, licking his lips.

"So, what now?" he whispered to Church.

"We wait for the others. They won't be long."

"And then what?"

"Oh, you'll love it," said Church excitedly. "We've been working on it all day."

He pointed a chubby finger vaguely past the photo frame.

"You can't see it but there's a sort of screen on the edge of this shelf. Stand behind it and it projects a huge image outwards. There's another one out there."

This information didn't really help explain much.

"But what will you want me to do?" Nick asked.

Jed and Church exchanged grins.

"You?" whispered Church cheerfully. "You just stand back and enjoy the show!"

*

It was nearly half an hour later when the lift door finally opened and Hercules, Varn, Ayisha and Mindi walked out onto the shelf.

Nick was taken aback. Ayisha was wearing some sort of black outfit with bones etched onto it, giving her the appearance of a long, delicate skeleton. Her face was made up to look like a skull, deathly pale and eerily frightening, even in the warm brightness of the room.

"Here," said Mindi, throwing a coat at Nick. "We need to hit the ground running as it were. We are, after all, on a tight, one hundred and eighty degree schedule."

Nick slipped the thick garment on, feeling even more confused.

"...And you'll need these," piped up Varn, shuffling in a large cloth bag. He straightened up, rubbing his back, and handed Nick some goggles.

"Whatever are these for?" he asked with a frown.

"Oh, these are great," said Church, helping to slip the goggles over Nick's head. "They'll help you see in the dark. If you adjust the little switch on the sides here, you'll be able to zoom in and see things really closely."

Nick felt dizzy as his eyes tried to adjust to the thickness of each lens, and the sudden heavy smell of rubber made him feel queasy. Both feelings subsided however as he stood there, swaying slightly and feeling a bit foolish in his big goggles and even bigger (and extremely unfashionable) coat!

"Now," said Church, fussing round, "is my little control panel in there?"

"Item 7B," confirmed Mindi, checking texts on her phone.

"Excellent," muttered Church, dragging out a black box with multitudes of switches and buttons on it. It wasn't an easy operation as his cloak kept getting in the way.

"Are we finally ready to commence objective one?" Mindi asked, her finger flashing across to constantly change the screen on another phone.

Everyone nodded.

"At last," said Hercules, striding to the lift door. Getting in was a struggle because the spear was a little large for such a small place. Finally, he wedged it in the corner, cutting himself only once this time in the process, and grabbed the door handle.

He paused and leaned out, a huge grin on his face.

"It's showtime!" he said happily, and shut the door.

*

The remainder of the group all put on their big, clumpy coats and Church crouched down over the box, his hands skimming across the controls.

At first nothing seemed to happen, but then Nick began to feel a definite chill in the air. After a few minutes the temperature had dropped so much that he could see his breath. He peered round the photo frame and adjusted his goggles.

"What the...?" muttered Dave, putting his plate down on the floor and rubbing his arms, but before he could stand up Church flicked a switch and the television went off; then came back on; then went off again.

"What the...?" repeated Dave, only this time his

voice sounded apprehensive. Duke, at his side slunk down closer to his master's legs, his eyes furiously flicking from side to side.

At that moment, Church switched the lights off, plunging the room into complete darkness.

Dave gasped.

Duke whimpered.

Nick re-adjusted his goggles. He now saw everything in varying shades of grey.

In the distance, out of the silent darkness, came the heavy clumping sound of footsteps slowly descending the stairs.

""D...D...D...Dominic...?" whispered Dave, squeezing over to the very edge of the couch.

Nick put his hand to his mouth, trying to suppress a sudden bout of giggles.

Thud. Thud. Thud.

Duke crawled across the floor, his belly nearly flat to the ground. He crawled slowly into a corner and curled up in a tight ball.

Nick zoomed in on the tiny figure of Hercules as he emerged from a door in the corner and carefully advanced on the huge, dark shadow of the dog, his goggles looking weirdly out of place with his robes and his spear.

Thud. Thud. Thud.

Even from so far above Nick could hear Dave's laboured breathing.

"This is where your friend Mr.Scoggins comes in," whispered Varn in his ear.

Nick glanced across. Above the grey figure of the cowering Dave, two hornets were silently hovering. They were connected together by a wire hanging down from each. At the lowest point at the centre of the wire hung a large black object that looked like a dismembered hand.

Thud. Thud. Thud.

The noise stopped outside the door. The sudden empty silence seemed even more terrifying in the darkness.

"Is…is that you Dominic?" stuttered a pitifully small voice.

The hornets descended, slowly at first, as though carefully aiming in on their target. They started to gain speed and the hand type object dropped directly onto Dave's shoulder. There was a piercing scream and the hornets shot back upwards before the trembling figure could grab the thing.

Over in the corner, Hercules had reached Duke. He pulled his arm back and launched his spear at the hindquarters of the dog. The spear disappeared into the blackness of fur and the dog leapt up, more in surprise than fear. The tiny spear could have been no more than a mere flea bite but the terrified dog howled and leapt up onto the couch where his master was cowering. The sudden movement brought another scream from Dave and another bout of giggles from Nick.

"Now watch," muttered Varn, pointing to Ayisha who strode across the shelf and stood behind the invisible screen.

Church pressed a couple of buttons and a dull glow began to form in the room. Dave's screams faded into a series of whimpering moans as the glow slowly intensified.

"No…" he mumbled miserably. "Oh…No…"

A skeleton with a thin, sad, skull like face shimmered in the centre of the room, floating in and out of view, little more than a haze in the darkness. Just to add to the effect, a subtle, soft moan floated out from hidden speakers.

The two grey figures on the couch began to stir.

"Come on," said Varn, grabbing the arm of Nick's heavy coat. "I think they're about to run. We'll have to move pretty fast."

He dragged Nick towards the lift door. Jed and Mindi were already there and Church was following, struggling with the control box.

Once inside Nick whipped off his goggles, his tousled hair sticking up in all directions.

"This is brilliant," he spluttered between bouts of laughter. "I can't believe all the work you've put in."

"Doozin' brilliant," agreed Jed, "and it gets better."

"We've had to do quite a bit of thinking outside the box so to speak," piped up Mindi, glancing anxiously at her watch.

"Is Ayisha making her own way?" asked Varn to Church.

"Oh yes. She's going round the top way."

The lift shuddered to a standstill and they emerged one floor below the living room.

"Quickly now," said Varn with uncharacteristic haste as he hopped onto what looked to Nick like one of those travelators they had at airports only this one had thick silver bars spaced out across it down its entire length. Nick and the others jumped on, squeezing between the bars.

"These are doozin' great," said Jed at his side.

"Hold on tight," shouted Varn from behind. "Grab the bar. These thing's go quite fast."

Nick grabbed the bar just in time as the travelator suddenly shot off. They travelled so fast that the air whipped through his hair and took his breath away. Above he could hear the heavy footsteps of Dave through the vast expanse of wooden floorboards. Obviously, the panic of trying to get out of the cottage overshadowed the fear of what may be lurking in the hallway.

Gradually the travelator slowed, then stopped and Nick staggered off, trying to catch his breath.

But there was no time to lose.

"Come on," cried the others, all squeezing into yet another lift. Nick jumped in, thinking, not for the first time, just how many tunnels and lifts there were in Hightower cottage. It was quite a disconcerting thought.

They shot upwards and emerged onto the shelf above the front door, where Marion's ugly pottery collection provided ample cover should it be required.

Nick pulled his goggles back on as they ran along the shelf in the darkness. By the time they'd reached the middle, which was now directly above the front door, he was quite exhausted.

He peered down, his eyes re-adjusting to the strange grey world. Ahead was the stairs going up to the bedrooms.

"What now?" he hissed into Varn's ear.

"Dave's tried to escape out the front door, but he's only got as far as the hallway here. We've locked the front door and the kitchen door...and there's no way he'll want to go back into the living room, not after Ayisha's little performance."

"So where is he now?"

Varn pointed directly below them.

"He's at the bottom of the stairs, wondering what to do."

Nick cautiously ventured as close to the edge of the shelf as he dared and stared down. The hunched shape of Dave and smaller hunched shape of Duke were cowering by the front door.

In the deathly silence, he wrinkled his nose. A horrid, earthy smell like old, rotting vegetables drifted on a gentle breeze. It was so rancid it even made Nick shiver nervously.

Jed patted his arm and pointed up the stairs. Nick looked up in time to see the vague outline of a huge black rat creeping stealthily down the steps, only this wasn't much like any rat he'd seen before. This had huge fang like teeth and enormous vicious talons for claws. A soft luminous glow emanated from it, making it seem to float in the darkness. Down its side was a long white patch that made its glowing aura even more surreal.

Nick grinned, knowing that Angel would be at the controls. It was sort of humbling to know that all these people were doing so much to help him.

"I've been in that rat," he whispered to Jed, "though it's been repaired and changed a bit since then!"

When Dave saw the rat he flung himself back against the front door, the glass rattling in its frame. Even Duke made no attempt to spring forward and attack, but just cowered there, whining softly.

The rat crawled down the stairs and stared at them, opening its mouth to display its impressively vicious fangs before, with an angry hiss it shot away into the living room.

"Now for Ayisha's grand finale," said Varn, nodding toward the top of the stairs.

They all stood there expectantly while Dave and Duke cowered fearfully.

For what seemed an age nothing happened, the still darkness hanging like an oppressive, forbidding cloak.

Varn and Church exchanged puzzled frowns.

Then slowly, gradually, a tiny distant light began to shimmer at the top of the stairs.

Dave emitted a soft, croaking sound below them.

The light intensified and as it did so, it seemed to drift forward and hang, hovering silently above the middle steps.

Dave's strange croaking sound trailed away into the icy darkness. For a moment he crouched there before suddenly lunging to the right. As frightened as he was of the living room there was no way he was staying at the bottom of the stairs. But even as he moved, the door crashed shut, as though pushed by invisible hands.

Dave let out a strangled, terrified scream and slumped back as the glowing light started to take shape.

Eyes! Piercing, intense eyes stared down, their glare softly illuminating the walls in a red glow. Nothing but eyes, for the rest of the face was cloaked within a hood.

"Oh, Ayisha's good," said Varn.

"Very good," agreed Church, standing up from the panel to enjoy the view.

The image hung there, shimmering menacingly. Behind the fearsome hooded figure seemed to be shadows, lurking silently in the background yet seemingly eager to get to the cringing figure below.

Suddenly, footsteps behind Nick made him turn.

"Sorry guys," said Ayisha, standing there in her skeleton outfit. She whipped off the skull hood and shook her hair free. "Couldn't get in. Someone had locked the door from the inside."

The others spun round, confused expressions creasing their faces.

"So who's...?" said Church, pointing at the apparition.

They turned back, just as the glow expanded, the writhing black army behind the main figure growing in size and intensity as though ready to swoop down on its prey.

"Tharll," muttered Nick, a lump growing in his throat. "He's helping us."

"You," corrected Varn. "He's helping you Nicky."

At that moment a new light flashed across the scene.

Two white bands drifted up the wall, over the ceiling and down the other side, accompanied by the roar of an engine.

"Quick Nicky," hissed Varn. "Your mum's here. You go back. We'll sort things out here."

"And do what?"

Varn smiled warmly. "You'll think of something."

Nick rushed back. The travelator began moving as soon as he stepped on it and stopped as soon as he reached the other side.

As he tumbled out of the door from the lift and rolled into the carpet, he could hear a car door slamming.

He dragged off his coat and goggles and used the shrinkage post as he staggered across the room. By the time he opened the door to the hallway his senses were pretty much back to normal.

Amazingly, the hallway was back to normal too. No foul smells, no apparitions, no bitter coldness.

What wasn't back to normal though, was Duke, who slunk past him with a pitiful whimper, and Dave, who stared at him in a wide eyed, petrified fashion.

"Dave? Are you all right?" he asked, as innocently as he could.

"You see it?" whispered Dave, his eyes wide and wild as he stared around fearfully.

"See what?"

"You know." The voice was high and quivering. "You must have seen it."

Behind him, a key was rattling in the lock.

"I don't know what you're talking about."

Dave moved with surprising agility. He leapt forward, his trembling hands grabbing Nick's T-shirt.

"This place," he yelled. "You must have seen it. Tell me you saw it."

He shook Nick hard, a maniacal fear radiating from his eyes.

"Tell me…"

"DAVID. TAKE YOUR HANDS OFF MY SON!"

It was the old voice. The confident, angry, totally in control voice. The one Nick always used to dread, but now it filled him with a happy relief. He hadn't heard that tone for such a long time.

The trembling hands released their grip.

"Marion, you wouldn't believe the…" Dave's unsteady voice trailed away under Marion's furious stare. Her eyes flickered to Nick for just a fraction of a second before returning to the broken, cowering wreck.

"Are you all right Dominic?"

"Yes Mum."

"Then go up to your room. I need to have a few words with David here. I'll be up shortly."

"Yes Mum."

Nick bounded up the stairs two at a time, trying as hard as he could to disguise his triumphant grin, but by the time he closed the bedroom door and sat on his bed it was no longer possible and he had a smile that seemed to stretch from ear to ear.

Downstairs he could hear loud voices coming from the kitchen. Or rather, he could hear his mum's voice very loudly. Dave appeared to be offering little resistance.

On the desk, his laptop screen suddenly flicked on. As the image strengthened Varn, Church, Hercules, Mindi, Ayisha and Jed appeared, standing against a backdrop of coffins, headstones and graveyards, something that was clearly the work of that great vampire Church!

"Bit of a row going on downstairs," said Varn with a grin.

"You can hear it then?"

They all nodded in unison.

"I think the whole world can hear it," added Nick happily as that familiar lump came back into his throat. "I just can't thank you all enough. You've all been so… so…fantastic. You're all absolutely fantastic."

The little group looked at each other and bristled with delight.

"It's a pleasure," mumbled Varn a little self consciously.

"Did you say we're absolutely fangtastic?" said Church, adjusting his cloak.

"What did I say about making awful vampire jokes?" warned Nick, trying to look stern.

"So did I," said Varn.

"And me," said Ayisha.

"Me too," cut in Mindi.

"Sorry. I'm starting to think it was a bit of a mistake to wear this outfit," Church replied innocently, though with heavy emphasis on the word 'stake!'

The shouting continued unabated downstairs. Nick tried to make out words but they were too muffled.

"Perhaps now my mum will go back to her normal self," he said hopefully. "If she does she'll see Dave for what he really is."

"Which is?" asked Varn.

"A bully… A bully and a wimp."

Hercules jostled forward amidst much nodding.

"Did you see that spear I threw Nicky?" he said grandly. "Did you? Why, I struck that loathsome brute to the very earth, that I did."

"Indeed you did," agreed Nick. "You were extremely brave."

Hercules puffed out his chest with pleasure and glanced at Ayisha, obviously hoping for looks of admiration. He didn't get them.

"What about the engine-heart?" Nick asked, turning

to Varn. "The spare one. What are you thinking of doing with that?"

Varn considered the question carefully before answering.

"Possibly just switching it off. We don't need another, and it's too dangerous to leave near any of the others."

"How about giving it to Tharll and the Deebers at the old home? I know they don't need one for light, but it might help for heating and stuff."

"A good point," cut in Mindi. "We could bring that up at our next meeting; run it up the flagpole as it were; push the envelope and see how the monkey runs, so to speak."

There was a moment's bemused silence. Varn rubbed his forehead as though he had a headache.

"What did you think of Mr.S then Nicky?" beamed Jed, changing the subject. "Did he come up with the doozin' goods or what?"

"He did. I'd like to go and see them again soon to say thanks."

"Sure. I'll arrange it."

"OK," replied Nick, "but try not to let Mrs.S put any food on!"

Downstairs, the volume level of Marion's voice increased, followed by the sound of a door slamming.

"Looks like things are happening," said Church, bending down to the control panel. "Go and have a look out the front window Nicky. We're going to help your friend on his way."

Nick ran round to the front bedroom window and cautiously peered out.

The haggard figure of Dave was trudging across the snow, dragging a large bag, Duke creeping along respectfully at his side.

Even before he'd levelled the key fob at the four by

four the hazard lights flashed once, the alarm beeped, and the engine roared into life.

Dave stopped, almost too frightened to move, but Mr.Scoggins soon managed to persuade him back into action!

From out of the sky four bats fluttered down, skimming round his head, their wings flapping furiously as they screeched, turning and diving, swooping and yelling.

Dave's shattered nerves could take no more. He flung the bag into the back, pushed the passive, trembling Duke onto the passenger seat, and hauled himself in.

The truck spun round effortlessly, snow spraying up from its wheels as it shot down the drive. Within seconds the red taillights turned out onto the lane and disappeared.

Dave was gone!

Nick's heart leapt as he returned to his bedroom. His mum was shuffling up the stairs, sniffling quietly to herself.

"You all right Mum?" he asked anxiously from the door.

"I think so Dominic. Are you?"

"Yeah. Has he gone?"

Marion barged into the bedroom without asking and sat down on the bed with a sigh.

"Yes, he's gone. I couldn't live with someone like that Dominic. He's not stable. I couldn't trust him."

"I'm sorry Mum," he replied, sitting down next to her. He did feel sorry for her because she was upset, but deep down he felt like jumping up and down on the bed in joy.

"Do you know, he'd got it into his head that this place was haunted. Terrified he was." She shook her head slowly. "What a wimp!"

"Yeah," agreed Nick, covering a smile with his hand.

"I know I've neglected you Dominic, and I'm sorry," she said, placing her hand over his.

"It's OK" he muttered.

"But I've decided to make it up to you," she said, her face brightening.

Nick started to feel apprehensive.

"You have?"

"Yes. You see, I know what's been wrong with you. Deep down, what's really been wrong with you."

"You do?"

"Yes. You've been bored Dominic. You've come here and I've not appreciated how quiet life is out in the country."

"You haven't?"

"No. So after Christmas we'll start doing things. Not stupid things like building hotels. Oh no, we'll leave this place just as it is. What we'll do is lots of interesting new things together."

"Right."

"It'll be great Dominic. Just you and me."

"Right," he repeated.

Suddenly she pulled him close and hugged him.

"Oh I'm sorry Dominic. I just didn't think. You've had no excitement since we came out here. Your life must have been so dull."

She squeezed him tighter and the bruises started to hurt.

He glanced awkwardly over her shoulder at the laptop. His friends all had happy, amused expressions on their faces.

He returned the smile.

Excitement…? Yeah like, that was something he reckoned he could do quite well without for a while!!

* * *